EXTRATERRESTRIAL SEX FETISH

EXTRATERRESTRIAL SEX FETISH

MATERIALS FOR THE CASE HISTORY OF AN ET S&M FREAK
A LITERARY PATHOLOGY BY SUPERVERT 32C INC.

Extraterrestrial Sex Fetish
© 2001 Supervert 32C Inc.
ISBN 0-9704971-0-5

Contact:
web: www.supervert.com
email: info@supervert.com

Text: Supervert 32C Inc.
Cover Design: Supervert 32C Inc.
Typesetting: Elliott Underwood
Printing & Binding: Printricate, Inc., New York

Manufactured in the United States of America.

FIRST EDITION

CONTENTS

OVERVIEW

I. Subject of the Case History

Mercury de Sade — male, Caucasian, thirty years old, unmarried, computer programmer. Affliction: *exophilia,* a monomania or fetishism whose object is the sexuality of extraterrestrials. Frustration of said fetishism frequently results in acts of sadism.

II. Content of the Case History

Alien Sex Scenes (ASS) — What Mercury de Sade wants. Pornographic visions of exophilia or sexual encounters between the fetishist and various extraterrestrials. Unordered series utilizing the faculty of imagination. Exploitation of aliens in fantasy.

Methods of Deterrestrialization (MOD) — What Mercury de Sade does. Narrative depicting the fetishist in the frustrated attempt to deterrestrialize or forcibly "alienate" Charlotte Goddard, a.k.a. Ninfa XIX. Ordered series utilizing the faculty of what Kant called practical reason. Exploitation of ninfas in reality.

Lessons in Exophilosophy (LIE) — What Mercury de Sade thinks. The history and analysis of *exophilosophy* or philosophical speculation on the nature of extraterrestrial life. Ordered series utilizing the faculty of what Kant called pure reason. Exploitation of philosophers in reason.

Digressions and Tangents (DAT) — Various commentaries, observations, and supplementary materials relating to the case history. Randomized series utilizing arbitrary faculties.

III. Organization of the Case History

Set theory is optimal for the description of sexuality, particularly its pathological forms. The virgin is {}, a null set, the curly brackets invoking the lips of a vagina that has yet to be penetrated. Monogamy is a set with one member. Heterosexuality is the union of male and female sets. Bestiality is the union of human and animal sets. Necrophilia is the union of living and dead sets. Pedophilia is a subset of heterosexuality—the union of male with a subset of the female set. Homosexuality occurs when a set becomes a member of itself.

Fetishism is a set whose members repeat. Exophilia is the union of human and alien sets.

Accordingly, the materials for the case history are organized utilizing methods from set theory, such that each section (ASS, MOD, LIE, DAT) is conceived as a set or sequence or series. In presentation the sets are interleaved. In content the sets display relations of order and randomness, convergence and divergence, intersection and union, reflection and redundancy. To read along the sets (e.g. MOD 01, MOD 02, MOD 03, etc.) is linear. To read across the sets (e.g. ASS 01, MOD 01, LIE 01, DAT 01, ASS 02, MOD 02, etc.) is non-linear or collage. To read as you will is arbitrary. To read like a computer is ideal. (See the appendix, "The Programmatic Structure of the Case History.")

Exophilia is a neologism coined by way of analogy with *exobiology*. Exobiology is the study (*logos*) of life (*bios*) outside (*exo*) earth. Similarly, exophilia is a love (*philos*) for that which is outside (*exo*) earth. In keeping with the traditional usage of the stem "philia" to indicate an abnormal passion often sexual in nature, as in pedophilia or necrophilia, exophilia should be understood as an abnormal desire for that which is outside earth—an extraterrestrial sex fetish. It is characterized by arousal in the presence of aliens or, less directly, representations of aliens. While the practitioners of other sexual deviations often reveal themselves in *flagrante delicto*—the pedophile groping the little girl next door, the necrophile robbing the cemetery—the exophile is rarely apprehended in the very act of satisfying his fetish. Evidently the reason for this is not the scarcity of exophiles but the lack of extraterrestrials themselves. Ironically, exophilia thus furnishes a new argument against the very existence of extraterrestrials, or at least against their visitation to earth. That is, if extraterrestrials were here, exophiles would fuck them. Consequently, the fact that exophiles are never caught in the act suggests (1) that extraterrestrials do not exist at all; (2) that extraterrestrials do not make contact with earthlings; (3) that, if extraterrestrials do make contact with humans, they invariably avoid exophiles. This last conclusion is corroborated by the fact that tabloids frequently report the rape of humans by aliens, but never the opposite—for if extraterrestrials did not avoid exophiles, the roles would be reversed. An exophile is a human who wants to rape an alien.

Because the exophile is rarely apprehended in the heat of the moment, in direct congress with a three-headed sex object from Mars, it is necessary to learn to recognize the exophile through indirect expressions of his abnormal passion. For example, an undue interest in science fiction is typical of the exophile. While in itself science fiction may be harmless, the exophile frequently fixates on certain characters or situations from novels or films. He may oblige his sexual partners to recreate, in the spirit of a psychodrama, key scenes from an episode of *Star Trek*. He may also, by way of compensation, develop fixations on actors or actresses associated with aliens in films: on Drew Barrymore, for her role in *ET the Extraterrestrial*, or Sigourney Weaver, for her admittedly erotic scenes in the *Alien* trilogy. Naturally, these fixations can extend beyond the world of science fiction to include real-world personalities closely associated with outer space. For example, an exophile might develop a homosexual attraction for a prominent scientist such as Carl Sagan or a famous astronaut such as Neil Armstrong. Other exophiles have performed sodomy with telescopes and incited astronomy clubs to perform group masturbation. In one notorious case, an exophiliac subject confessed to a sexual obsession with astronaut Christa McAuliffe, a schoolteacher killed in the explosion of the space shuttle *Challenger* in 1986. He would arouse himself with fantasies of the woman doing a striptease with her spacesuit and then watch a videotape of the seventy-three second shuttle flight, naturally timing his climactic release to the sudden bursting of the vehicle in the sky.

It cannot be overemphasized that these are all compensatory mechanisms. The exophile does not truly desire congress with rockets or astronauts but with extraterrestrials. However, precisely the seeming impossibility of this desire makes the exophile unique even among fetishists. While the devotee of feet or hair may have to plot and scheme to obtain satisfaction for his fetish, he at least has various means of recourse. After all, feet and hair are everywhere to be found, but where are there extraterrestrials? If, as psychological theory proclaims, the fetish is a substitute for normal sexual relations, such that the fetishist prefers a shoe to a vagina, the exophile must make a substitution for a substitute. That is, in the stead of a vagina, he prefers an alien orifice. However, this alien orifice being practically unobtainable, he must instead satisfy himself with a prostitute made up to look like a Martian. The exophile thus finds himself two generations away from gratification—substituting a vagina for an alien, which is itself a substitute for a vagina. How can he possibly satisfy himself? Here emerges the sadism typical of the exophile. The exophile is inevitably discontented by the way in which the basic humanity of a sexual partner asserts itself through the cheap trappings of a Martian costume and will therefore be sure to humiliate, abuse, even murder the girl. While it is commonly thought that aliens are superior to mankind, the exophile interprets this to mean that mankind is intrinsically inferior, and thus does he—the exophile—justify his every act of cruelty. It is comparable to the view that the rape victim "asked for it." Being an inferior type of being, does mankind not deserve to be maltreated? Does he not ask for it?

The way the abduction myth has it, hicks driving their cars along lonely roads surrounded by cornfields suddenly experience vehicular weirdness and temporal distortion. Extraterrestrials swoop down on them like hawks on mice, taking them aboard their flying saucers for invasive medical examinations. Proctologists from Polaris probe the rectum with metal instruments not designed for human bodies, gynecologists from the Crab nebula insert speculums intended for crab vaginas, thus causing unspeakable damage to earthly orifices—bizarrely, unspeakable damage that disappears the next day, except for the psychic wounds, horrible traumas that appear under hypnosis, "And then the gray felt my cervix with his claw, it was terrible…" That's the myth, a nice myth, a myth that Mercury de Sade likes to fantasize about, though he's not sure which role to assume. On one hand, he prefers the active, sadistic role of the alien probing the human body with gynecological instruments from Mars. On the other hand, Mercury de Sade is not really interested in the human body. What he wants is something new. To obtain this he plainly has either to redesign the human body—which is not so easy to do, given that it would take thousands of years of evolution to outfit the old bag of meat with a really new orifice—or to find new bodies, alien anatomies, extraterrestrial sex organs.

And this isn't so easy either. Practical restrictions on space travel make it impossible for the fetishist to travel to other worlds. And though rumor has it that aliens do come to earth, their visits are, to say the very least, unpredictable. What is the exophile to do—put out a little sign, "Aliens welcome?" You almost can't blame Mercury de Sade for his compensatory strategies, which consist largely of trying to jam humans into alien molds. Ninfa XVIII, for example, he compels to don a white body stocking, which he then soaks in a green fluid, Lime Gatorade. The idea is to make her resemble a Little Green Man—except that she's not really green, nor is she a man, except in the broad sense that she's human, which, from the vantage point of Mercury de Sade, is precisely the trouble with her. She is little, anyway: a fifteen-year-old girl picked up in the public atrium of the Citicorp Building, where a lot of high school kids hang out after class. He brings her back to Casa de Sade, gets her stoned, ties her up, prepares to have his way with her—but Lord, that smell. You ever fuck a giant lime? It's hard to convince yourself that the object—and she is an object—of your affections hails from outer space when she smells like an advertisement for citrus fruit. It takes a lot of concentration to put Anita Bryant out of your head and concentrate on the girl to hand. The ironic part is that Anita Bryant was a great opponent of the homosexual lifestyle, and yet Mercury de

Sade avails himself of Ninfa XVIII as though she really were a Little Green Man—which is to say that he fucks her the way one man fucks another. It may not be a new orifice but, from the girl's vantage point, it certainly is a new sexual organ.

Perhaps, then, it really is possible to redesign the human body without evolution—or at least to reassign the functions normally allocated to its various parts. The ass can make a nice cunt, at least for the active partner. The cunt, liberated from its duties, can be used by the passive partner for something else—a purse, makeup kit, or trash can. If the passive partner is a man, his ass can still be a cunt, and his penis can be used as a pen protector, eyedropper, or, with a little creativity, tire-pressure gauge. (Testicles could swell to indicate air pressure.) It is not only "nether parts," however, that can be repurposed. The face can easily be made into a sexual organ. Oral sex, for example, is so common that you forget what a perversion of purpose it really is—after all, putting a penis in the mouth is as weird as inserting food in a vagina. Swallowing semen is as much a short circuit of anatomic function as fertilizing an egg with a potato chip. For the exophile, though, such perversions do not go far enough. Even if it becomes a cunt, the mouth remains an earthly orifice. For this reason, Mercury de Sade tends to finish every encounter with a cum shot. Why? Because to bury something inside a human body is an admission of defeat. Unless aliens descend from the sky, kill the passive partner, and extract the semen from her body during an autopsy, there is no way sperm in a human body will ever achieve contact with extraterrestrials. But to ejaculate on the surface of a body—that holds out hope of contact. It's like putting cookies out on a plate for Santa Claus.

INDEX   LIE 01 Alpha
ABSTRACT   Exophilosophy

Buried within the canon of philosophy are the histories of numerous other philosophies, repressed systems of thought that sometimes emerge like cerebral ghosts to haunt the rational, daylight world of the *lumen naturale.* Plato's transmigration of souls, Descartes' pineal gland, Berkeley's tar water, Nietzsche's eternal return—these are the notions that embarrass philosophy, that are explained away with reference to ignorance of the times or idiosyncrasies of the thinker. But sometimes these cryptophilosophies refuse to go away: they appear again and again, in the work of thinker after thinker, a mass hallucination that occurs not in a crowd in space but in a series over time. Such is the case of *exophilosophy.* What is it? Like its peer exobiology, exophilosophy is the study of life beyond earth—specifically the philosophical study of life beyond earth. In the broadest sense its objects include all theological entities (gods and angels and demons as extraterrestrial life forms) and the thousand other alien figures that populate philosophy: the daemon of Socrates, the Übermensch of Nietzsche, the Other of phenomenology. Not only advocacy but also the critical analysis of supramundane entities pertains as well, and thus the ghosts scorned by Spinoza and the spiritualists exposed by Schopenhauer also take their rightful place in the history of exophilosophy.

In its most restricted sense, however, exophilosophy does not concern itself with the paranormal in general but only with the study of alien life. In broad outline, exophilosophy begins in antiquity with the gradual attempt to separate exophilosophy proper from theology. Two competing conceptions of extraterrestrial life emerge: the materialist, for whom extraterrestrial life is a consequence of a plurality of worlds, and the idealist, for whom extraterrestrial life results from the eternity of the soul. After this the basic terms of the problem are not significantly altered until the Enlightenment, when developments in science (Galileo, Kepler, Newton) initiate an exophilosophical golden age: Descartes, Leibniz, Berkeley, Voltaire, Hume, and Kant all write enthusiastically about the plausibility of extraterrestrial life. With the advent of the nineteenth century, however, another transformation occurs. Philosophers still argue pro (Peirce, Bergson) and con (Hegel, Kierkegaard) about extraterrestrial life, but at the same time the very question itself becomes an object of consideration. While scientists assume the lead in considerations of existence and non-existence, relating the problem of extraterrestrial life to discoveries in physics, chemistry, and biology, philosophers submit it to various kinds of meta-analysis: John Stuart Mill criticizes the analogical reasoning behind the belief in extraterrestrial life, and Ludwig Wittgenstein approaches it from a linguistic vantage point.

The history of exophilosophy can thus be divided into three stages. The first, encompassing antiquity and the Middle Ages, concerns itself with three basic problems: the plurality of worlds, the relation of the cosmos and the soul, and *exomorphology* or the form and appearance of extraterrestrial beings. The second stage, which begins with the Enlightenment and extends through the nineteenth century, is the heyday of exophilosophy as such: nearly every major philosopher of the period directly participates in the debate concerning extraterrestrial life. New problems are formulated, theology is slowly disentangled from exophilosophy, and in general there emerges an awareness or self-consciousness about the status of belief in extraterrestrial life *qua* belief. The third period, which begins around the turn of the century, witnesses the gradual appropriation of exophilosophy by various branches of science. Many of the problems remain the same, but their solutions come to depend on technical arguments concerning planetary formation, the chemical origin of life, and so on. In reaction, exophilosophy retreats to various kinds of meta-analysis, which remain within the traditional philosophical purviews of logic and epistemology. Exophilosophical issues continue to conceal themselves in sublimated form in other areas of philosophy—is the Other of phenomenology not an essentially alien being?—but not without new possibilities for exophilosophy already making their appearance on the horizon.

Aliens, it would seem, are the rapists of the universe. Frequent are the claims that extraterrestrials come to earth, abduct human beings, molest them in a flying saucer, then return their victims to a car in the middle of a cornfield, where they gradually recover from a post-coital daze to realize that they cannot account for the last several hours of their time. But are human beings really so desirable that extraterrestrials would travel thousands of light-years in order to fuck them? Mercury de Sade threaded a CD-ROM onto each nipple of Ninfa I and, securing them in place by inserting pins through her nipples, proceeded to tell her a little parable: On earth there was once a man who claimed to have been kidnapped and raped by a beautiful alien. Everyone scoffed at his story: the man must be crazy, he must want attention or publicity, and so on. But back on the spaceship, the alien held its tongue—not for fear of being disbelieved, but for fear of being derided. In space, to fuck another species is as taboo as on the big blue marble: aliens with sexual longings for humans are no better regarded by their peers than humans with sexual longings for animals. Outside earth, the love that dare not speak its name is love of man.

At the heavily guarded customs checkpoint of Beta, each visitor was interrogated by a mercenary species of squid-like creature feared for its ruthless perfection in violence and combat. Stepping forward, Mercury de Sade was wired to a lie detector that monitored alpha waves directly, so that it perceived not only spoken but cogitated acts of deception. Mercury de Sade tried to answer questions as automatically and unthinkingly as possible. His reason for visiting was scientific. He was a member of an academic commission already established on the planet. Had he undertaken the surgical procedures upon which admission to Beta was contingent? Here a slight flutter disrupted the otherwise smooth flow of Mercury de Sade's alpha readout. He knew that, were he to answer this question unbelievably, he would be subject to an invasive bodily examination. And physically it was impossible to fake this one entrance requirement: Beta was the only planet in the universe that required every male visitor to be castrated in order to set foot on its shores. Mercury de Sade did his best to think and to feel embarrassment, so that the guard would interpret his alpha flutter as discomfort rather than deceit. The tactic worked, and Mercury de Sade soon found himself riding in the back of a propulsion taxi toward his hotel.

Beta had instituted the castration policy because it was the most raped planet in the universe. Both the men and women of Beta were so intoxicatingly attractive to all other species of creature that no measure seemed capable of preventing the frequent violations to which the planet was subject. This had in fact been going on for so many hundreds of thousands of years that the inhabitants of Beta had evolved certain unique types of self-protection. Like many animals on earth, the Betas developed camouflage mechanisms, so that they were essentially sexual chameleons. It was impossible to tell a male from a female, not because they looked alike, but because they were liable to transform into one another at any random moment. A pederast would try to rape a boy, only to find himself rolling on the floor with a girl, or vice versa. Moreover, a further mutation occurred whereby false, misleading genitalia appeared all over the Beta body. There were vaginas that led nowhere like doors opening onto brick walls, penises that poked up out of trap doors in the skin only to disappear in whirlpools of flesh that would become pulsing pink pussies. The putative rapist would try to insert himself into a vagina, but then fall to the ground blubbering and rubbing his blunted erection. However, much as the prospect of long prison sentences never stopped the rapists of earth, neither did this camouflage and its consequences prevent exophiles from trying—and sometimes succeeding—to taste the exotic pleasures of Beta.

In his hotel room, Mercury de Sade tied up a young Beta. Though he thought it was a female, he couldn't be sure. Regardless, the thing was fascinating to watch: genitalia would burst on its face like a time-lapse film of a flower, only to disappear and blossom somewhere else, on its stomach or leg. A plain patch of pinkish skin would grow moist like exposed tissue, and then it would cave in to simulate a vagina, or bulge up in imitation of a penis. Mercury de Sade wondered if this evolutionary defense mechanism hadn't worked at cross-purposes, since he found the sight of it highly arousing, a pornographic movie acted out in the flesh of a living creature. At the same time, it also had a teasing effect: just when you started to fixate on one piece of anatomy, it disappeared or transformed and you were left titillated but suspended, unsatisfied. It was like watching a stripper: you could look but you couldn't touch—or, in the case of the Beta, everything you tried to touch would vanish beneath your fingertips. Finally, when Mercury de Sade could no longer stand to be teased, he prepared a pot of coffee. This he forced the Beta to drink, and then he prepared another pot. After three generous helpings, caffeine not only caused the thing to quiver in frantic genital oscillations, but to emit a viscous stream of fecal matter from an orifice that could neither conceal nor disguise itself. "Is it piss or shit? Does it come from the cunt or the ass? I don't know," said Mercury de Sade to himself, "but whatever it is, it's a genuine hole and I intend to fuck it."

Historians have written of the "privatization of excrement" that has occurred since the nineteenth century. The bathroom was not always the Fort Knox of crap that it has become today, with individuals locking themselves inside as though they were shitting out bars of gold. ("Look, I got the Midas tush!") Only with the modern period were bodily functions such as excretion separated from the public sphere, so that the bathroom was to become a fecal citadel in which the individual protected his excrement from the prying eyes of the public. However, once the bathroom acquired the impenetrability of a bank vault, it unintentionally acquired a new function as well. Not only could it hide the shitter, it could protect him as well. It is for this reason that insecure individuals often develop a proclivity for spending abnormally long hours in the bathroom. Feeling less vulnerable behind locked doors, they take long showers or cultivate constipation. And although this security can always be compromised through transparent mirrors and other tricks of the espionage trade, the so-called "digital revolution" has brought about especially effective ways to violate occupants of the bathroom. For example, it is a simple matter to plant surveillance cameras behind mirrors or vents, inside air fresheners or the handles of toilet brushes. These cameras can be linked by radio transmitter to computer terminals that buffer the video streams to disk for exploitation or enjoyment. This technology is not of the future: how many stepdaughters are already the unwitting stars of surveillance movies shot from the bowls of toilets?

A victim of precisely this false sense of security, Charlotte stands in the shower wearing a black bra and panties. If she thought her image were being disseminated, she would be subject to a real dilemma. Would she remove her bra and panties? On one hand, this would expose her naked body to view. On the other hand, to wear her underthings in the shower is obviously expressive of some abnormality. Which is worse to expose—her tits or her psyche? In truth, Charlotte is more confident of her body than herself and thus might well opt to remove her bra and panties. Her nakedness would defend her psyche. The reality of the situation, however, is the reverse. Her body is clothed but her psyche is naked. Charlotte, like most people, reveals herself for what she is in the bathroom. An interesting analysis could be made of the relation between truth and the bathroom: in the privacy of the fecal citadel, one does not put on airs. The bedroom is a place of lies: men promise love and women fake orgasm. But in the bathroom, truth is naked as an ass. "If only my truth were as nice as my ass," Charlotte would think, if she were aware of the issue. The truth is that she has a firm, pert ass shaped like an upside-down heart. This is apparent even in a pair of wet black panties, bikini cut. These were bought at Victoria's Secret as part of a set and given to her on her sixteenth birthday by her father—the father explaining to the clerk (who must have sensed a slight impropriety) that, since Charlotte's mother passed away, he felt an obligation to fulfill the duties of both parents, including occasional forays into the normally maternal role of clothes shopping. Certainly this elicited sympathy from the clerk, a black girl with a pushed-up bust, whom the father imagined feeling up.

So why does Charlotte wear her bra and panties in the shower? It is not because she is fat or ugly or deformed. It's just that, to her, it is precisely bodily charms that—well, it's like this. Tiffany's takes the diamonds out of its display cases at night, for the obvious reason that it doesn't want to expose itself to trouble. Tits, however, can't be taken out of their display case and locked away in the safe. They're always on display, even if you try to flatten them by wrapping an Ace bandage around them. People still notice—especially the wrong kind of people, the sexual equivalent of safecrackers. Is it not almost obvious what psychic abnormality is expressed by a girl who wears her under-things in the shower? In school Charlotte had learned that the Greeks personified fate as three women—but perhaps, she thought at the time, they saw it only from afar. In close-up, fate can also consist of women's body parts, magnified, exaggerated beyond all proportion, a future determined by buttocks or breasts.

The materialist conception of extraterrestrial life begins in antiquity with the recognition that the earth may not be the only world hospitable to life. After all, earthly life is not concentrated in Athens alone, so why should universal life be restricted to earth? Traditionally the Greek philosopher Anaxagoras (500-428 BCE) is credited with developing the theory of a plurality of worlds. He believed that the moon was inhabited and that life came to earth by falling from the sky—a notion of life's origin that scientists, speculating that primitive organisms may literally have "fallen from the sky" by riding to earth aboard comets and asteroids, would later call *panspermia.* For Anaxagoras, the point was not only that human life began elsewhere, but that there were other worlds from which it could come. That Anaxagoras did believe in such a plurality of worlds is beyond doubt. When asked about his notorious indifference to human affairs, he replied "I am greatly concerned with my fatherland" and gestured toward the stars.

But what convinced the philosopher that life existed in other worlds? Probably it was a consequence of basic metaphysical hypotheses. Anaxagoras held that mind or *nous* existed independently of matter. The Greek word *kosmos,* now synonymous with "universe," originally meant *order.* Mind was that which gave order to the universe, and therefore was coextensive with it. Matter, conversely, was a continuous, flowing, amorphous substance capable of infinite combination and recombination. In this belief Anaxagoras was prescient: modern chemistry has shown that cosmic admixture is the rule. Even the human body is literally comprised of particles originating in the stars: in the Milky Way, every star more than six billion years old has contributed at least one hydrogen atom to the constitution of every living person. Might it not be for such a reason that Anaxagoras considered the stars his homeland? Might he not have been the first to recognize a blurring of the lines between earth and other worlds? In a man there is already a bit of the extraterrestrial, and in a philosopher this bit becomes aware of itself.

Anaxagoras was thus the first to formulate what has since become a paradigmatic argument for the existence of extraterrestrial life. If the universe is consistent, must the conditions that enable life to prosper on earth now allow life to prosper elsewhere? The atomist philosophers who followed Anaxagoras went on to elucidate this principle materialistically. Leucippus (flourished ca 440 BCE) and Democritus (ca 460-370 BCE) believed that the universe was comprised of small indivisible particles swirling in a great empty space or void. A world forms when a collection of these atoms separates from the surrounding atmosphere. This collection becomes a vortex, repulsing smaller atoms and drawing larger ones toward the center. Subsequently the vortex becomes a sphere, and a surface or membrane encloses it. Such a process, because atoms are infinite and ubiquitous, may repeat itself indefinitely, thus giving rise to a plurality of worlds. In the *Refutatio* Hippolytus clearly implies that Leucippus and Democritus conceived of these worlds as habitable: "there are innumerable worlds, which differ in size... There are some worlds devoid of living creatures or plants or any moisture." (*Ref.* I, 13, 2) But if only some of these worlds lack life, the majority must possess it. Certainly later atomists believed this. Epicurus (341-270 BCE) declared that there was no way to prove that such worlds are not inhabited (cf. "Letter to Herodotus" in Diogenes Laertius, X, 74). And in a text explicitly intended to popularize atomism, Lucretius (99-55 BCE) put the matter even more forcefully: "When there is plenty of matter in readiness, when space is available and no cause or circumstance impedes, then... You have the same natural force to congregate them in any place precisely as they have been congregated here. You are bound therefore to acknowledge that in other regions there are other earths and various tribes of men and breeds of beasts." (*De Rerum Natura*, II, 1023-1089)

Advocates of alien life frequently dabble in philosophy or, in cases where their speculations are too crazy to qualify as philosophy, pseudo-philosophy. Mercury de Sade inverts this paradigm insofar as he shows that philosophers have frequently dabbled in extraterrestrial life as well. His program is to extract the history of a new philosophy, exophilosophy, from the works of the great thinkers. However, whether this history itself is really philosophy or pseudo-philosophy is difficult to determine. On one hand, it does gather together a previously subterranean theme in the works of philosophers generally acknowledged as great or important. To whatever extent these philosophers are considered authoritative, the new history in which they participate must also be considered legitimate. On the other hand, does the very attempt to compose such a history not emerge from the same fetishism that motivates the historian sexually? Plainly Mercury de Sade does to philosophers intellectually what he does in imagination to aliens and in reality to ninfas: he uses them, distorts them, fucks them. Must his history, even if it includes well-reasoned pronouncements by authoritative thinkers, not therefore be biased and illegitimate? Is it not simply an attempt to rationalize a perversion by implying that it is shared in some way by the greatest minds of all time?

Then again, is it not just possible that there exists an intrinsic connection between philosophy and the question of extraterrestrial life? And if so, is a man obsessed with extraterrestrial life not bound to approach it philosophically? That there is an intrinsic connection is suggested by the nature of the prevailing myth of alien life. That is, aliens are normally reputed to be of a higher order of intelligence than man. Were justice at question (are aliens fairer than man?), then extraterrestrial life would be inherently linked to ethics or perhaps politics. Were sanity at question (are aliens crazier than man?), then extraterrestrial life would be inherently linked to psychology. Were perversion at question (are aliens more debauched than man?), then extraterrestrial life would be inherently linked to sexuality. Rarely, however, is the subject considered in these terms. The question of extraterrestrial life is invariably posed in terms of intelligence—and what if not philosophy is concerned with intelligence? Moreover, even if aliens are not superior, even if they are not intelligent, the question of their existence or non-existence remains eminently philosophical. Why? Because hitherto there has been no empirical proof whatsoever of the existence of alien life. The entire question is so far a construction of the mind, and what if not philosophy concerns itself with the nature of mental constructions?

When the original inhabitants of Gamma killed themselves in a military apocalypse, they left behind a race of intelligent replicants who were perfectly content to take over the planet. These industrious creatures occupied cities, set up councils and legislatures, and subsumed all facilities necessary for the sustenance of biological life into a new infrastructure dedicated to the maintenance of robots: supermarkets were converted into warehouses of spare parts, new power plants were constructed, farms were replaced with battery factories and silicon manufacturers. Gradually, however, a serious problem emerged. Malfunctioning parts could be replaced without pain, power failures culminated not in the grave but in the repair shop, and yet the replicant Gammas were not immortal. Sometimes a robot suffered a severe enough injury—melting, freezing, drowning, shattering, exploding—that it was impossible to repair him. In this way death reasserted its rights, and the robots acquired the desire for self-replication. But how could they perpetuate their race into the future? For the first time in history a race had consciously to answer this question for itself. Normally species perpetuation just happens, and sometimes intelligence evolves on top of it. On Gamma, however, the situation was the reverse: intelligence existed prior to any impulse to procreate, and the robots found themselves in the unique situation of having to decide on a method of self-replication. Should the government set up research laboratories for the production of new individuals? Should market conditions be allowed to hold sway, presuming that demand for new individuals would somehow create supply? Should clusters of robots form family units to perpetuate their programmatic genealogy?

At first it may have seemed illogical for the robots to choose sex, and yet, regardless of the woes it caused earth man, sex had proven itself by evolution to be a robust method of species perpetuation. Consequently, the robot society of Gamma decided to create a series of controlled reproduction facilities called *pornodromes*. Upon entrance, a robot would be programmed to experience lust. Upon departure, he would be deprogrammed. But during his stay, he was to throw himself into a bizarre procreative act that was part fornication and part deconstruction: the robots would kiss and touch in simulation of human lovemaking, all the while removing from each other's body a small number of parts with which to fabricate a little fetal replicant. For an exophile participating in such practices, the danger was obvious: a robot might stick a screwdriver into his back or clip a vein with a pair of needle-nosed pliers. A Gamma could caress a man fondly while extracting a vital organ with vice-grips. A human heart could be soldered to an alien logic board or a kidney riveted to a memory chip in a fruitless meeting of man and machine. To circumvent such a horrible fate, Mercury de Sade donned a green bodysuit lined with fake circuits and wires. Looking very much like a human motherboard, he gained entry to the pornodrome and set out to engage a partner. Passing through dark rooms with the sterile iron ambiance of bank vaults, he eyed robots fucking in groups of two and three. Initiating a reproductive act with a girlish replicant, Mercury de Sade felt her hands running over his body: one settled on his joystick, the other probed his back for screws and bolts.

The challenge for him was to obtain pleasure while simultaneously dismantling her. However, while one of her own would only take a few key components, Mercury de Sade had to break her down entirely in order to prevent her from working underneath his circuit suit and thus fatally wounding him. As he kissed her, Mercury de Sade removed a screwdriver from his tool belt and unfastened a protective plate on the back of her metal cranium. At the same time, he felt her snipping at wires on his back using artificial fingernails sharp as scissors. Slipping his left index finger into her vagina, a vinyl pocket lined with lubricated sensors, he probed with his right hand into the circuitry in her head. Acting on a hunch, he pulled a wire from its contact. This caused a short circuit whose outward effects resembled the orgasm of an earth female: shaking, twittering, gasping and grasping. She looked up at him, eyes flashing like the lights on an ambulance, a programmer's notion of ecstasy surging up into the code that controlled her face. But just then Mercury de Sade felt her fingernail pierce his bodysuit and draw a line of blood across his back. He had little time to act. Concentrating, he jabbed a screwdriver into her right eye while thrusting between her legs. Twisting the tool, he felt her body spasm against him, then she slumped to the floor and lay there with wires poking like hair from her head.

Mercury de Sade is an aficionado of electronics stores. Or to be precise, his interest is not in electronics stores per se. Rather, he is possessed of various sexual compulsions, one of which has the secondary effect of causing him to frequent electronics shops the way other men visit X-rated video outlets. Radio Shack is not to his taste. For whatever reasons of gender—whether nature or nurture—it is men who go for the guts of gadgets, and because Radio Shack stocks so many wires and switches and relays and capacitors, the store tends both to employ and to attract the bearded human. And while there may well be electronic fetishists who engage in secret foreplay with ham radio kits in the aisles of Radio Shack, they cannot count Mercury de Sade among their members. Mercury de Sade prefers The Wiz. This store puts the wires and switches off to the back or side and thrusts forth its electronic goods in all their gleaming glory: televisions, camcorders, walkmans, computers, stereos. Radio Shack has all these things, but they're mixed in with the nuts-and-bolts stuff. The Wiz separates them, and thereby lures in the breasted human. In this lies its appeal. In much the same way as a Playboy photo spread conveys the idea of lesbianism simply by posing two girls beside one another, so too does The Wiz tickle an unnatural libidinal itch by coupling electrical devices and sexual objects. In the mind of Mercury de Sade, every device suffers the electronic equivalent of blue balls, unspent electrons backing up into its system and threatening to explode, until the female shopper makes an appearance, lusting to form a circuit with the device, to suck off the pent-up electrons and swallow them in an orgy of listening to the radio or talking on the telephone. The electricity makes the speaker vibrate and a sound wave slaps at her ear like a cum shot...

There are in fact two kinds of girls to be found at The Wiz: salesgirls, often attractive, and customers, who desire a fulfillment that can only be achieved through the acquisition of technology. In turn, customers can be further broken down into girls who can and girls who cannot afford the object of their desire. These latter reveal their vulnerability in the biting of a lip or the regretful return of a Sony Discman to the hands of a salesperson—and this vulnerability, readily apparent to the connoisseur, can be easily exploited. Is it not one of the clichés of romance that girls like to be spoiled with candy and flowers? Why not also circuits and silicon? Which kind of girl is Charlotte? Her image is fractured across a quartet of monitors at the guard station, which Mercury de Sade is able to observe by pretending to interest himself in the coaxial cable hanging nearby. Can she afford what she wants? Although her clothing—charcoal skirt, navy sweater, white shirt, argyle socks, black loafers—

defines her as a student, probably of a prep or religious school, she does not quite give the appearance of a class president, prom queen, cheerleader, or girl next door. There's almost something film noir about her, like a gun moll. She has black pearls for eyes and her hair, dyed a synthetic bronze hue reminiscent of tanning lotion, tangles about her head like the tape of a cassette disemboweled by a malfunctioning gear. Which kind of girl is she? Mercury de Sade sees that she is about to pocket a beeper, so he distracts the guard with a question about signal splitters and follows her out of the store.

There are many reasons teenagers turn to theft. It might be kleptomania—but this would itself require explanation. It might be peer pressure—perhaps in her little head Charlotte hears the Nirvana song memorializing the teen practice of bonding through petty crime: "I arrest myself/I wear a shield/I go out of my way to prove that I steal." It might be a desire to defy authority or, conversely, a desire to be caught and punished. Which kind is Charlotte? Mercury de Sade trails her into the Graybar Building on Lexington Avenue, follows her down the stairs into the underground passages leading to the subway, extracts a homemade gizmo from his pocket, points it at Charlotte, presses a button and sets off the beeper she's just stolen. She freaks. Has she been followed? Would they beep her to find her in the crowd? She pulls the beeper out and throws it down on the subway tracks. A Latino guy offers to get it for her, but she walks away without answering. He jumps down on the filthy iron tracks, kicks a Gatorade bottle out of the way, gets the beeper, follows her. After all, she's a pretty girl. Finally she takes it, mutters thanks, and stands by herself. Mercury de Sade sets the beeper off again. She takes it out and starts pushing buttons, trying to squelch the thing. "Thought you beat The Wiz, didn't you?" intrudes Mercury de Sade. She looks up at him in fear and hostility. "What're you, a guard?" He makes a smile intended to suggest complicity. "Do I look like a guard?" he asks. She takes in his casual dress and bald head. "If you're not a guard, what do you want with me?"

If the materialists of antiquity argued that a human was created from particles of universal matter, another strain of thinkers held the essentially religious belief that a human would return to the stars upon death. In the first case, a human was born of stellar material, in the second case, he returned to stellar material. According to Plato (ca 427-347 BCE), God created the universe and then made "souls equal in number to the stars and assigned each soul to a star." (*Timaeus*, 41d) However, only the good or pure souls would return to their home star after corporeal death. "He who lived well during his appointed time was to return and dwell in his native star, and there he would have a blessed and congenial existence." (*Timaeus*, 42b) For these thinkers, consequently, the question of extraterrestrial life was not "Are there inhabitants of worlds beyond earth?" but rather "How should a man live so that in death he returns to the stars?" The notion of extraterrestrial life was intertwined with that of terrestrial death—or rather, death was reconceived as a mere shedding of skin that enabled the soul to take its proper station in the heavens. If the materialist conception of alien life thus discovered a bit of the extraterrestrial within man, the idealist discovered that every man has the capacity to become extraterrestrial—by dying.

Yet another strain of thinkers, also idealist in inspiration, held that it was not the soul of man that returned to the stars. Rather, it was stars themselves that were possessed of souls. Extraterrestrial intelligence was imagined not as life *in* other worlds but rather as life *of* other worlds. Although this "psychocosmology" seems to have originated with the Pythagoreans, it was a belief that persisted into the middle ages. The early Christian theologian and scholar Origen (ca 185-254) held that when "the saints have reached the heavenly places, then they will clearly see the nature of the stars one by one, and will understand whether they are living beings or whatever else may be the case." (*De Principiis*, 2.11.7.241-4) The Jewish philosopher Maimonides (1135-1204) wrote that "The enunciation that the heavenly sphere is endowed with a soul will appear reasonable to all who sufficiently reflect on it... The circular motion of the sphere is consequently due to the action of some idea which produces this particular kind of motion; but as ideas are only possible in intellectual beings, the heavenly sphere is an intellectual being." (*Guide of the Perplexed*, II, ch. IV) That this is not one of the deliberate obfuscations embedded in the *Guide of the Perplexed* is evidenced by Maimonides' reiteration in the "Letter on Astrology": gentile philosophers, he writes, "maintain that the spheres and the stars possess souls and knowledge. All these things are true. I have already made it clear, with proofs, that all these things involve no damage to religion."

But if heavenly bodies are living beings endowed with souls, just what is a soul? In *De Anima,* Aristotle (382-322 BCE) argues that the soul is to the body as an impression is to wax. Thomas Aquinas (1225-1274) interpreted Aristotle to mean that, although the soul needed the body to think and feel, it differed because it was abstract. In this sense the relation between the soul and the body is comparable to that between a computer program and the hardware used to run it. In *The Anthropic Cosmological Principle*, John Barrow and Frank Tipler argue that the classical definition of the soul is "astonishing" in its resemblance to computer theory: "The essence of a human being is not the body but the program which controls the body; we might even identify the program which controls the body with the religious notion of a *soul,* for both are defined to be non-material entities which are the essence of a human personality. In fact, defining the soul to be a type of program has much in common with Aristotle and Aquinas' definition of the soul as 'the form of activity of the body.'" But what does this have to do with extraterrestrial life? Certainly the implications with regard to heavenly bodies—that is, if the soul is a program, the star that possesses a soul must be a fantastic computer—are farfetched, and yet the theory does point to a more plausible scenario. Many experts argue that only robots could withstand the vast distances of interstellar travel, and thus if aliens ever do come to earth, they will be robots. And what is the soul of a robot if not a computer program?

If the goal of the exercise is to use object-oriented programming techniques to create a model of an alien being, it is necessary to begin with the recognition that "being" is the more fundamental object and that "alien" functions as a property—thus an "alien being" is a being that possesses the property of alien-ness. Furthermore, "alien" is a relational property in the sense that it is only meaningful in contrast to some other property—for example, in contrast to humanity or terrestriality. In light of this, the logical way to proceed with the program is to define "being" as a very general ancestor and then, using methods of inheritance, derive objects which model not only "being with the property of alien-ness" but also other properties from which "alien-ness" may differentiate itself. The following sequence, using traditional philosophical distinctions between forms of existence, suggests itself first:

> I. Non-Being (property: lack of existence)
> II. Being (property: existence)
>> A. Inorganic (property: lack of life)
>> B. Organic (property: life)
>>> 1. Plant (properties: immobility, photosynthesis)
>>> 2. Animal (properties: mobility, consumption)
>>>> i. Man (property: reason)
>>>> ii. Alien (property: ???)

While at first pass it would appear logical to add "alien" to the sequence as a second item in the class of animals, in fact this raises a conundrum. If man is distinguished from animal by his ability to reason, what other property would serve to distinguish alien from man? Would the alien not need to possess telepathy or immortality or some other trait foreign to mankind? Furthermore, the alien is already as existent, living, mobile, and hungry as man—what if he also possesses the ability to reason? Would this not require that he be included in the class of rational beings, i.e. men? Certainly the creator of a flying saucer must be able to reason, and yet it would be absurd to identify man with alien. Therefore the sequence must be adjusted:

I. Non-Being (property: lack of existence)
II. Being (property: existence)
    A. Inorganic (property: lack of life)
    B. Organic (property: life)
        1. Plant (properties: immobility, photosynthesis)
        2. Animal (properties: mobility, consumption)
            i. Unreasoning (property: lack of rationality)
            ii. Reasoning (property: rationality)
                - alien (property: lack of terrestriality)
                - human (property: terrestriality)

However, the potential error here is that the model characterizes the alien as an existent, living, mobile, hungry, reasoning creature that distinguishes itself from man only insofar as it hails from a planet that is not earth. In other words, it equates a difference in origin with a difference in kind, and this equation is not reliable: according to this, a human born in an artificial habitat on Mars would be alien, while a purple brainfish with eyes on ten-mile stalks would be human if only it were born on earth. Ironically, the implication is that differences of origin do sustain differences of kind, but only so long as the cultures fail to meet. "Contact" between man and alien is thus not an innocent touching of civilizations but the harbinger of a destruction of differences between the two. Consequently, as it is probable that, even when men are born on Mars and aliens are born on earth, there will remain significant differences, how are these to be modeled programmatically? Perhaps genetic lineage is really the determining factor:

    I. Non-Being (property: lack of existence)
    II. Being (property: existence)
        A. Inorganic (property: lack of life)
        B. Organic (property: life)
            1. Plant (properties: immobility, photosynthesis)
            2. Animal (properties: mobility, consumption)
                i. Unreasoning (property: lack of rationality)
                ii. Reasoning (property: rationality)
                    - alien (property: lack of DNA)
                    - human (property: DNA)

To be clear, aliens may not lack the actual acid so much as they may simply belong to a different long-term sequence of it. However, genetic differentiation poses two further problems. First, to define man and alien genetically is to run the risk of promoting genocide (genetocide?) or ethnic cleansing on a cosmic scale. It is not difficult to imagine a Martian Hitler wanting to rid the universe of the soft, white, and—if aliens really are superior beings—inferior worm of a creature from earth. Second, genetic differentiation is susceptible to the same problem of convergence as mere differences of origin. Once man and alien do make contact, they will begin to crossbreed. Their genetic lineages will converge, and this will once again eradicate the characteristic distinctions between man and alien. In fact, this implies that humanity as such will not survive contact with alien beings: they will kill man through hatred, or they will absorb him through love. (However, is it really the distinction between man and alien that is difficult to maintain? Or is the distinction simply an impossible thing to program? While in the first case the result would be a convergence between the terrestrial and the extraterrestrial, in the second case the result would be a divergence between the technical and the extraterrestrial. That is, many theorists hold that aliens must be robots, for the simple reason that only mechanical entities could withstand—both physically and "mentally"—the prolonged rigors of travel through deep space. However, if a robot is by definition a programmed being, and if it is impossible to program an abiding distinction between man and alien, then an "alien robot" is an oxymoron. It cannot exist.)

The still dewy grass would soon be dried by the bright yellow sun that had just risen in the lustrous blue sky. Strange birds twittered in the treetops, greeting the dawn with an alien song the sound of a synthesizer. Mercury de Sade breathed deep, filling his lungs with the oxygen-rich air of Delta, and strolled through the orchard marveling at the cock trees. These were essentially enormous oak trees, except that their trunks were shaped like gnarled penises. It looked as though a platoon of giants had castrated themselves and left their penises sticking upright in the soil. In the stead of bark there were veins lining the shaft of each tree, and at the base were not roots but testicles which anchored the trees in the ground. At their tops the trees did not grow thinner but rather sprouted a kind of bulbous head, at the crest of which was a small slit. Often sap would leak from this slit, particularly in the spring when it would run down the tree trunks, an arboreal pre-cum. Later in the year the trees would sprout acorns, inside of which were tiny male fetuses. The shell of the acorn protected the fetus from most predators, and when it matured it reached the approximate girth of a watermelon. At this point it dropped to the ground and cracked open, revealing a developed male baby. This was how reproduction of males occurred on Delta. The right testicle was extracted from an adult and planted in fertile ground. If conditions were right, the testicle grew to become a cock tree, and then its fruit—the giant acorn—contained a bouncing baby boy.

Emerging from the orchard, Mercury de Sade found himself in a field of manicured rows stretching to the horizon. Before him a hundred acres of vaginas hung like tomatoes from green vines. The fields had been tilled and the vaginas planted in late spring. The farmer had cared for his crop all summer long: weeding, watering, spraying the vaginas with pesticides to ward off pernicious insects, spraying the vaginas with liquid Monistat to prevent yeast infections. Many an old-timer could tell of entire crops wiped out by uncontrollable rampages of yeast: the vaginas would become red and inflamed, white flour-like paste would ooze out of them, and the poor things would suffer so from itching that their vines would try to bend back in the breeze to scratch them. But the crop that stretched out in neat rows before Mercury de Sade had suffered no such calamity. These were beautiful vaginas. Some were plainly more mature than others—some vaginas had menstruated, brown blood leaking down their twisting tubers, while others were still small and green—but these differences in maturity had been cultivated to serve the variegated tastes of consumers. Some men preferred their vaginas green and firm, others ripe and red, while still others preferred them on the borderline of rot and decay. And although they were best fresh, it was not unheard-of that men sometimes even kept vaginas in the freezer, taking them out in the winter and heating them in microwaves and convection ovens.

Walking out among the rows, Mercury de Sade stooped and picked a vagina at random. In his hand it felt soft like a water balloon filled with warm water. Turning it over, he saw a small dark welt on its side. The flesh there was abnormally soft, like a bruise, and when he pushed at it with his finger a brackish fluid emerged. Taking his utility knife from a pocket, he cut the vagina open and saw the cause of the welt: small black insects had colonized the cunt's innards, consuming its substance. Perhaps this one was simply hanging too low, he thought. If they hang too low, their bottoms sit in ground water and begin to rot, allowing bugs to infiltrate. Dropping the vagina in the dirt, he walked out further among the rows admiring the blossoming lips and blooming vulvae. Stooping to pick another, he squeezed and examined it like a matron in the supermarket. It was a beautiful vagina, slightly on the green side but still firm and full. Raising it to his mouth, he bit into it, the sweet red fluid gushing into his mouth like that of a country-fresh peach. He sucked and savored its flesh, and when at last he came to its engorged clitoris, it burst like a white grape in his mouth. Excited, he then picked several of the best-looking vaginas. Licking and sucking a green one, he pushed himself into a ripe one and worked at it as though trying to core an apple... Afterward, he carried it back toward the orchard. He did not want to drop it on the ground, for fear of fertilizing the soil, so he hurled it against a tree and watched it explode in red and white fluids against the giant penis.

What does Mercury de Sade want from Charlotte? In a way, he wants what any man wants from a woman—except that he wants to be done with mankind. Really, according to the stringent requirements of his fetish, Mercury de Sade does not even want Charlotte. He wants an extraterrestrial. He wants to take a gray in his arms, stroke its cold, felt-like head, insert his manhood into a far-out orifice—but obviously this is not so easy to accomplish. Granted, every fetishist must resolve the dilemmas involved with the acquisition of his desiderata. Shoe freaks often steal. Necrophiles dig up cemeteries or break into funeral parlors. But what about exophiles? If it seems difficult to pick up a girl at The Wiz, imagine how difficult it is to pick up a gray or a Martian on earth. There are plenty of gay bars, but where are the gray bars? Is the desperate exophile condemned to go around wearing a sign that says "abduct me?" And even if he did, what alien would pick up such a pathetic human? Desire works that way. You want that which seems unattainable. Aliens want humans who aren't interested in aliens. That's why there are abductions rather than pick-ups. If somebody willingly goes with an alien, it's not an abduction, is it? There's no point in Mercury de Sade tattooing "abduct me" on the top of his bald head. It would only be a cosmic turn-off. So what's he to do? A necrophile can pay a hooker to wear pallid makeup and lie still as a corpse. The exophile could do this too— but is the morphology of alien beings not a great mystery? What does an extraterrestrial look like exactly? He could wrap a hooker in tinfoil or put antennae on her tits—but how could such cheap tricks pass for real? Fucking tinfoil, how could he possibly believe he's fucking an alien?

     Another approach might be through the mind rather than the body. What if Mercury de Sade could inculcate an alien psyche in a pretty girl? This changes the nature of his problem. The immediate goal is no longer to obtain an extraterrestrial but rather to transform a human. But what does it mean to transform a human? This is the expertise of cults: brainwashing, operant conditioning, mind control. There are negative techniques that involve deprivation: cut a person off from friends and family, deprive her of information about the outside world, withhold food and drink and sleep. Conversely, there are also positive techniques: initiate into rituals and practices, induce new beliefs, require participation in acts that bind the individual to the cult group. Although Mercury de Sade is obviously no cult—in fact, as a loner he is deeply creeped out by the group dynamics of cults—nevertheless the programmer in him feels right at home with such techniques. They are essentially algorithmic, an instruction set such as would be fed to a computer, except that in the case of brainwashing they are applied to a person. Effectively they transform the person into a robot or machine—and yet, were Mercury de Sade to brainwash Charlotte, would she not just become an alien robot? A simulation of an alien rather than a bona fide gray? And for that matter, what instruction set could even serve to make her an alien? He could train her to say, like Mork from Ork, "Nanu nanu"—but again, how could he possibly fall for such cheap tricks? Fucking a sitcom character, how could he possibly believe he's fucking a real alien?

But what is a real alien? Are aliens even real? Does the question of the reality of aliens not ultimately boil down to the first question in the philosophy textbook: What is reality? Thinking about it, Mercury de Sade decides that there is only one answer. Fucking makes reality. This could be called the Argument from Copulation: reality is connection to the outside; sex connects a person to the outside (in the form of another person); ergo sex is reality. However, if fucking really does determine reality somehow, then the reality (or unreality) of extraterrestrial beings must depend upon their sexuality. If they do not have sexual relations, they do not have reality. If they do have sexual relations, then they must no doubt exist—at least for each other. But how then could man know of their existence? The necessary conclusion is that for man to ascertain the reality of aliens, he must have intercourse with them. The tabloid press frequently reports the sexual abuse of human beings by extraterrestrial creatures. Is it not just possible that these are the true demonstrations of the reality of alien beings? And if so, why are they given such little credit? Why is it that no one takes seriously the report of a hairdresser in Anaheim who claims to have been gang-raped by Martian sex fiends? Perhaps the denial directed at these reports has this as its cause: it is not that aliens do not exist, but that sexual relations are suppressed. Ergo wherever reality depends on sexuality, the moral majority will be sure to see unreality. And vice versa: the same majority will posit the greatest reality in that entity with the least sexuality, i.e. God.

What do aliens look like? Do they have eyeballs at the end of their fingertips? Do they have fingers? To what extent does their appearance compare to that of earthlings? Such questions fall under the purview of *exomorphology,* the study of the physical form of extraterrestrial beings. Exomorphology seems to have begun with speculations about the nature of lunar beings in particular—perhaps for the obvious reason that, of the heavenly bodies, the moon is nearest to the earth and hence most promising for study. Pythagoras, Anaxagoras, and Plato all believed that there was life on the moon, but it was Aristotle (382-322 BCE) who first speculated about the morphology of lunar beings. An enthusiastic naturalist and biologist, Aristotle hypothesized that there was a class of animal corresponding to each of the four elements: earth, water, air, and fire. "Plants may be assigned to land, the aquatic animals to water, the land animals to air… The fourth class must not be sought in these regions, though there certainly ought to be some animal corresponding to the element of fire... Such a kind of animal must be sought in the moon." (*De Generatione Animalium*, III:20) Because at the time the moon's luminescence was attributed to an igneous effect, it was natural for Aristotle to conceive of lunar animals as creatures consisting of fire.

Lunar exomorphology did not advance very far past such vague correlations until the appearance of an astonishing work by the Greek biographer and moralist Plutarch (42-120). *Concerning the Face Which Appears in the Moon,* a text nearly contemporaneous to the New Testament, depicts a group of thinkers discussing the moon's habitability. Theon, a general man of letters, argues that the moon is not habitable. First, he doubts that the gravity of the moon is sufficient to prevent "men" from falling off it: there is reason to wonder "how it is that we are not forever seeing countless 'men falling headlong and lives spurned away,' tumbling off the moon, as it were, and turned head over heels." (*De Facie Quae in Orbe Lunae Apparet*, 938A) Second, he argues that the moon does not possess an atmosphere capable of supporting life: since it has nothing to protect it from the sun, "is it really likely that the men on the moon endure twelve summers every year?" (*De Facie*, 938A) Lamprias, a vaguely Platonist thinker, responds to the arguments. First, the rotation of the moon may "smooth the air" so that "there is no danger of falling and slipping off for those who stand there." (*De Facie*, 938F) Second, and most important for exomorphology, Lamprias argues that harsh lunar conditions need not prevent life from developing there. Rather, it may simply result in a different kind of life. "It is plausible that the men on the moon, if they do exist, are slight of body and capable of being nourished by whatever comes their way." (*De Facie*, 940C)

This debate expresses a fundamental tension in the history of exomorphology. Theon really argues that *manlike* beings could not survive harsh lunar conditions, and Lamprias responds that the improbability of human life is no proof against life as such. In repudiating this obvious anthropocentrism Lamprias discovers the epistemological quandary at the heart of exomorphology itself. "We have no comprehension of these beings... nor of the fact that a different place and nature and temperature are suitable to them." (*De Facie*, 940D) In other words, is it possible to describe the morphology of alien beings without human projections? Are we doomed to see no more than ourselves in extraterrestrials? Is it certain that mankind would be able to comprehend or even recognize alien life if he found it? For example, there is no agreement among biologists as to whether a virus is really a living or merely a self-replicating entity. Hence if a virus-like entity were to be encountered on Mars, would it be recognized as a form of life? Only if the discoverer *wanted* to think of it as such. Consequently, it is a rule that recognition of a life form is inseparable from a subjective element of decision. And if that is the case, if it is impossible to divest perception of an alien entity from obvious human projections, how is it possible to assert that it exists at all?

Such an inherent absurdity may well inform the parody of exomorphology by the satirical philosopher and philosophical satirist Lucian (ca 115-200). The exomorphology that emerges in his "true" story of a trip to the moon focuses rather disproportionately on scatology: "Moonmen have artificial penises, generally of ivory but, in the case of the poor, of wood... They don't urinate or defecate. They have no rectal orifice so, instead of the anus, boys offer for intercourse the hollow of the knee above the calf, since there's an opening there." (*Verae Historiae*, 1.22-24) For Lucian the fundamental premise of exomorphology—describing the nature of beings that have never been seen—is so ridiculous that the descriptions themselves ought to attain to a level of absurdity. Lucian imagines that a race of "tree people" inhabit the moon as well: "The procreation of tree people is as follows. A man's right testicle is cut off and planted in the ground. This produces a huge tree of flesh with a trunk like a penis. It has branches and leaves and, as fruit, bears eighteen-inch acorns. When ripe, these are gathered, the shells cracked open, and men are hatched from them." (*Verae Historiae*, 1.22) By pushing anthropocentrism to an extreme, Lucian arrives at a point where exomorphology appears to be nothing but the projection of human minds. It is no longer a matter of there being a bit of the extraterrestrial in man. Rather, there is nothing but man in the "extraterrestrial."

To overcome such skepticism requires a mind accustomed to speaking concretely about abstract entities—a religious mind. In this regard, in what may be the most remarkable statement of exomorphology during the middle ages, Nicholas of Cusa (1401-1464) arranges extraterrestrial beings in a spiritual hierarchy. That there are such beings he has no doubt: "none of the other regions of the stars are empty of inhabitants." (*De Docta Ignorantia*, 172) In the earthly region, moreover, aliens are arranged in a gradient of grace: "in the solar region there are inhabitants which are more solar, brilliant, illustrious, and intellectual—being even more spiritual than [those] on the moon, where [the inhabitants] are more material and more solidified... We believe this on the basis of the fiery influence of the sun and on the basis of the watery and aerial influence of the moon and the weighty material influence of the earth." Nicholas thus follows Aristotle and Plutarch in correlating alien beings to their planetary atmospheres, but he differs radically by attributing different levels of reality to them: "these intellectual solar natures are mostly in a state of actuality and scarcely in a state of potentiality; but the terrestrial [natures] are mostly in potentiality and scarcely in actuality; lunar [natures] fluctuate between [solar and terrestrial natures]." In Nicholas of Cusa, reality is made to depend not on matter but on spirit. It is not fucking that makes reality, but rather reality that must be desexualized. It is as though the lunar sodomites of Lucian so perverted exomorphology that, to redeem it, Nicholas sought to cleanse it of all sexuality, and this he could only achieve by emptying it of matter as such. After all, if aliens were composed of pure spirit, how could they possibly have erections?

Attempts to prove the reality of an *ens extramundanum* are not unique to ufologists, alien abductees, or flying saucer buffs. For centuries already theologians have struggled to formulate rationalistic proofs of the existence of an otherworldly being superior to man. Traditionally these proofs have sought to reinforce the *theologia revelata,* the "revealed" or mystic understanding of God, with a *theologia rationalis,* a "philosophical" or rationalistic apprehension of God. Because knowledge by revelation is intrinsically personal, subjective, and unverifiable, the aim of these rationalistic proofs is to demonstrate the reality of God in a manner that approaches the objective or, that being impossible, the suprapersonal. Similarly, because the quasi-mystic reports of contactees or abductees are in principle unverifiable, should not alienologists also strive to prove the existence of extraterrestrial life utilizing the techniques of rationalism? And to begin, might they not determine what is salvageable in the traditional arguments for the existence of God? That is, if the traditional arguments seek to prove the existence of an extraterrestrial deity, might the religious element not be removed and thereby leave as remainder a demonstration of extraterrestrial life?

The most fundamental of the traditional arguments—according to one philosopher, it secretly underlies every proof of God—is known as the Ontological Argument. Formulated early in the twelfth century by St Anselm, it reasons that

> God is the greatest thing it is possible to conceive
> It is greater for a thing to exist in reality than in thought
> Hence God *must* exist in reality (else He wouldn't be the greatest)

If the conclusion were not true, it would be possible to conceive of a being greater than God—a being who, possessing the greatness of existence in reality, puts to shame any divinity that merely dwells in man's thoughts. In other words, if God is perfect, He must exist, for it is illogical for a being to be both perfect and non-existent. By the same token, if alien beings are in fact more advanced than humans, their existence is guaranteed by a parallel ontological proof:

> The alien being is greater than the human
> The human being exists in reality
> Hence the alien *must* exist in reality (else he wouldn't be greater)

Plainly, however, both the divine and alien syllogisms depend on the definitions advanced in the major premises: God is more perfect and the alien more intelligent than man. How is it possible to justify, in either case, the inferiority of humankind?

In the divine proof, the first premise assumes that it is possible to know something about the nature of God—to wit, that He is exceedingly great in all things. Such an assumption is, in other contexts, questioned not only by atheists but by theologians as well. Their doctrine of the *via negativa* states that it is impossible to know anything positive about the nature of God. All descriptions of God, even those advanced in scripture, only indicate what He is not, and thus use human attributes to describe in a metaphorical fashion a being whose essence remains unknowable. By consequence, were the *via negativa* rigorously applied to the Ontological Argument, the first premise and with it the conclusion would collapse: it would be impossible to affirm that God is the greatest because it is only possible to know that which He is not (i.e. non-human, non-terrestrial, non-material, etc). In fact, the assertion that

God is the greatest thing it is possible to conceive

conceals a very subtle act of deception. Because the subject immediately implies the common conception of an omnipotent being, the predicate only seems to reconfirm it ex post facto: "an omnipotent being"—here one already thinks of a ne plus ultra—"is the greatest thing which it is possible to conceive." However, if the phrasing is inverted, it becomes clear not only that the predicate does not confirm the subject, but that there is no necessary relation whatsoever between the two:

The greatest thing it is possible to conceive is God

Is "God" a necessary conclusion? Might it not be equally possible that—while granting that greatness requires existence in reality—the greatest thing it is possible to conceive is a mutual orgasm during the collapse of a neutron star?

This objection against the first premise is also critical for the alien ontological proof. How are we to know that the alien is superior to man? Certainly it might be inferred from empirical data. To travel the universe, UFOs would require technology superior to that of man, and therefore an extraterrestrial dumber than mankind could not possibly visit earth. An alien landing in a cornfield in Wyoming would really be superior to the hicks he raped, at least technologically. However, such empirical confirmation of the superiority of aliens is inadmissible in the formulation of a rationalistic proof because it introduces an a posteriori claim into an a priori demonstration. Much as Anselm thought that the greatness of God proceeded from the very definition of Him, so too would the superiority of aliens have to be deducible from their nature—but how would this be possible? After all, "alien" can only be defined negatively, in opposition to man. What is the alien? We do not know. All we can say for certain is that he is not-man. Where does he come from? We do not know. All we can say for certain is that he hails from not-earth. What does he look like? We do not know. Here we cannot even say that his appearance is not-human, for it is entirely possible that his body would be as familiar as Gray's anatomy. How, then, would it be possible to demonstrate the alien's superiority if all that we can guarantee is his non-humanity? The only way to proceed would be to prove not that superiority flows from the essence of alien-ness, but that inferiority belongs to the very definition of humanity. If man is absolutely the basest entity alive, then any other creature in the universe would of necessity be superior to him. And this is quite simple to prove, since introspection alone ought to demonstrate to anyone the intrinsic inferiority of humankind.

Only two virginal girls survived when the spaceship piloted by their parents crashed on the moon. Then spooks from the Dark Side Pentagon transferred them to a holding area to protect them, for it was discovered that aliens from Epsilon were unusually sensitive to telekinetic transmissions. Given a direct line of sight between sender and receiver, the girls could be made to walk, talk, sing, or dance, just by impelling the thought toward them. And while this tele-kinetic ability might have appeared to be a great advantage to the earthling who envied such powers, it was a liability in present circumstances. In a telepathic culture, everyone is capable of receiving thoughts and thus there is a balance of power. Nobody seeks to harm anyone else: the intended evil can easily be picked up by its potential targets—and even if it is not, even if some harm is done, it is impossible to hide one's guilt in a society of telepaths. Justice is always served. However, when telepathically receptive creatures are surround-ed by mute, isolated, remote individuals such as earthlings, the balance of power is disrupted. The opaque individuals can victimize the telepathically sen-sitive without fear of reprisal.

Entering by himself into the holding area, Mercury de Sade found the Epsilon girls huddled together in a corner, as though trying to protect each other from his intentions. Standing directly in front of them, he sought to test their receptivity to his thoughts. He wasn't sure whether he should issue mental com-mands, which subsequently they would follow, or whether he should imagine them acting out various scenarios, thus causing them to imitate these visualiza-tions. *Stand,* he thought, directing himself toward the girls. Nothing happened, so instead he simply imagined them standing side by side in front of him. Immediately they stood up and assumed their positions in the mental tableau he had created. After experimenting for a few moments, Mercury de Sade under-stood that his telekinetic power over the girls functioned much like the anima-tor's technique of tweening: he had only to imagine key points, and the girls would automatically fill in the movements required to progress from one point to the next. In a way, he thought, this is the rationalist's dream come true. My thoughts are no longer confined to the monkey cage of the brain. They enter into actuality and become real. It's almost a weird kind of "cogito ergo sum": my personal reality does not depend on the fact that I think; rather, reality itself comes to depend on the substance of what I think. In short: I think, therefore it is.

Once he had the two girls standing, Mercury de Sade was able to get a good look at them. They were still wearing their Epsilon spacesuits, silvery jumpsuits and soft white tops that clung to their bodies like 1950s sweaters. The older girl was about fifteen by earth standards, her sister approximately twelve. Both had fine long hair the hue of caramelized sugar, and small oval faces with delicate noses and pouting lips suggestive of plums in both color and curvature. The older girl was about two inches taller than her sister, and also fuller of figure: she had sleek round breasts and gently curving hips that suggested aerodynamic streamlining, as though her body had been formed not in a uterus but a wind tunnel. Using a series of imagined projections, Mercury de Sade moved their bodies through a series of lesbian maneuvers. Soon they levitated directly up into the air, adolescent angels literally hanging on his next thought. Spinning and moving them, he floated the girls through a ballet of zero-gravity sexual positions, culminating in a yin-yang symbol, each girl's head between the legs of her sister. At this juncture he was ready for the projection of his mind to be accompanied by a projection from his body. Orgasm, however, distracted him, interrupted his thoughts, and so the girls crashed to the ground, breaking their necks. Virgin birth is the prerogative of God, he thought, looking at the damaged bodies, but virgin death even a man can accomplish. "Too bad for them I'm a man," he sighed, pulling up the zipper of his spacesuit.

At the end of the subway platform there is a booth with MTA employees in it. Trolls in blue uniforms, they manipulate a decrepit instrument panel that has not been updated since the 1950s: silver switches, black knobs, red and green lights protrude from the yellow metal surface. There is also a black-and-white monitor so old that its picture looks filtered through seawater. The monitor cuts between four different cameras positioned in the subway stop: one at the off-hours waiting area, one at the concrete stairs leading to the street, one at the token booth, and one that gives a panoramic view of the entire platform. Unless they are bored, none of the subway workers watch it. Even if they did observe some heinous crime on it, a schizo who signed himself out of Bellevue pushing a twenty-nine-year-old assistant editor in front of the train, the best they might do is call the cops. Why leave the booth and get your ass shot? This is the reigning principle: fear. Or maybe it's laziness—who wants their ass shot off because what else is there to sit on all day? Either way it's too bad, because they miss a lot, snatches of real life that they wouldn't have to watch on talk shows or "mockumentaries." For example, there in blurry black and white a Caucasian man—cotton trousers, clean Oxford shirt, shaved head that projects the appearance not of a neo-Nazi skinhead but of a hygienic surgeon—confronts an attractive girl wearing a school uniform. She looks a little young to be his girlfriend, so it's probably not a lover's quarrel. Maybe he's trying to pick her up? She looks a little young, but maybe not *so* young—after all, with that music television and everything they grow up so quickly nowadays.

Naturally the video image itself is ambiguous. Film theorists demonstrated this in the early part of the century. Splice an image of a gun into the scene—don't even dwell on it, just flash a black weapon in the midst of an otherwise static shot of a couple—and automatically the audience will have a sense of foreboding. Is the man going to hurt the woman? Splice in another shot of the escaped Bellevue schizo, and maybe they'll think the bald man is going to save the woman from the menacing loony freak. Splice in a few more shots and it would even be possible to build sympathy for the schizo: after all, he's not bad, he's just sick, so what right does the bald guy have to shoot a sick person? Such manipulation of meaning is not irrelevant because, although there is no schizo to pose a danger to Charlotte, Mercury de Sade utilizes a similar technique to transform her interpretation of the situation. Look at it from her perspective: having just shoplifted a beeper from The Wiz, how could she not presume that Mercury de Sade is a plainclothes guard or cop? Now look at it from his perspective: in order to have the opportunity to program the mind inside the girl's body, must he not remove her suspicions and fears, anything that would close her down to him? "What do I want with you?" he repeats. "Let's put it this way. When I saw you were about to pocket that beeper, I distracted the guard who was watching you. Why do you think I would do that?" She shrugs her shoulders. "I don't know," she says. "Why would you do that?" One of the reasons Mercury de Sade is an effective manipulator is that, in such moments, he doesn't even need to feign embarrassment. He's genuinely a shy enough person that he feels awkward, although at the same time he's shrewd enough to calculate the effects of flattery. "Well," he stutters, "you're an awfully pretty girl."

The silver train pulls into the station and the doors open, releasing a stream of people who flow past Charlotte and Mercury de Sade in a formation reminiscent of a flock of geese. After the doors of the train hang open for an unnaturally long moment, the conductor announces that the train is being held in the station. People roll their eyes and sigh. A lethargy like a Mexican siesta sets in. A chubby brunette in professional attire withdraws a cell phone and makes a series of monosyllabic grunts, as though there's a trained monkey on the other end of the line. "Yeah, it's me. What? I don't know. Uh-huh. Yeah. Yeah. Yeah, right. All right. I don't—no, not me. Ok. Uh-huh." As she speaks, her eye wanders out the door of the car and settles on a couple speaking on the platform. She thinks the guy is cute: his clothes are casual but professional, so she figures he probably works for an internet startup. The bald head strikes her as pretentious, but she would overlook it for a date. Suddenly she grows self-conscious of her body. She looks at her reflection in the silver wall of the subway car. She is not exactly fat, but at thirty-one she's too "broad in the beam" to get a guy like baldy out there. Is she getting a double chin? The attraction she feels is transformed in the furnace of her self-consciousness into a hot contempt. That guy doesn't want chunky paralegals, he wants girls like that little blonde—that *bottle* blonde. What a creep, picking up on schoolgirls. She starts to build a mental sorority with Charlotte, identifying with her in the hopes that she will reject the bald guy and give his ego a good kick in the cajones. "Stand clear of the closing doors," comes the conductor's voice over the loudspeaker, and as the subway jerks back into motion she watches with disappointment as the girl fails to get on the train.

Although a mere century and a half elapses between Nicholas of Cusa and René Descartes, it is this period that initiates an entirely new turn in philosophy—and hence also in exophilosophy. At first this may seem strange, since Nicholas' conception of extraterrestrial life was in fact far bolder than the evasive, ambiguous position of Descartes. However, it is precisely this retreat on the intellectual front that signifies a great advance on another: Nicholas was a thinker so deeply mired in religious times that his piety was beyond question—a fact which, ironically, granted him the speculative liberty to undertake his exophilosophical inquiries. With Descartes, however, the social background has changed: the church has suppressed Galileo and burned Giordano Bruno at the stake. The thinker has become a persona non grata, a subversive. In response, Descartes plays both sides of the fence: sometimes he gives outright lip service to the church, at other times he sends it the intellectual equivalent of a letter bomb. *I think, therefore I am* is a taunt hurled at so many centuries of religious obfuscation. Its emphasis comes to be not only ontological (I *exist*) but polemical: I *think,* assholes, so don't try to deny that I and by implication my ideas *exist*. In this respect it's comparable to the slogan chanted by gay activists: "We're here, we're queer, get used to it." I *think,* therefore I am, so get used to it.

Early in his career Descartes is enthusiastic about the prospects of the telescope for determining "whether there are animals on the moon." (Letter to Ferrier, 13 November 1629) Later, however, it is not technology that aids but rather theology that ensnares exophilosophy. Writing three years before his death, Descartes asserts that "I do not see why the mystery of the Incarnation and all the other advantages which God bestowed on man preclude that He may have granted an infinity of other very great advantages upon an infinity of other creatures. And though I do not thereby infer that there are intelligent creatures on the stars or anywhere else, I also do not see that there is any reason to prove that there are not." (Letter to Chanut, 6 June 1647) Why was the Incarnation, the manifestation of God in the human form of Christ, inimical to the conception of extraterrestrial life? Because it seemed to make a mockery of Christ's sacrifice. If there are rational, intelligent beings in other worlds, why would man be the only creature God would care to redeem? Conversely, if extraterrestrials need to be redeemed, would Christ be condemned to die on the cross repeatedly, in world after world, year after year? It was inconceivable that Christ would be subject to such torture, and yet really there was only one other alternative: a Martian messiah, a Saturnian savior, a Jovian Jesus on the cross...

Rather than engage the point directly, Descartes prudently considers the more general question of the purpose of man in God's creation. If in other worlds there are other beings upon whom God has bestowed various advantages, need that lessen the significance of man in the eyes of God? "Indeed the advantages which all the intelligent creatures of an indefinite world may possess are of this kind: they do not diminish those that we possess." (Letter to Chanut, 6 June 1647) By way of proof, he adduces three arguments. First, man possesses such "advantages" as virtue, knowledge, health. If an extraterrestrial also possesses virtue, does that reduce man's virtue? Second, Descartes alludes to the fact that, according to scripture, man already shares creation with an extraterrestrial creature—the angel. And if angels, which are more perfect than men, do not lessen the significance of humanity in God's eyes, why must other aliens? Third, Descartes draws an analogy with astronomy: though the stars are larger than earth, this doesn't diminish the planet in our estimate, so even if aliens are smarter than man, why should this diminish him in God's estimate? On the surface, it would thus appear that Descartes strives to remain within the proper bounds set by theology. But in this case is it not perhaps warranted to discover within this solicitude a secret willfulness, a refusal to concede what is really the point? For in the final analysis, the thrust of Descartes' entire argument amounts to this: if in the universe there are other beings, perhaps even a supreme being, it is still man—the thinking man—that remains most important. So get used to it.

Everything is black as the void before birth until I fix the circuit breaker. The computers come back on and the clocks all blink 12:00 over and over, as though there are only two times: midnight and midday. In fact, my own thoughts are like this: the midnight of sex and the high noon of philosophy. Like a broken clock I don't know any of the hours in-between. And weirdly, much as the actual numbers on the clock are the same for both times, somehow sex and philosophy fuse in my mind—also in my body. I do not experience the mind-body dichotomy. I think like a nymphomaniac and I fuck like a syllogism. Exophilia and exophilosophy are the physical and mental expressions of the same fetish. At root, I'm not sure that there isn't something profoundly right about this. After all, "Greek" refers not only to the birthplace of philosophy but to a "perversion" of sexuality. In Plato's *Symposium* sodomy is portrayed as the physical complement of philosophy itself. The argument is that there are two ways of making oneself immortal: one has either children of the body (real children, babies with green eyes and diapers) or children of the mind (ideas, poems, artworks). In consequence, those who have children of the mind take their physical pleasures in a way that is non-reproductive, as in sodomy. (Implicitly, those who have children of the body take their mental pleasures in a way that is non-reproductive—in other words, they have the cognitive equivalent of anal sex: thoughts that fail to become "memes" because they are stillborn in the sphincters of the intellect.) It follows, therefore, that Greek sex and Greek thought are of a pair—the *philos* and the *sophos* that make up philosophy itself.

Although I think this goes a long way toward demonstrating that the mind-body dichotomy is an illusory problem, it does leave open the question of immortality. According to the argument, the philosopher (poet, artist, etc.) has the potential to become immortal through his works. It was natural for Plato to believe this, since the concept of eternity was not yet compromised by scientific knowledge. Today, however, we know that the earth and sun have predictable life spans that fall far short of eternity. What kind of longevity can be attributed to a mere book when it is certain that the sun is a fat man exhausting itself in the cosmic marathon? The inescapable conclusion is that the creative work has to be capable of exiting at least the solar system. Its longevity is directly proportional to its success in communicating with beings beyond earth. Conversely, I wonder if the superior intelligence of extraterrestrials isn't related to this. If a book gains in longevity by being extraterrestrial, then perhaps the extraterrestrial gains in intelligence by being exposed to such "classic" books. If shitty ideas and books and artworks never make it beyond their solar system of origin, intergalactic space becomes an elite library or museum. The extraterrestrial being is constantly exposed to the creations of the greatest minds in the universe, and it is only when he approaches a backwater planet like earth that he is subject to the detritus of provincials such as man. This already happens in miniature on earth: those living in major cities have access to great art, and it is when they venture out into the provinces that they are exposed to the crappy paintings sold as art in shopping malls. Why shouldn't the same be true in space?

If all of this is true, however, it follows that extraterrestrials should be not only beings of superior intelligence—"philosophers," as it were—but also sodomites. If their minds are the cosmic equivalent of Greek, then so should their bodies be fond of the "Greek" passions. In this respect, it would stand to reason that the reports in the *Weekly World News* and other supermarket tabloids of women being raped and impregnated by aliens must be false—not because aliens fail to come to earth, not because they fail to rape humans, but because wisdom demands that they fuck earthlings in the ass. I suppose it is possible that women are in fact raped but fail to perceive that it is not their cunt but their ass that has been violated. Therefore they presume they are pregnant, perhaps they even experience phantom pregnancies, when in reality the semen of extraterrestrials has nestled itself inside their anus. Then again, it should not be ruled out that the assholes of human beings are capable of being impregnated by the sperm of alien beings. Who knows? There may be an acid in the ejaculate of Martians that eats its way through the intestinal lining in order to wiggle into the human uterus and glom onto an egg. On the other hand, it also occurs to me that, if aliens are in fact sodomites, they must be exclusively "tops" or "dominants," since there are never reports that a man was abducted by an alien being—who subsequently forced the man to fuck it in the organ of excretion (whatever that may be in the Martian anatomy). It is always the human being who is getting poked by the alien, and thus one is forced to conclude that aliens are like queers who pride themselves on their manliness. "I'm not your bitch," spits the Martian to the man who would embugger him.

Following a guide rope down the incline leading from the spaceship to the customs area, Mercury de Sade prepared for the inspection. On Zeta a passport was not necessary. Photo identification was useless. Documentation in the normal sense was obsolete. To pass through customs it was necessary to submit to a process indistinguishable, to an earthling, from casual sex—or from something more extreme than casual sex, since it came at the hands of a weird being shrouded in utter darkness. Perhaps it was more like rape—but then again, Mercury de Sade being an exophile, it was in principle impossible for an alien to rape him. Giving himself over to the palpitations of sexual organs reaching out from space-like blackness, Mercury de Sade took the encounter for what it was: a perfunctory identity check. If he could not actually see the organs, could not determine their color or gender, he could still detect the relative disinterest with which they touched him. These were aliens doing a job. They were doing to him what they did to the previous traveler, and what they would do to the traveler after that. They were not taking pleasure from him, nor trying to give him pleasure. Instead, they were simply utilizing sex as a means of obtaining the same information earthlings obtain from the barcode on a passport. They were scanning him with sex.

　　When the sun of Zeta exploded, eyes became useless. There was no longer any need for an organ that gathered light rays, and yet the organism itself retained a basic need to gather information. As one sense faded into obsolescence, another had to arise in its place. On Zeta, the new sense was sex. In a darkened world, touch gains dramatically in importance, and what is sex but an extreme form of touch? Or to put it another way, what is the organ most sensitive to touch? The genital organ. In this respect it is but a short step from the sensual pleasure of a genital to the sensory input of a finger. When the inhabitants of Zeta lost their sight, their sex rose to fill the void. Naturally this had profound social consequences. Everything that spoke to the eye had to be replaced by something that touched on a genital. Various forms of photo ID gave way to analytical handjobs. Paintings and sculptures gave way to static orgies ensconced in museums. All forms of knowledge acquisition had to be transmuted into fornication. A marine biologist could not merely observe the alien equivalent of a dolphin: he now had to enter into the water and embrace it. A doctor could not merely inspect a rash or a wound in order to decide on a cure: he now had to lick it, kiss it, rub himself on it like a dog on a chair leg. Of necessity, veterinarians became zoophiles and pediatricians became pederasts.

　　Desirous of a sexual experience less perfunctory than the customs inspection, Mercury de Sade remained on Zeta until he was able to cultivate a relationship with a local. He was careful to pursue one who was articulate enough to explain—or at least try to explain, since it was essentially describing color to a blind man—what she perceived when fucking him. Finally they compared notes. For Mercury de Sade, the encounter had been weirdly epistemological. It was like having sex with a mind reader, or a psychologist whose intent was not to enjoy herself but to discover the root of his sexual pathologies. She seemed not just to have sex but to gather data. He felt as though his semen were being sent to a laboratory for analysis. Pleasure had been invaded by information. Even in utter darkness, it was like fucking with eyes open and lights on. For the Zeta, however, it was the opposite. She felt that Mercury de Sade lacked a dimension. Whereas the important thing for him was simply to take pleasure, for her it was to take pleasure in understanding. Fucking him was, she said, like trying to have a conversation with someone deeply self-involved. "When we Zetas have sex," she explained, "it's like knowing the other person entirely. It's a long, raw, open discussion, a sharing of secrets, a spiritual communion as well as a physical process." Mercury de Sade thought for a moment. "But the senses lie," he said. "If sex is perception, you can't separate it from deception."

Leaving the subway station with Mercury de Sade, Charlotte imagines her therapist giving an interview on the evening news. She likes to think of him as a "talking head," not only because he has an opinion on everything but because the image deprives him of any body parts that could do her harm. In her mind's eye she sees him inhabiting a world of monitors and screens, a super ego achieving ubiquity through broadcast television. Anchorperson: Why would Charlotte allow herself to go off with a bald-headed stranger? Talking head: Charlotte feels compromised by the fact that Mercury de Sade witnessed her theft of a beeper from The Wiz. Is it not humiliating to display one's kleptomania to a stranger? However, once Mercury de Sade confesses his own complicity in her crime (having, that is, distracted the security guard), her sense of compromise is transformed. Added to it is a sense of obligation: because he performed a favor for her, she is now indebted to him. Although this obligation could also give rise to wariness—why would a stranger perform a favor for her?—any suspicion is dampened by Mercury de Sade's insinuation that his interests are romantic. Naturally this flatters her. She assesses him no longer from the vantage point of the prey but rather from that of the prize. This gives her a certain sense of power: her disadvantage turns to advantage by means of her femininity. She notes his boyish mouth, wet eyes, his apparent sensitivity, and her power assumes a benign, intrigued aspect. The impulsiveness of hormones gives energy to this psychological vector, and the result is recklessness.

Question: but what about that paranoia that causes Charlotte to shower in her underwear? How could she respond to a man whose attraction to her follows the laws of fate dictated by the Bell curve of her breast? Talking head: here it is necessary to understand the psychology of a girl who has been violated. Her relation with her body is as tangled as her legs in a sheet during a nightmare. On one hand, she recognizes that her body can serve as a source of power. On the other hand, precisely because her body is desirable, she remains aware of the potential that she might be brutally dispossessed of it. For this reason she acquires the wary attitude of the society lady who doesn't wear her jewelry in public. Why exhibit your pearls if some punk is just going to rip them off your neck? Furthermore, because the body founds relations of gender, Charlotte's relation with her body extends to her relation with men. On one hand, she has the romantic interests natural for a girl her age. Pictures of the popular film actor Johnny Depp are taped to the wall beside her bed, and she enjoys the racier parts of *Cosmopolitan* magazine. On the other hand, her behavior also expresses a hostility toward the opposite sex. Since she is in no way a materially deprived child—her father is the chief executive of an international telecommunications company—to steal that which she can plainly afford suggests that the psychological function of theft is not to acquire things but rather to strike at someone or something. In her case, the target is not the Wiz but her father, insofar as secretly she desires to get caught and thereby shame him.

Futhermore, this psychology does not exist in isolation. It must be placed against the background of a society in which everything happens with increasing rapidity. Social life comes to follow the mathematical law developed for silicon chips: exponential increases of velocity are achieved in ever briefer periods of time. Life plummets headlong into the wind tunnels of bandwidth. Kids like Charlotte grow up with a rapidity that astounds their parents—though note that "grow up" is usually associated with the acquisition of sexual knowledge. It is not a matter of kids becoming engineers at the age of fourteen. It's a matter of them becoming libertines. In the past, grown men have been imprisoned simply for writing of the things that teenagers now know from firsthand. Certainly this is true of Charlotte, although it would be wrong to paint her as a libertine. For Charlotte, sex is basically atonal, a chore like washing dishes or cleaning a room. Romance, however, retains its girlish fervor, since it has not been flattened for her the way sex has. No one has ever forced her to have romance before. And really this is why she allows herself to leave the subway platform with Mercury de Sade. Some girls sleep with a guy after a first date, thus accelerating from romance to sexuality, but for Charlotte it's the reverse: love at first sight appeals to her because it accelerates from sexuality to romance. Or at least she hopes it does.

An esoteric question lying somewhere between theology and epistemology—to wit, if God revealed a new idea to a man, would he be able to explain it to another?—leads Locke to an analogous question: could a human being with five senses understand the ideas of an alien being with six? "And supposing God should discover to any one, supernaturally, a species of creatures inhabiting, for example, Jupiter or Saturn, (for that it is possible there may be such, nobody can deny,) which had six senses; and imprint on his mind the ideas conveyed to theirs by that sixth sense: he could no more, by words, produce in the minds of other men those ideas imprinted by that sixth sense, than one of us could convey the idea of any color, by the sound of words, into a man who, having the other four senses perfect, had always totally wanted the fifth, of seeing." (*Essay on Human Understanding*, IV.iii.23) It is therefore Locke's innovation to introduce a question of profound general importance in exophilosophy: is it possible for man and alien to communicate? This is not only a technical question—one which today involves issues of interstellar distance and maximum transmission rates (defined by the speed of light) for information—but a philosophical problem of the highest order. It leads away from theology straight into the fundamentals of epistemology and language.

Locke's primary assumption is that all ideas derive from experience. There is nothing in the mind that was not first in the senses. However, this seemingly common-sensical assertion is not without its difficulties. What if two men do not possess the same senses? For example, is it possible to explain color to a blind man? "Red is an aggressive color, angry, the color of blood, the sun, the Nazi flag." Conversely, an exactly opposite description is equally descriptive. "Red is the color of love, the color of a strawberry, a rose, a valentine, a woman's lips." What is a blind man to think of a color that is part fascist and part passion? The necessary conclusion is that it is impossible to convey literally the information of a given sense to a person who lacks that sense. If this is true, however, does it not only lead to further difficulties? For example, is it not absurd to assert that two men ever really possess the *same* senses? One always perceives differently than another, so that even if quantitatively two men possess the same number of senses, qualitatively they still possess essentially different senses. In red one sees spilt blood, the other rouged lips. Furthermore, to the extent that higher order or "complex" ideas are amalgamations of lower order or "simple" ideas, differences that occur in sensation flow through to create differences in conception. Consequently, it may not only be red that we perceive differently: it may also be God, or knowledge, or life, or other higher order abstractions. And if we understand these differently, can we really communicate?

In short, though Locke clearly believes in the plausibility of extraterrestrial life, he inadvertently furnishes a powerful argument against communicating with it. All knowledge derives from experience; aliens perceive unknown worlds with unknown senses; is it not likely that man and alien will fail to understand one another? Suppose, for instance, that an alien lacks a key human sense—sight, as in the conjecture of the blind man—and in its stead possesses a sense entirely inhuman, such as receptivity to magnetic fields. Immediately huge domains of experience become incommunicable: the alien does not know the fascination of sunlight shimmering on water, but the human does not know the splendor of strong magnetic fields butting into each other like sumo wrestlers. Perhaps this alone would not be such a hindrance to communication, but potentially devastating effects emerge as these sensory differences are reinforced as conceptual ones. For example, the human conception of "understanding" is easily reverse-engineered into simple ideas based on vision: insight, viewpoint, looking into a matter, seeing eye to eye, seeing what something means, "I see." Lacking sight, the alien will have no human understanding of "understanding," and owing to its magnetic sense it may well possess a conception more like "mutual attraction" or "alignment of poles." Where the man sees or fails to see, the alien is attracted or repulsed.

To the casual observer, Mercury de Sade did not give the impression of a fashion statement. He favored cotton trousers, standard issue from Banana Republic or the Gap. He liked oxford shirts, button-downs, generally blue, white, or occasionally plaid. If the weather demanded it, he would wear crewneck sweaters—usually black, gray, or dark green. For footwear he preferred bulky black shoes, especially old-fashioned styles such as wingtips. These outfits were basically straight from the advertisements of the day and were thus not particularly remarkable. The body beneath these clothes was fit, broad-shouldered, tall. If Mercury de Sade had cared for athletics, he would have been barrel-chested, even a football player, but since his concerns lay elsewhere, he had the body of a solid but not burly man. In this too, his appearance was unremarkable. In fact, the only irregularity in his appearance was his bald head, which he had begun shaving in his early twenties. Rather than give him the look of a skinhead, a cancer patient, or a holocaust survivor, this gave him a certain cleanly air. However, it was not hygiene that inspired Mercury de Sade to shave his head. Really he had been deeply affected by popular depictions of extraterrestrial beings, in which they were never shown with such amenities as hair and fingernails. Consequently, Mercury de Sade came to conceive of these as symbols and expressions of a uniquely terrestrial anatomy, and if he trimmed his nails and shaved his hair it was to disavow the humanity that grew like a mildew on his body.

Mercury de Sade floated on a pleasure buoy near the shore of a bright green lake. The Tahiti of the cosmos, Eta was known for its tropical climate, limpid oceans, and easy-going natives. Though human in anatomy, the inhabitants of Eta were kaleidoscopic in color: skin the midnight purple of blueberries, pinkish eyes with black pupils, and hair a subtle silver, owing to certain sparkling metals in the local diet. The Eta girls splashing and swimming near him were purple counterparts of their pubescent cousins on earth: lithe bodies with the sleek muscles of deer, breasts lying on their chests like two halves of a pink grapefruit. Slipping off the buoy into the carbonated water of the lake, Mercury de Sade paddled underwater to where they were playing. In the peppermint green of the water he could see the motion of a rump, a bare knee flash up into view and then disappear, a purple hand tug at the top of a bathing suit not properly filled out by breasts the size of a scoop of ice cream. He surfaced for air amidst an archipelago of pretty heads that laughed at his sudden appearance. The natives of Eta were invariably trusting of strangers, and for good reason: there was no robbery, because an Eta would give someone whatever he asked for, and there was no rape, because a girl would give a man whatever he asked for.

Paddling back to his pleasure buoy, Mercury de Sade removed a small bottle of pills from his kit and inserted half a dozen into his mouth, where he held them between cheek and gum. Keeping his mouth tightly closed against the water, he swam back to the girls. In turn, he kissed each one and used his tongue to push a pill into her mouth. They continued to play for a few moments, tossing a glittering ball back and forth, until the pill began to make itself felt. One of the girls frowned and vomited a bit of ochre fluid. Mercury de Sade stroked the back of her head with one hand whilst pushing another girl down under the water, directing her to nibble like a little fish at his scrotum. He pushed his erection into the rectum of another girl, but was violently expelled by a stream of amber diarrhea. Soon every girl was puking and shitting into the effervescent green water, and Mercury de Sade went from each to each inserting himself into a vagina, an ass, a mouth. The entire lake bubbled with excrement and vomit, the girls convulsing in the middle of it, some caught in the heaving motions of expulsion, others attaining climax over and over again. Mercury de Sade himself had begun to feel the effects of the pill, except that in him it produced not sickness but synesthesia. His entire circuit board of sensation had been crosswired. He could hear diarrhea against his skin and taste urine in his nose. Just looking at the girls flopping about in the brackish water caused a distinct excitement in his penis, and conversely when he would insert himself into a snug little orifice his eyeballs would tingle with distinctly genital pleasure.

Mercury de Sade imagined that the girls must experience the same cross-wiring. Did they vomit from their cunts and orgasm in their throats? Shit from their mouths and tingle in their intestines? He could only assume that they did, but he had little time to think about it. He had himself begun to orgasm, spewing heavy cream into the defiled green waters. Three of the girls hurled him in the air in "for he's the jolly good fellow" fashion. Each time his body reached the top of an arc, he spurt gobs of white semen into the air like tracer bullets. The girls thrashed about in the water, vomiting and vying with each other to catch the flying gusts of sperm in their mouths, which felt as though it were being shot into their rectums. Before long the pill itself climaxed inside all of them simultaneously. There was a jumble of arms and shit and faces and genitalia and vomit and the synesthesia reached transpersonal proportions. Mercury de Sade felt himself puking from his fingertips as a girl climaxed in his asshole. He felt himself shitting semen and crying tears of urine and getting fucked in the vagina by a penis attached to his ear, so that each thrust resounded like the crack of a wet towel. He and the girls had become a single throbbing mass of fuck and excrement floating in the bubbling green waters of an extraterrestrial lake. Their pains were his, his pleasures were theirs, and every fluid traversed them equally in a single tube of flesh that could have been intestine or esophagus or vagina on the inside but only cock on the out.

A regular camera captures the scene before it. From the street, a camera would show the window of a Starbucks espresso bar, the reflections in that window, and, depending on lighting conditions, the two people sitting at the counter inside: a blond girl wearing a skirt and sweater, and a guy wearing cotton trousers, a blue shirt, and a Los Angeles Kings baseball hat. But what if a camera could capture the images in a person's mind? What collage would ensue from the intersection of images in the minds of Charlotte and Mercury de Sade? She is aware of the reflection of her own face in the window. She looks at it with the scrutiny of an auto mechanic. Is her lipstick crisp? Is the slight pimple on her forehead covered without being obvious? Does he find her pretty? For his part, he is not at all aware of his own reflection, in spite of the fact that he has to look through his own face to see anything outside. He is aware of her, a bunny rabbit beside him, but he directs his gaze to the skyscraper across the street. "It's really an arrogant building," he says, motioning with his head to the Modernist structure. "Why?" she asks. "Look at how it refuses to blend in with its environment," he explains. "It stands there like an arrogant glass prick in the midst of these marble buildings." She looks at the tower and has to agree. It's glass but it's not fragile. "Well," she says, "that's my dad." Mercury de Sade raises an eyebrow. "He designed it?" Charlotte shakes her head. "No, but he paid for it."

Ironically, the lover and the manipulator want the same thing: to be bound together with the object of their affections. Or maybe it's not exactly the same. What the lover has in mind is to be united with the object of love in a mutual osmosis. It's the old dream "to be two souls as one"—to think the same thoughts, to feel the same feelings. The manipulator wants this too, except that it's his thoughts and his feelings that are to be "shared" by the object of his attentions. In the lover's dream, there is a balance of power. Neither party reigns over the other because their interests are identical. Conversely, in the manipulator's psychodrama, his interests are to become the interests of his subject— which is to say that their interests are not identical at all, since the interest of the manipulator is for himself while the interest of his victim is for the manipulator. The tricky thing, naturally, is to keep these separate. While the one-sided bond of manipulation rarely slips over into the mutuality of love, the opposite often occurs: love degrades into manipulation. In fact, much as a spy might go under-cover in order to gain access to confidential information, so too can the manip-ulator pose as a lover in order to gain access to the ties that bind. It makes his job much easier, doesn't it? Rather than do the active work of binding, he has only to incite her desires to bind. That's how this crazy idea came about. Mercury de Sade spoke about how her shoplifting binds them, how criminal complicity becomes romantic entanglement. It's crazy, but young girls are apt to be influenced by such talk. Bonnie and Clyde, you know. It was Charlotte's idea. "Ready to go up?"

No stranger to the guards at the front desk of the skyscraper, Charlotte leads Mercury de Sade into the sleek silver elevators. When the doors open, a corporate ghost town presents itself: empty desks, pictures of wives and children, a cup of cold coffee with red lipstick stains, a computer monitor left on for the night. "Wait here," she warns, ducking into her father's office. "Ok, coast's clear." They enter the sanctum sanctorum. Across from the door is a handsome wooden desk with a computer. To one side is a wall of windows looking out on the city: in the fading sunset distant lights blink on like bulbs on an instrument panel. To the other side is a wall of electronic equipment: computers, video projection devices, a satellite tracking system. "What should we take?" Charlotte asks. They don't really have a plan. Or rather, since their tacit plan is to bond, they hadn't thought of anything in particular to steal. Seating himself at her father's computer, Mercury de Sade scans it for anything interesting. "Why don't you keep a lookout?" he suggests. He skims through financial spreadsheets, internal memoranda, logs of email. Accessing a remote server he discovers a directory named "SATDATA" which contains positions, times, and access codes for a series of telecommunications satellites. Rummaging in the desk, he finds a box of blank Zip cartridges and inserts one into the computer. "Someone's coming," Charlotte hisses. In the remote arctic of his programmer's mind, the information sounds distant and abstract. He is reticent to abandon the data he has found. "Quick, we've got to hide," she says, pulling at his arm. At the last moment he drags SATDATA to the Zip and leaves it copying as they dash to conceal themselves.

The individual as a monad that mirrors the universe—the *characteristica universalis* or universal language that would enable all intelligent beings, terrestrial or otherwise, to communicate—the plurality of worlds, full of "compossibles" and "incompossibles"—the stuff of exophilosophy so saturates the thought of Leibniz that his actual remarks about extraterrestrial life seem circumstantial in comparison. In discussing the potential impact on theology of the discovery of lunar life, he writes: "If somebody else came from the moon by means of some extraordinary machine... we might grant him citizenship and all its rights with the title of man, though he were a complete stranger to our globe; but if he asked for baptism and wished to be accepted as a proselyte of our law, I believe you would see great disputes arise among the theologians." (*New Essays on the Understanding*, §22) Leibniz imagines the great dispute from a Catholic viewpoint: "Several would no doubt maintain that the rational animals of that country not being of the race of Adam have no share in the redemption of Jesus Christ; but others would say perhaps that we do not know enough about where Adam has always been or what has happened to all his posterity, there having been theologians who believe that the moon was the place of Paradise." Finally, he suggests that Catholics would baptize the lunatics, though without thereby allowing them to become priests. That Leibniz is thus able to treat with levity a subject that all but muted Descartes indicates the gradual deflation of the church, which had left off terrorizing intellectuals, witches, and Jews in order to bludgeon the natives of the New World instead. Certainly Leibniz's parody acknowledges this. What would the church do with the inhabitants of a *really* new world? Homogenize them. Make them join the "flock."

  Ironically, in spite of the originality and diversity of his intellect, Leibniz did follow the party line on most questions of theology. In fact, it may have been precisely this combination of creativity and credibility that enabled him to advance one of the most eccentric defenses of Christian dogma in the history of thought. The dilemma involves the responsibility of God for a morally ambivalent universe. God is good, says the church—but if God created the universe and everything in it, and if there is evil in the universe, does it not stand to reason that God is evil or at least as malicious as He is jealous? To counter this argument, Leibniz invokes the possibility of extraterrestrial life. He begins by citing what has since come to be known as the Large Numbers Hypothesis, i.e. the theory that there are so many stars that at least a few of them must be inhabited: "Today," he writes, "whatever bounds are given or not given to the universe, it must be acknowledged that there is an infinite number of globes, as great and as greater than ours, which have as much right as it to hold rational inhabitants, though it follows not at all that they are human." (*Theodicy*, §19) However, while most proponents of the Large Numbers Hypothesis would simply assert that the inhabitants of these other worlds are non-human, Leibniz makes the additional theological claim that these aliens would not necessarily be, like man, damned. "It may be that all suns are peopled only by blessed creatures," he writes, "and nothing constrains us to think that many are damned, for few instances of few samples suffice to show the advantage which good extracts from evil." This argumentation is clever, insofar as it brushes over a questionable premise (the population density of the universe) with an accurate point of logic (the illegitimacy of inferring a universal conclusion—the damnation of being—from a statistically small number of known cases or, as Leibniz puts it, "a few instances of a few samples").

In other words, just because human life is miserable does not mean that extraterrestrial life is miserable too. In fact, Leibniz insinuates that extraterrestriality is practically equivalent to beatitude. Why? Because it implies that the universe is not full of evil, as might be thought based on the sample of humanity. Consequently, if the universe is full of good—full of beatific Martians who lead lives beyond evil, sin, and discontent—then two conclusions must ensue. First, it is not God but man who is evil, man who creates a lake of malignancy in an otherwise praiseworthy cosmos. Second, because the universe is—with one notable exception—full of goodness, it follows that its creator must therefore be good as well. While certainly this attempt to reinforce theology with exophilosophy is tenuous, it shows that Leibniz did not, as is often claimed, conceive this as the best of all possible worlds. Rather, this is the worst of all possible worlds in the best of all universes. And in this respect, might he not have been right? Certainly popular mythology portrays extraterrestrial life as more intelligent, virtuous, and peace-loving than man. Might it not be that no alien has made official contact with humanity for the obvious reason that, in comparison, we are nothing but drunken slobs, ignorant bigots, self-satisfied idiots, wretched mortals? "Take me to your leader" may also mean "protect me from your average man." We worry about making contact with aliens—but ought we not worry about the first impression we make as well?

The myth takes the form of a low-budget sci-fi movie in which aliens land in a flying saucer shaped suspiciously like a hubcap and announce to earthlings: "Take me to your leader." The locals oblige by taking the aliens to the White House, but is the President really *the* leader? Who has the authority to represent all of earth to an extraterrestrial culture? Mercury de Sade obliged Ninfa VII to profane the Microsoft Corporation—"Fuck Windows! Shit on Word!"—while he ejaculated in her face and formulated a little parable: Aliens once landed on earth, and it so happened that their first contact was with a little boy. "Take me to your leader," they said, and the boy promptly took them to his father. After making certain inquiries, the aliens decided that the father was not the true leader of all mankind, so they boarded their UFO and flew to a different part of earth. This time their first contact was with a working man. "Take me to your leader," they said, and the working man promptly took them to his employer. After making certain inquiries, the aliens decided that the employer was not the true leader of all mankind, so they boarded their UFO and flew to a different part of earth. This time their first contact was with a religious man. "Take me to your leader," they said, and the religious man promptly took them to his clergyman. After making certain inquiries, the aliens decided that the clergyman was not the true leader of all mankind, but rather than board their UFO they asked the clergyman to take them to *his* leader. In response, the clergyman tried to explain to them about God, and when the aliens asked to speak to Him, the clergyman showed them how to pray. The aliens perceived this as local custom, similar to kneeling or bowing before a king, so they assumed positions of prayer and began to tell God their message: "We have come to enslave your people. If you do not respond to our terms within three earth days, we will annihilate your planet with our cosmic death ray..."

Mercury de Sade and Ninfa VIII waited at the airlock. Soon there was a swoosh-ing sound and a feeling of falling backwards through an air vent. The airlock slid open, and on the other side stood the rustler in anonymous protective cloth-ing. He conducted the two through gray metal corridors with iron grates on the floors to the Theta snake pit. Off to one side was a separate room that gave the appearance of an intensive care unit. Mercury de Sade gestured for Ninfa VIII to wait for him in the room, and she settled herself obediently on a gurney with white fiber sheets. Mercury de Sade completed a transaction with the rustler, who suggested that he have a look at a Theta snake before proceeding. Opening a large metal door reminiscent of a bank vault, the rustler slipped out of the room for a few moments and then returned with a Theta snake curling around his arms. It had roughly the appearance of a vacuum hose, and its dark red body was segmented like an earthworm. "It's a brain living in the body of a snake," the rustler said affectionately. He went on to explain that, in the Theta snakes, the brains are not concentrated in a single locus but are rather distributed throughout the creature's body. This made it a long, thin, tube-like creature remarkably difficult to kill: to chop off a part of it was not to amputate a vital organ but rather to cause the creature to split into two independent, fully func-tional units.

"It's like being fucked by pure brain substance," the rustler said. "You know how when you take peyote everything looks like it's a plant? Being fucked by a Theta snake is the same thing. Everything starts to look like it's made out of neural tissue: toaster ovens turn to gray matter, your shoes become cytoplasm, your fingers look like brain stems waving in the air... It's a real trip, man." Mercury de Sade refused a local anesthetic and directed the rustler to begin insertion. At first he felt as though he were being fisted without lubrica-tion: he was certain his rectum was being torn apart, and in spite of the pain he wondered in the back of his mind if he'd have to get a colostomy afterward. Soon, however, the snake wiggled its way further inside, and the sharp toothache pain became a dull but almost pleasant sensation, the ache of a tired muscle. It seemed to have filled up every nook and cranny of his inside—not just his anus or his intestine, but his arms and legs, his forehead, his fingertips, his toes. He wasn't even sure anymore which was the greater part of him—man or snake.

Mercury de Sade had arranged beforehand to be locked in the side room with Ninfa VIII, so the rustler guided him to the chamber and sealed the door. His idea was that the orgiastic sensation of Theta snake invagination would be augmented and amplified by fucking the ninfa simultaneously. Once in the room, however, Mercury de Sade found himself in a bizarre mental state. Though he felt lucid and had been prepared for the drug-like effects the snake would inspire, seeing Ninfa VIII transformed into a fuck doll made of brain tissue was still disarming. He tried to remember her hair, her complexion, her body, but what he saw before him was zombie-like. It smiled at him, but there was something obscene about the way it curled its lips, as though someone had stuck a hand inside several pleats of a cadaver's brain in order to perform a gruesome puppet show. To focus, he ran his hands over the ninfa's breasts, which were firm and round as a pair of occipital lobes in a brassiere. He felt a stir of excitement and leaned over to kiss the girl full on the central sulcus. Against his lips it was warm and salty, reminding him of miniature hot dogs. He contemplated them for a moment, then was surprised when something pushed back into his mouth. Was it a tongue or a hippocampus? He felt a sudden upsurge of excitement and pushed the pretty brain back onto the gurney, which seemed to be made of a pasta-like organic substance. He pulled out his penis, consciously avoiding looking at it for fear it would now be his corpus callosum, and pushed it into the ninfa. He felt it slide into the thalamus, and as his frenzy increased he held the brain in his hands and gnawed on its dura mater.

The enemies of the fetishist, like those of the drug addict, derive their powers from the law of supply and demand. On one hand, much as the drug addict has to fight the increases in tolerance which cause him to crave ever larger doses, so too does the fetishist have to fight against boredom and exhaustion. It's the Law of Diminishing Kicks: the dosage that thrilled yesterday falls short today. On the other hand, because the fetishist is terrorized by this constant and often increasing demand, anything that stands in the way of supply is automatically his enemy. And is there not always something in the way? When your fetish is the sexuality of aliens, what stands between you and the pulsing pink pussies of pretty young things from Polaris? All of space. So you compensate. You pursue human girls instead. What stands in your way then? All kinds of nasty little unpredictable things. You never quite know. You try to kidnap a college girl (Ninfa VIII) in the parking lot of a K-Mart, and all of a sudden the poor jerk who gathers the shopping carts decides to play the hero. There you are, minding your own business, which is to satisfy your fetish, and a teenage kid in a red polyester vest tries to knock you to the pavement. It's a real bitch. Charlotte invites Mercury de Sade to burgle her father's office, and naturally the father shows up.

Like masochists in a psychodrama, Mercury de Sade and Charlotte view events from the viewpoint of the boot. Two sets of feet cross the floor in front of them: those of her father, wearing charcoal trousers cuffed at the hem, and the feet of a younger man, also wearing gray trousers in imitation of the older executive. "But our job is nothing more than sleight of hand," Charlotte's father pontificates. "It's like pulling a quarter out of somebody's ear. We take a voice, bounce it off a satellite, stick it in your ear, and then pull a response back out of your mouth." The older man laughs, but the younger responds in a supplicating tone: "But to make sure we brand the project I don't think we should even send out an RFP." There is a pause, as though the father is weighing the proposition. "Were you using my computer, Johnson?" asks the father. In his mind, Mercury de Sade can see the status bar indicating the progress of the satellite documents copying to disk. "Not today," protests the young man. "Maybe the tech guy set it up for a virus scan." The younger feet move toward the computer desk. "That's funny," he says, "it looks like your machine's performing a file copy. Do you have automated backup software?" The older feet approach the younger ones from behind, as though attempting to see the computer monitor over the young man's shoulder. Suddenly the young man emits a funny sound. "Mr. Goddard," he hisses. "Again?" His feet turn around. "I'm putting out an RFP right now," the older man deadpans, "a Request For Penis." Charlotte stirs uneasily. "Ok, but would you please turn off the cameras this time?" asks the young man. "Why, you don't like saving your posterior for posterity?" quips Charlotte's father. "Please," the young man pleads. They hear the older man phoning the guards downstairs. "You can kill the video, Joe."

A rash of outrage spreads across Charlotte's body as she hears the distinct, sickening sounds of kissing—sounds like a cat being stepped on, like a foot being extricated from mud, like a plunger unclogging a toilet. This glare of emotion blinds her to the obvious fact that strikes Mercury de Sade: a security guard named Joe has taped their foolish larceny. "Goddy," says the younger man, apparently introducing a hiatus into the older one's ardor. "Can I ask you a question?" The father teases: "What is it? A raise? A promotion? What does my little Johnson want?" The younger man's voice grows serious, wary but at the same time hopeful. "Talk is," he pouts, "that you're banging the blond girl in marketing." The father's voice grows hard and defensive. "Of course I am," he says. "So what?" Johnson is surprised less by the confirmation than by the belligerent attitude in which it is delivered. Mercury de Sade imagines the father blowing cigar smoke in the younger man's face. "So what?" the young man repeats, indignant. "It's just that—I thought—you know, it's not the money." The father maintains a truculent tone. "You think I don't like broads?" he bellows. "I like everything, except *you* maybe. You whine worse than any broad I ever laid." There is a brief sound of scuffle, the young man's shoes are covered by his trousers, he grunts like an animal—and the legs suddenly acquire a penis and an ass. You can't see them, but you know they're there. It's a musty smell, mildew in damp underwear... Afterward, after interminable gasping and grunting and groaning and groping, the father phones for a reservation at a steakhouse and the pair leaves. Stretching and rubbing their limbs like athletes, the stowaways emerge from their hiding place, and Mercury de Sade retrieves his Zip.

Berkeley echoes Leibniz's notion that the universe may be populated by alien creatures happier than man: "for aught we know, this spot, with the few sinners on it, bears no greater proportion to the universe of intelligences than a dungeon doth to a kingdom. It seems we are led not only by revelation, but by common sense, observing and inferring from the analogy of visible things, to conclude there are innumerable orders of intelligent beings more happy and more perfect than man, whose life is but a span, and whose place, this earthly globe, is but a point, in respect of the whole system of creation." (*Alciphron*, IV.23) However, this speculation immediately invokes the epistemological problem at the heart of Berkeley's philosophy. How is it possible to know that these "orders of intelligent beings" exist? How is it possible to distinguish them from mental representations such as hallucinations or dreams? Berkeley had positioned *esse est percipi* (to be is to be perceived) as the first principle of his entire philosophy, and ontologically this requires that the very existence of a thing depends on its being perceived. It is intrinsically impossible to demonstrate the existence of a thing without touching upon it by means of a perception—in this, a daylight hour, is it absolutely beyond doubt that the moon exists? Might it not have been exploded by a renegade nuclear warhead whose shockwaves have yet to rattle the earth? Is it possible to say with absolute certainty that the moon exists without actually seeing it? At the limit, existence would not be accorded to an unfelt pain, so why should it be granted to an unseen sight?

From this line of thought Berkeley draws the conclusion that reality is not a thing external to subjectivity—a thing "out there," autonomous, indifferent to the incessant voyeurism of human senses. Rather, reality is more like a man staring into his navel: perceiver and perceived form a single actuality. Perception is less a means for a subject to observe a world than for the world to turn back on itself. But if this is true, what of extraterrestrial life? Do we not conceive of the alien as a being "out there?" Berkeley writes that "it is plain that we cannot know the existence of *other spirits* otherwise than by their operations, or the ideas by them excited in us." (*A Treatise Concerning the Principles of Human Knowledge,* §145) In other words, what the mind perceives is not alien beings, external realities, objective entities. The mind only perceives its own ideas, thus it is always by means of the intervention of an idea that an entity makes itself known to us. We "see the color, size, figure, and motions of a man, we perceive only certain sensations or ideas excited in our own minds; and these being exhibited to our view in sundry distinct collections, serve to mark out unto us the existence of finite and created spirits like ourselves. Hence it is plain we do not *see* a man—if by *man* is meant that which lives, moves, perceives, and thinks as we do—but only such a certain collection of ideas as directs us to think there is a distinct principle of thought and motion, like to ourselves, and accompanying and represented by it." (*Treatise*, §148)

In short, we do not see a man but a collection of ideas that we take for a man, and so too with extraterrestrials: we do not see an alien so much as a collection of ideas that we take for alien. This is a dramatic reconceptualization of the notion of extraterrestrial. It no longer portrays the alien as a being from another world, but as a being who is *perceived* as strange or other. In this regard the very term "alien" is less a description than a judgment, more along the lines of "nigger" or "queer" than "neutrino" or "quark." When a man says, "You are a nigger," it is not an accurate description of a person but an admission of prejudice. Similarly, "alien" is not an accurate description of an extraterrestrial being but an admission of ignorance on the part of a terrestrial one. "You are an alien" means that I possess a limited number of cognitive categories for the recognition and description of living beings, and that I discovered this limit when faced with a being with green skin and wraparound eyes. Berkeley's achievement thus consists of a profound relocation of the threshold between man and alien. The dividing line is no longer between this planet and others. Because that which is "alien" is simply a collection of human ideas, the only truly alien existence is that which is never touched upon by the human mind. In other words, *the only true alien is not extraterrestrial but rather extra-mental.* And by definition it would be impossible to know anything about it.

As a fetishist whose lusts focus on extraterrestrial sex objects, I could not help but wonder whether there was any tangible connection between my sexuality and outer space. Are the flows of my desire connected in any way to events beyond earth? To investigate this question, I decided to focus on the possible relation between my sexuality and the moon. I specifically chose the moon for several reasons. First, it is the celestial body closest to earth, hence presumably its effects would be more apparent than those of Venus or distant quasars. Second, the periodicity of the moon provides a backdrop of regular variation against which I could compare the vagaries of my sexuality. Would I find a cor-relation between lunar cycles and sexual activity? Third, although I am aware that most scientists reject the hypothesis of "lunacy" or lunar influence on human behavior, at the same time popular opinion and anecdotal evidence speak in favor of it. Might I not find some truth to the clichés of the common man? Would the full moon intensify the wanton cravings of my fetish? Fourth, I was attracted by the idea that, since the body is composed primarily of water, the moon might exert an influence on it comparable to that which causes the tides of the oceans. Admittedly, research into this area suggested that no such con-nection exists. One team of investigators concluded that "gravitational mechan-ics... offers no support for the ideas of biological tides." And yet, fully aware of these negative conclusions, I wanted to test the hypothesis for myself. The liquidity of sex itself seemed to demand it. Might the moon not cause the sem-inal tide I feel so urgently inside?

Using data obtained from NASA, I set up a spreadsheet. The first col-umn listed the dates for an entire year of observations. I began with January 1st and continued by day until December 31st of the same year. The second column listed the distance of the moon from the earth on each given day. Naturally this distance varies in accord with well-understood mechanics. The third column listed the age of the current cycle of the moon. For example, on January 1st the moon was 21.3 days into its cycle. The fourth column listed the phase of the moon as a decimal. A full moon was thus 1.0, as occurred on March 24th of the year under investigation, and a new moon was a small decimal approaching zero as on April 7th, when its phase was 0.003. The fifth column was labeled L.D.V.C., meaning Lunar Direct Visual Contact. I thought it significant to note whether I had actually made eye contact with the moon on the day in question. The sixth and seventh columns noted my latitude and longitude on earth. While usually my observations were made in New York City, during the course of the year my latitude and longitude sometimes changed significantly, as during a trip to Arizona. Because this altered my relation to the moon in various ways, it seemed important to record. The eighth column was labeled S.H.I., standing for Subjective Horniness Indicator. This was a frankly subjective index I utilized to record my apparent level of sexual desire. I used −1 for a day of decreased desire, 0 for a day of normal desire, and 1 for a day of enhanced desire. In the ninth column I kept track of the number of times I masturbated per day, and in the tenth column the number of times I engaged in intercourse per day. Each of these was defined by the successful completion of the act: only orgasms counted.

At the completion of the year, the data were parsed in various ways. A total number of orgasms (with subtotals for masturbation and intercourse) was obtained, thus also providing a mean number of orgasms per day. The S.H.I. was calculated and, in accord with expectation, resulted in a value only very slightly above zero. (Zero being the indicator of a "normal" amount of horniness, the mean for the year should naturally approach zero.) These sexual data were then compared to lunar data. Days of peak S.H.I. were compared to lunar distance, age, and phase, with the result being that no correlation was evident. Days of maximum orgasmic activity were also compared, with the result being equally negative. Subsequently all days of orgasmic activity above the mean were compared to the lunar data, again with no significant result. Adjustments in the latitude and longitude of the experimenter also failed to indicate any change in the pattern of climactic activity. For example, the orgasmic mean of the trip to Arizona was almost identical to the daily orgasmic mean of the year. Finally, all these data were also compared with an astronomical calendar listing various events such as eclipses, apogees, perigees, perihelions, aphelions, conjunctions, and so on. The only interesting result concerned September 16th, a day when the S.H.I. was a factor of 1 and the orgasmic total was more than double the mean. Lunar events of this day included a rare combination of eclipse, perigee, and full moon. Might there have been some correlation between the enhanced sexual activity and the combination of lunar events? Perhaps, although it should be pointed out that by themselves eclipses, perigees, and full moons failed to correlate with climactic activity. Further experiments would be necessary on days repeating the combination of lunar events.

In sum, the data obtained during a year of observations strongly suggest that there is no significant interaction between the moon and sexuality. Cycles of lunar activity failed to correlate to a regular pattern of sexual activity and, with the one exception noted above, notable events in the lunar cycle did not meaningfully coincide with deviations in either sexual desire or activity. The obvious conclusion is that lunar cycles and sexual activity are two separate, unrelated patterns of occurrence. In no way can the moon be said to cause fluctuations of desire. In a certain sense, this is a liberating conclusion, because it means that sexuality is not subjugated to the impersonal movements of a celestial body condemned for eons to repeat the same orbits around the earth. (Then again, would it be surprising if sexuality were tied to these celestial mechanics? After all, human sexuality has changed as little as the lunar orbit: in and out, round and round, in and out, round and round... Man has evolved, but sexuality has stagnated.) As for exophilia, the disjunction between lunar and sexual activity implies that the cause of an extraterrestrial sex fetish is itself, in all probability, terrestrial. Although exophilia may take a creature from outer space as its object, it derives from an earthly point of origin. The question that will remain open, however, is this: How is it that a terrestrial impulsion cannot find satisfaction on earth? And is a man suffering such an insatiable impulsion not ultimately doomed? The moon may not induce orgasm, but the frustration of desire is certain to induce lunacy.

Because the alien was one hundred and twenty thousand feet tall, it was neces-sary to approach it by means of a small helicopter. Staring out through the wind-shield, Mercury de Sade noted the coordinates of a surface feature resembling a mountain chain on its side. These mountains, which stuck out horizontally from the upright body supporting them, were the only place to land besides the tops of the feet. Careful to guide the helicopter away from the cleavage between the mountains, Mercury de Sade felt very much like a mosquito landing on the breast of a giant. Settling down on the globular surface, a soft peat beneath his black shoes, he began the descent down the vertical face of the alien's midriff. Digging into the flesh with hooks and ropes, he moved down the incline with the grappling motions of a spelunker. A thicket of light hairs, which would hard-ly have been noticeable on the belly of a human, tangled his ropes and imped-ed his progress. As he moved downward, it was like approaching the equator: the heat seemed to rise, the smell of the body grew danker, a drop of perspira-tion crashed by like the monster in a horror movie, *The Blob That Ate Manhattan.*

While climbing, Mercury de Sade reviewed the math that explained the incredible stature of the alien. A being one hundred and twenty thousand feet in height is nearly twenty-three miles tall, compared to the average height of a human female, which is about sixty-four inches. If the bellybutton of an earth woman is half an inch in depth, the corresponding bellybutton of the alien would be about three hundred yards deep. Were he to fall into the bellybutton, the impact alone could kill him. Mathematically, the girth of his destination was also astonishing. If the average earth female is sixty-four inches tall and the actual slit of her vagina is an inch, then her vagina is one sixty-fourth her height. Consequently, if the alien female is one hundred and twenty thousand feet tall, her vagina would be a sixty-fourth of that: one thousand eight hundred and sev-enty-five feet, or more than six hundred yards—a vagina a third of a mile in aperture! As he computed these numbers, Mercury de Sade descended into the pubes, a forest blown every which way by an incredible wind: tangled trees, branches thrown everywhere, curling onto one another, black and shiny like the eyes of an insect. The smell was overwhelming, jungle rot. Perspiration ran in rivulets the size of earthly rivers. Beneath him he could make out the clitoris, larger than a football stadium. Then suddenly he saw a great finger coming toward him: like a genital crab causing an itch in the pubes of a human, his grap-pling hooks had brought this great scratching wrath from the hand of the alien. Digging in, Mercury de Sade hung on for dear life as a great earthquake shook the forest of pubes around him. Huge shafts were battered and twisted like toys, and one hair the size of a redwood was shorn from its moorings by a fingernail.

When calm returned, Mercury de Sade reviewed the possible dangers of entering into the vagina. A penis the size of a skyscraper could come pounding in, pummeling him against the cervix. A glob of yeast could catch him like quicksand. A great menstrual flow, a tidal wave of brown blood, could sweep him away. If he were lucky, he would land in a sanitary napkin the size of an airplane landing strip. If he were unlucky, he would land in a toilet the size of Lake Ontario and be flushed away into alien sewers. Were these great risks worth the reward? Scaling over the clitoris, Mercury de Sade waded through the muck covering the labia: the natural moisture of the vagina formed a thick slime that reached to his knees. Entering the vagina itself, he looked about with a flashlight, half-expecting to see cave paintings. Mindful of the life-threatening dangers of sex, infection, and menstruation, he decided to satisfy himself as quickly as possible. Dropping his trousers and positioning himself before the moist interior wall of the vagina, the image of Jonah tickling the whale with a feather crossed his mind... Afterward, he wondered whether he really had experienced sex with the alien. On one hand, his penis had ejaculated inside an extraterrestrial vagina. Was this not the very definition of genital intercourse? But on the other hand, the act had not felt like sex in any usual sense of the word: it was like rubbing oneself on the Great Wall of China. Perhaps, he reflected, there is an intrinsic scale to sexual relations. If the vagina is significantly larger than the penis, intercourse becomes frotteurism, masturbation. And if the vagina is significantly smaller, it becomes violence.

"Yeah?" retorts Mr. Goddard drunkenly, a chewed gob of half-raw steak falling out of his mouth and landing with a bloody splat on the white tablecloth. "My dick is bigger than your tits." The waitress turns in disgust as Charlotte's father bursts out laughing and sprays a toxic combination of beef, wine, and spit across the breadbasket in the center of the table. He punches Johnson on the shoulder as a sort of exclamation point to his humor. He leers at the others at the table and makes goo-goo eyes intended to camouflage his lurid audacity in a fake, childish innocence. His companions drain their glasses and guffaw in unison like synchronized swimmers in the cesspool of their boss's vulgarity. "Sweetheart," he yells over the heads of a professional couple striving to finish their calamari, "hey sweetheart, come back here." The waitress pauses, torn between her pride and the basic necessity of her livelihood. "I'm sorry," Mr. Goddard spits out in a slobbering drawl. "I don't know what I'm saying when I'm drunk. Let me make it up to you." He pulls his billfold from his rear pocket and withdraws three hundred-dollar bills. The waitress eyes them, experiencing a moment of religious epiphany: her bruised pride undergoes a miracle cure, trumpets blare in the sky and a little cartoon cloud appears before her eyes, heralding the purchase of a leather jacket and a pair of red pumps that she had wanted to buy at Daffy's for several weeks. "This will be your tip," he slurs, waving the bills in the air like a fan, "if you just let me slip it between your tits." She has already sustained so much abuse—is a final insult tolerable given the reward? "Well, all right," she agrees, looking to make sure her manager is out of sight.

The waitress holds the collar of her white shirt fast as Mr. Goddard reaches over and, with a display of excessive cautiousness, pushes the folded bills down into her gelatinous cleavage. Just as he finishes, however, he digs his index finger into her brassiere and gives a hard yank, ripping her shirt and forcing a boob to flop up out of its cup like a fish flipping out of a net. "You son of a bitch!" she cries, stamping her foot and shoving the tit fish back into place. "Oh, I'm *so* sorry," yells Mr. Goddard, a fake remorse covering his sarcasm like a thin film of scum. She makes a move as though to spit at him, and he jumps down on the floor in a position normally reserved for men about to propose marriage. "Go ahead and spit," he shouts with glee, "I'll catch it in my mouth." She kicks him in the ribs and he tips over like a statue, breaking as he hits the floor into a thousand pieces of convulsive laughter. She scoops up the hundred-dollar bills and hustles off, leaving Mr. Goddard hiccupping in a fit of hilarity. When the tears finally clear from his eyes, he looks up to see a Mexican dishwasher standing over him with a baseball bat. "Aren't you too big for Little League," he cracks. The Mexican glowers at him, the bat poised in his hand. "Wait," he mocks, "don't tell me. I remember you. You play shortstop for the Wetbacks, right?" He climbs to his feet to assist his companions, who are remonstrating with the maitre d'. "Pierre," he calls to the man, whose name is Tony, "how about you get rid of the wetback here and take a few greenbacks along with you." He removes a thin brick of bills from his wallet, and the maitre d' retreats.

"I don't know what she was so uptight about," frowns Mr. Goddard, returning to his seat. "The way I see it, it's not how big your equipment is, it's how good your connection is." Reaching to pluck a strawberry from the whipped cream adorning his dessert, Johnson dares to mumble: "If your dick were a modem, the connection would only last a second." Hearing the remark, Mr. Goddard reaches over with a fork and jabs it in the back of Johnson's hand. It balances there for a long minute before the fast withdrawal of the hand causes it to topple backward in the direction of motion. A drop of blood falls down into the whipped cream. Johnson cries out in pain, but Mr. Goddard shoves a cloth napkin into his mouth. "Can it," he commands. "What kind of sissy are you? I'm talking." In a belligerent effort to continue the jocular tone of the evening, Mr. Goddard resumes his line of joking. "I judge every orifice the same way I judge a phone line. It's all bandwidth to me, all just a matter of how much I can *ram* through it." He grabs his crotch and shakes it with the frenzy of an Indian with his tom-tom. His companions force themselves to laugh through the pall cast over them by the humiliation of Johnson. Had this evening of drunken comedy not taken a frightening and violent turn? Their lips grin and their throats gurgle with mirth, but their eyes pass from face to face with a silent question: Who would be next? Who would suffer the drunken abuse of this rich, powerful, obscene man? Who would allow a wine bottle to be broken over his head in order to keep his job? Who would drink urine from a stem glass in order not to be deprived of a stock option? Who would be next, they wonder, looking from one to the other like the occupants of a sinking lifeboat.

Voltaire writes frequently about extraterrestrial life. It recurs in the philosophical dictionary, it furnishes the vantage point for the *Treaty on Metaphysics,* it
appears as a near-certainty in the *Ignorant Philosopher:* "I suspect, I even have
grounds to believe, that the planets orbiting the innumerable suns which fill up
space are inhabited by thinking, feeling creatures." (*Le Philosophe Ignorant*, ch.
1) It is in *Micromegas,* however, that Voltaire parodies the entire history of
exophilosophy. In the tale, two "philosophers"—Micromegas, from Sirius, and
another from Saturn—stumble across the planet earth and undergo a close
encounter with man. In the process, no tenet, no speculation, no hypothesis of
exophilosophy remains standing. Exomorphology is the first to fall: Voltaire
portrays Micromegas as one hundred and twenty thousand feet tall, as though to
point up the fact that exomorphology remains fundamentally of "fish story"
character. Because exomorphology consists of descriptions of beings one has
never seen, its methodology is inextricable from tall tales and exaggeration. The
Saturnian, accordingly, possesses seventy-two and Micromegas "nearly a thousand senses." However, this quirk of exomorphology leads to no epistemological quandaries of the type imagined by Locke. To the contrary, rather than
emphasize the impossibility of communication between beings of different sensory capacities, it reveals a "universal law of nature" best expressed by the
Saturnian: "We find that with our seventy-two senses, our ring, and our five
moons, we really are much too limited, and despite all our curiosity and the
quite considerable number of passions which derive from our seventy-two senses, we still have plenty of time to get bored." (*Micromegas*, ch. 2)

If it is a universal law that, regardless of the bounties of their worlds
or the amplitude of their senses, beings are invariably susceptible to boredom,
the thesis of Leibniz and Berkeley cannot stand: the universe is not populated
with "blessed" creatures happier than man. Even Saturnians, who live fifteen
thousand years, and Sirians, who live one hundred and five thousand, bitch that
life is too short. Conversely, if this is not the best of all universes, might it not
be that this is also not the worst of all possible worlds? While life on earth is at
first too small for the travelers to detect, eventually the alien visitors discover a
shipload of men returning from a scientific expedition. Initially Micromegas is
struck by the contrast between the expansive intelligence and diminutive stature
of humankind. This causes him to wonder whether life on earth is not in fact the
best: "having so little material substance and being apparently all mind and spirit, you must spend your lives loving and thinking—the true life of the spirit.
Nowhere have I seen real happiness, but no doubt it exists here." (*Micromegas*,

ch. 7) However, when a theologian affirms this by telling the aliens that God made everything especially for man, it merely causes them to burst out laughing: "He looked the two celestial inhabitants up and down and told them that everything, their persons, their worlds, their suns, their stars, had been made uniquely for man. On hearing this, our two travelers fell about, choking with that irrepressible laughter which, according to Homer, is the portion of the gods."

Although Voltaire seems personally to have believed in the plausibility of extraterrestrial life, his satire is strictly corrosive. To be clear, Voltaire's skepticism is directed not at extraterrestrial life but at man—at the follies expressed by man when his thoughts attend to suprahuman beings. Exophilosophy had begun with speculation about the nature of extraterrestrial beings, and now with Voltaire it was able to go a step further: it was able to turn its gaze back at man himself without thereby becoming a form of humanism. The question was no longer simply "What do aliens look like?" but rather "What does man look like to aliens?" What kind of first impression would we make? What does man look like from the vantage point of outside? In comparison to a being over a hundred thousand feet tall, man looks small, very small, and insignificant. His philosophy is a mere squeaking, and it is laughable to think God made anything for him. With *Micromegas,* Voltaire thus invents an entirely new type in exophilosophy—the alien interlocutor, a view of man from without. The alien becomes a figure like the demon of Descartes, a Devil's Advocate, a personification of perspectives beyond the human. Even when the standard themes of exophilosophy come to be taken over by twentieth-century science, the interlocutor will remain to remind man that he is less bad than small, less human than homunculus.

I sometimes wonder whether I am less a sexual than an ideal perversion—or rather, a perversion of the ideals of my forefathers. What I mean is that the generation before me espoused exploration, individualism, freedom. Love, for example, was to be free. And yet, however liberating this must have been at the time, when it is the amniotic fluid in which the individual develops, it becomes something else entirely. You take it for granted. It's not liberating, it's boring. Free love—you get what you pay for. The intense eroticism energizing the tight sweater of the 1950s is exhausted by the burnt brassiere of the 1970s. Who wants to see Gloria Steinem's tits anyway? The Law of Diminishing Kicks sets in—thrills that were thrilling under the suppression of sex fail to titillate under the conditions of unmitigated liberty, so you turn to increasingly weirder, more explicit kicks. Where the curve of a breast used to suffice, now it takes fornication with animals and corpses and children. It takes whips and chains and piercings and bloodlettings and all manner of psychodrama. The burning of the brassiere is transformed into a lit cigarette held tight against the pink nipple of an abused teen. Nothing less will do. If the sleep of reason produces monsters, so too does the awakening of perversion, whose monsters are jaded and bored, Frankensteins of frustration, futility, and fatigue.

I have come to realize that my obsession with sex is an expression of a more profound boredom with it. The Marquis de Sade, it is thought, suffered from a dysfunction that made it difficult for him to ejaculate. It is easy to see how "sadism" may have sprung from this soil of frustration: missionary position won't do the trick, doggy style is no good, blowjobs suck, anal sex is a no-go. Boys bore, girls gall, beasts gore, people appall—what more is there to ball? Poor Sade is compelled to invent a thousand nasty variations on the act, their outrageousness increasing in proportion with his difficulty in ejaculating. Similarly, I find myself dispensing with each fuck as though it were an item on a grocery list. Ninfa XVIII, Ninfa XIX, Ninfa XX... But what do you do when you get to the bottom of the list? Suppose a man were to live forever. In an infinite period of time, he would be able to fuck every member of humanity, exhausting every conceivable position and perversion. What could he possibly do to continue to get off? Evidently he would have to turn his sexual energies toward the non-human. He would fuck goats and raspberry bushes and igneous rock formations. But what next? What if—as is possible in an infinite amount of time—what if he exhausted everything on earth? Would he not have to turn his fuck energies toward that which is neither human nor earthly? To get off would require extraterrestrials.

But what kind of proposition is this? Where do you come up with willing extraterrestrials? Or, for that matter, unwilling ones? Tell me the address of a Martian bordello, please. Point me to a whorehouse nearer than Uranus. Can't think of any? You're starting to grok—so perhaps you can also understand a temporary measure. It's like this. Each human forms a stop on an underground waterway of body fluids: everyone is connected by a dank braid of sperm and egg and lubricant, such that the definition of man should not be "rational animal" but rather interlude of jism, node of cum, juncture of juices. A human is no more than an interval in the great chain of fuck—but isn't there someone who remains *hors commerce* like the proof of a coin or stamp? Someone who has not been spent or licked or fingered by the anonymous greedy hands of humanity? Who has not been perforated by the circuit of reproductive sexuality that bonds and multiplies the human animal? Who has not voted in the democracy of fornication, has not pledged allegiance to the flag of small pleasures, has not signed the social contract of reproduction? Extraterrestrials may be impossible to find, but there is another sex object that enables me to "boldly go where no man has gone before." That sex object is the virgin.

Looking faintly surprised at the sight of Mercury de Sade, the father stooped slightly to introduce himself and then, adopting a stiff-upper-lip attitude, showed the visitor into the ballroom. The birthday party was well under way, but the arrival of Mercury de Sade stopped all the singing and games. The children, aged mostly around twelve, smiled and twittered and stared at him. The father leaned close to Mercury de Sade and, gesturing, said: "There's my daughter, the birthday girl." The girl beamed at him, embarrassed and flattered and excited. She had sparkling hair the color of ginger ale, a brownish complexion, and green eyes. Wearing a royal blue party dress, she stood with a cock to her hips, a posture derived from a fashion magazine. Mercury de Sade winked, and she lowered her eyes bashfully. "Look here," said the father to him, quietly and awkwardly, "you aren't quite, um, what we were expecting." Mercury de Sade nodded. "Would you mind if we go have a look at your equipment before proceeding?" Mercury de Sade smiled confidently. "Of course," he said. Entering the next room, he unzipped his trousers. "Rather large, aren't you?" said the father. "Don't worry," soothed Mercury de Sade. "I've done this many times before."

While on earth sexual excitement caused the organs of reproduction to swell with blood, on Kappa it caused the entire organism to swell. More specifically, size on Kappa was correlated with sexual history. The more an alien fucked, the bigger he grew. Celibate people were naturally tiny, while sexually active adults stood taller than basketball players. Disparities in size thus dictated the sociology of sexual relations on Kappa. When an inexperienced hence smaller male would attempt coitus with an experienced hence larger female, the results would not be pleasurable for either. The discrepancy in size made it impossible for either to feel the act of penetration: the male member was simply too small for the enlarged female orifice, and would hang there inside it like a child's hand in an adult's glove. Conversely, coitus between an experienced male and an inexperienced female was not pleasurable—at least not for the female—for the exact opposite reason: the male member being too large, it would invariably tear the female orifice, causing bleeding and pain. The ideal coupling, therefore, was between partners of approximately equal size and sexual drive. This was true of all cases except for children, who needed to be forcibly "maturated." In order to ensure that their children matured at a proper rate, it became the custom for parents to throw birthday parties—but in the stead of clowns or puppet shows, the parents would invite child molesters to come and make their children grow.

The father seemed reluctant to admit that Mercury de Sade was not too large for his daughter. "You've just got the jitters," said Mercury de Sade. "It's often difficult for fathers. I mean, if your kid was having surgery, you'd have a hard time watching, wouldn't you?" Mercury de Sade slapped him on the back, and the father allowed himself to be cajoled into acceptance. After all, the girls were already waiting. He conducted Mercury de Sade back to the party, and the daughter was quickly laid out on the table in front of her friends. Mercury de Sade undressed and began what he pretended he was paid to do. Afterward, getting down from the table, the mother greeted him with a piece of birthday cake. "You must be famished," she said. But as she handed him the titanium plate, she glanced at her daughter and noticed the red between her thighs. "What is that?" she shrieked, pointing. The father took on a threatening mien, and Mercury de Sade worried that he was going to be exposed—since, after all, he was an exophile, not really a state-certified molester. Affecting calm, he licked vanilla frosting from his fingers. "She's menstruating," he bluffed. "Often happens. Catalytic acceleration of sexual characteristics brings on spontaneous menses." He bit into his cake and, as the parents resumed the party, ate it too.

Back in Casa de Sade, Charlotte balances on the edge of a chair as though preparing to skydive. The blue glow of a computer monitor casts a reflection like that of a swimming pool across her face. Her fingers claw at the air with a furious, unconscious automatism, trying to scratch out the eyes of ghosts. A thief can always steal data, thinks Mercury de Sade, watching her, but sometimes the data gets its revenge and rapes you. It stabs into your consciousness like a giant cock and ejaculates all kinds of things you never wanted to know into your brain. Take Charlotte. After the death of a parent, most children have enough difficulty adjusting to the prospect that the surviving parent may remarry. Charlotte, however, has to face the prospect that her father has found not only one replacement for her mother but an entire series of them—an entire series of random subordinates of varying gender. Her father is not a respectable widower but a fag and a whore. Ouch. Isn't that the kind of information that really hurts? Hurts like a big red info-cock being rammed into a little gray data-brain? It's all a matter of perspective, though. What is data rape for Charlotte is something else entirely for Mercury de Sade. For him, it is deciphering Charlotte's PIN code: he knows about her kleptomania, her father—he's putting two and two together, rage directed obliquely at a father who's a sexual pig… It stands to reason, doesn't it? Are the first digits of her psychic PIN not coming into focus? "It must have been really weird," he says, faking sympathy, "to see your father like that. I mean, dogging another man…"

"I wasn't really, like, too surprised," she whispers. Her speech breaks down into resentful sputtering, an audio stream broken by the data spikes of rage. "I was—I mean—you know—I don't—it's not like...." Recalling that, when children cannot speak directly of a traumatic event, psychologists give them stuffed animals and instruct them to show with the animals that which they cannot say with their mouths, Mercury de Sade leans in to Charlotte's ear. "Tell it," he says, "tell it like a video game." Puzzled, she looks up at him. "It didn't happen to you," he asserts. "Nothing ever happened to you. You're fine, you're sitting here with me right now, safe and sound. But one time you played a video game, didn't you? Something happened, didn't it? Something with you and your father…" She pushes herself back in the chair, breathes deeply, draws into herself, finds the eye of the storm, the calm of confession inside the bluster of anger. "The target is in the shower," she says. "It's not a very fair position for a target, is it, when she's naked? Suddenly she realizes Player One is standing in the doorway… What's he doing? What does he want? He reaches out and opens the shower door." Mercury de Sade interrupts: "Does he get points for doing this?" Charlotte nods. "He gets points for doing stuff. He tells the target she's pretty and that he couldn't live without her since mommy died. She misses her mommy but she feels proud. She's a big girl and she can take care of her daddy."

Mercury de Sade imagines the scene mapped out in pixels the color of neon tubes: there's PacMan at the bathroom door, his yellow mouth yapping open and closed in anticipation of gobbling up the pixilated girl in the shower. "Does Player One get points with the target when he makes her feel proud?" he asks, fishing for signs of complicity on her part. "No," she snaps. "You can't get points *with* the target, only *against* the target." PacMan moves down the corridor of Mercury de Sade's imagination in a frenzy, swallowing ninfa after ninfa. "And does Player One get a good score?" he asks her. "A good score," she repeats, trying to remember. "It's not bad—not bad the first time. It doesn't hurt. It's kind of fun. But every day he wants to play again. He seems to want a better and better score." The words convey powerful images to Mercury de Sade: there's PacMan crawling into bed with Charlotte when she's sleeping. "And does Player One," asks Mercury de Sade, "ever get the—the *all-time* score?" Charlotte hesitates, biting her bottom lip. "No," she says finally, "he doesn't. I almost get the impression he doesn't want to… Like the game would be over if he got the all-time score and he doesn't want the game to end. He wants to keep playing and playing and playing." PacMan has liberated himself from the machine. It is impossible to turn him off: there is no power switch, no plug to pull, no battery to die. He gives a licking, thinks Mercury de Sade, and keeps on ticking.

It is in the course of a polemic against the teleological argument for the existence of God—commonly known as the argument from design—that Hume broaches the subject of extraterrestrial life. To counter the proposition that the universe exhibits design, Hume argues that the universe is incomparably vast, and empirical evidence indicates that intelligence occurs only in an infinitesimal portion of it. Consequently, if it is improbable to extend intelligence to other life forms, it is even less probable to attribute the origin of the universe to any intelligence capable of pursuing a design. "So far from admitting," writes Hume, "that the operations of a part can afford us any just conclusion concerning the origin of the whole, I will not allow any one part to form a rule for another part, if the latter be very remote from the former. Is there any reasonable ground to conclude, that the inhabitants of other planets possess thought, intelligence, reason, or any thing similar to these faculties in men? When Nature has so extremely diversified her manner of operation in this small globe; can we imagine, that she incessantly copies herself throughout so immense a universe? And if thought, as we may well suppose, be confined merely to this narrow corner, and has even there so limited a sphere of action; with what propriety can we assign it for the original cause of all things?" (*Dialogues Concerning Natural Religion*, part II) However, although Hume makes use of an exophilosophical argument essentially as a means to undercut a theological one, his proposition concerning extraterrestrial life is in fact more consequential than it may at first appear.

Traditionally the argument for extraterrestrial life is based on an analogy: earth is a planet that is inhabited, so if Mars is a planet, might it not be inhabited as well? Within every analogy there resides an inference—in this case, that Mars is inhabited—which immediately calls for scrutiny. Hume had devastatingly criticized a similar inference in causal relations: there is no necessary connection between a cause and "its" effect, he argued. There is contiguity in space, succession in time, and a conjunction of objects or events in experience, but the connection between cause and effect is merely a perceived connection. In other words, every time a UFO is sighted a mysterious crop circle appears in a desolate field, so we infer that the UFO causes the crop circle. But is this inference not solely on the part of the mind? Is it not simply habit to say that one thing always follows another? Certainly it may happen that tomorrow events occur in an unconjoined fashion different than today. It could even happen that the sun won't rise. It is only we, having experienced the rise of the sun day after day after day, who presume that it must rise tomorrow.

Consequently, every causal relation is in truth a mental association imputed to reality. And the same is true for an analogical inference: every analogy is a mental association projected onto an empirical state of affairs. That two objects agree in one respect (i.e. both earth and Mars are planets) is no guarantee that they will agree in another (in being inhabited).

Hume further subjects analogy to his "microscope," a procedure involving the reduction of complex to simple ideas and the reduction of simple ideas to empirical sources. But what is the empirical source of the logical procedure of analogy? For Hume, it is part-whole relations: earth and Mars are two parts whose "whole" is the conclusion that planets are habitable. If this is true, however, Hume is immediately able to expose two further inferences lacking necessary connection: first, it is impossible to infer from a part to its whole, and second, it is impossible to infer from one part to another part. While the first fallacy refers to the teleological argument—humanity is an intelligent part of creation, on the basis of which it is inferred that the whole of creation exhibits intelligence—the second pertains specifically to extraterrestrial life. Is it possible to "form a rule" for one part (intelligent life on Mars) based on the rule of another (intelligent life on earth)? Hume gives two empirical grounds for the impossibility of this procedure. First, though causes are always imagined, the more proximate things are—the closer objects are in space, the closer events are in time—the more likely it is that they have some genuine causal interaction. Second, Hume argues from the empirical observation that while there are thousands of forms of life on earth, only one appears to possess conscious intelligence. Consequently, though life may be plentiful, intelligent life is genuinely rare. It is a "special" part and hence no model able to furnish rules for other parts.

Hyper-intelligent beings with abstract, streamlined bodies visit earth in order to save mankind from the perils of his own idiocy—that *this* is the myth ought alone demonstrate the quasi-religious character of belief in extraterrestrial life. It is equally possible that aliens are obese green beings who fart and visit earth in hot pursuit of human excrement, a delicacy in other worlds. Or that aliens are deformed purple dwarves who copulate by inserting their tongues into the humps on each other's backs and ejaculating seminal fluid into their spinal columns. Anything is possible—even that extraterrestrial beings, although this may be difficult to conceive, are *dumber* than mankind. Are there any better grounds for extraterrestrial intelligence than for extraterrestrial ignorance? Adherents of the intelligence myth argue that, if aliens manage to visit earth, they must have achieved faster-than-light travel, and this plainly implies an intelligence superior to that of man (since man has yet to develop supra-light-speed spacecraft). And yet, in the absence of intelligent beings, there remain no good grounds for this argument. It is just as plausible that a completely stupid alien accidentally discovers that lighting his farts in the vicinity of a black hole creates a space-time vortex that sucks the farter into another dimension. In short, considering the matter from the vantage point not of myth but of episte-mology, what really are the prospects for extraterrestrial intelligence?

　　　Until relatively modern times, philosophy conceived of reason as extraterrestrial in nature. The entire thrust of Platonism consists in the notion that reason can attain to realities beyond the "prison house of the senses" that constrain thought to earthly things. Reason is a means to bring about an align-ment between the inner soul and the outer cosmos. When I conceive the formu-la for the radius of a circle, do I not effectuate a coordination between my thoughts and the motions of the heavenly bodies? No one expressed this more forcefully than Anaxagoras: the universe itself, he claimed, is mind. *Nous* (mind) and *kosmos* (order) are coextensive—therefore the universe is rational, and reason is extraterrestrial. But if this is true, what are the prospects for the novelty of extraterrestrial intelligence? Relatively the same as those for the nov-elty of human intelligence. If reason is universal, the minds of man and alien share the same fundamental constraints. Consequently, just as laws of nature result in cosmological constants such as the speed of light, so too will con-straints on the operations of thought result in *conceptual constants*. But just what kind of constants or constraints might there be? It is not difficult to local-ize bottom-up, empirical constraints. In political philosophy, for example, all forms of government will consist ultimately of a variation on one of three possibilities (empirically determined insofar as the givens are a group of people and a need for leadership): all rule (democracy), no rule (anarchy), some rule (tyranny, oligarchy). The probability is relatively low that aliens will reveal to mankind any genuinely new form of political organization. And yet, precisely because such constraints are determined empirically, and because empirical conditions necessarily vary in alien worlds, it is impossible to state with certainty that earth-based constraints will pertain on planet alpha or beta.

Conversely, to whatever extent reason is universal, top-down constraints pertinent to reason as such will necessarily apply to all intelligence terrestrial or extraterrestrial. No doubt it was Immanuel Kant who most profoundly delineated the limits of such "pure" reason. In the *Critique of Pure Reason*, he portrayed two basic kinds of limit. First, in the transcendental aesthetic, Kant showed that the mind "legislates" sensory perception by processing it through primal filters such as the "intuitions" of space, time, and causation. Is it possible to think outside these intuitions—to conceive of flowers that occupy neither time nor space? If it is not, as Kant maintained, then these constitute parameters proper to cogitation as such. The intelligence of aliens cannot exceed them: they may breed fantastic anti-gravity flowers with unknown colors and unforeseen smells, but they will not conceive flowers that do not exist in space-time. Second, in the transcendental logic, Kant showed that the same legalities apply to reason in its "pure" form, devoid of sensory or terrestrial input—which is why, for instance, the ideal constructions of geometry accord with the real solids and planes of experience. However, the emphasis in the transcendental logic is less on the limits (or what Kant called the "discipline") of pure reason than on the possibility for rational novelty. Can reason innovate without sensory input? The answer, which depends on Kant's controversial proof of the synthetic a priori, is complex but affirmative. For the purposes of extraterrestrial intelligence, the consequence is that empirical factors may not suffice to distinguish the thinking of man and alien. If pure reason is universal and capable of novelty, it doesn't matter what globe the thinker calls home. Intelligence is not only extraterrestrial, it is altogether extra-planetary.

An epistemological analysis of the capacities of reason—its constraints as well as its possibilities—thus reveals a curve of convergence between the thought systems of alien and human beings. And if this curve unites the trajectories of reason, its exact point of convergence is at *truth*. Why? Because truth is by definition a point of intersection, a commonality. It is not relative to any one planet, least of all earth: "true on earth" would mean *not* true as such. In fact, this accords with a logical definition of truth espoused by philosophers from Leibniz to Tarski: truth is *truth in all possible worlds*—and a fortiori, truth is therefore extraterrestrial. Augustine once developed a clever argument to demonstrate this, though naturally he assimilated the supramundanity of truth to God. Reason, according to a philosophical tradition already old by the time of Augustine, is the greatness of man. But truth, thought Augustine, must be higher than reason, since it is reason that is judged by truth (and not vice versa). From these two premises a crystalline syllogism ensues: reason is the greatness of man; truth is higher than reason; ergo truth is suprahuman, possibly divine. Clearing the hierarchy from the deduction removes the divinity but not the extraterrestriality: reason is the defining characteristic of man; truth is separate or different from reason; ergo truth is exohuman, extraterrestrial. In the final analysis, even the basest platitudes confirm it: to err is human—thus to be true is alien.

The rusting hulks of decommissioned rockets thrust up into the air from the abandoned launch pad like monuments to a space dark age. Their shadowy recesses provided shelter to sidereal bums, intergalactic winos, and dope fiends from the Crab nebula. Drug deals negotiated in telepathic grunts would be consummated in the dark seclusion of their decrepit engine rooms, and hookers with iridescent purple eyes and self-replicating fingers would pickpocket the has-been astronauts they fucked on the rotting bulkheads of antebellum sputniks. It was here in the ruins of a deteriorating Cape Canaveral that the auction of sex slaves was to take place. Mercury de Sade made his way past the chrome husks of abandoned escape hatches and the wreckage of second stages that had failed to detach. Here and there drunken engineers and dirty, homeless computer technicians stood huddled around fires that had been lit in upside-down nose cones. Reaching the end of the launch pad, Mercury de Sade saw the spectral figure of the extrasolar pimp hovering over his charges, who were shackled to a rusty scaffold. No other bidders were present yet, and the pimp was made wary by the premature arrival of an unknown visitor. "I just wanted to have an opportunity to inspect the merchandise," Mercury de Sade reassured him, but by the time he finished the sentence he had already disemboweled the exotic pimp with a razor.

Leaving the other captives to be devoured by bidders yet to come, Mercury de Sade made off with a Lambda princess and her young handmaid. He scarcely dared even look at them until they were all safely ensconced in Casa de Sade. Superficially the women of Lambda looked exactly like those of earth: the princess might have been a college girl, a cheerleader for a university basketball team, and the handmaid her little sister. Each was dark and Italianate: black eyes, lustrous hair, a complexion the color of brown sugar. The princess was distinguished by a curvaceous figure, with large breasts and a straight stomach giving her the silhouette of a question mark, but the childish body of the handmaid also possessed a delicate allure, like a grace note or an after-dinner mint. "It's amazing," said Mercury de Sade, running his fingers along their necks, shoulders, wrists, thighs, looking for signs of conjunction. For the women of Lambda, although they looked like those of earth, were in fact made up of autonomous organisms. Arms and legs were independent entities that attached themselves to the trunk by means of tendon-like tethers. The head was a creature that, unattached, scampered about on leathery bird legs that poked out the bottom of the neck. The breasts were separate organisms as well. They did not shake when the girl moved or walked, but rather each breast gave rise to independent motions, squirming around in the brassiere like a hamster.

To fuck one of these aliens was rather like trying to organize an athletic team. Not every organism wanted to have sex at the same time. The mouth might want to kiss while the cunt wanted to piss, and thus the woman would say "fuck me" but in order to do so the cunt would have to be raped. Or often it would be the reverse: the mouth would say "no," but the cunt would latch onto its object like a lamprey. On occasion parts would even bicker amongst themselves, one or another of them would decide to defect right while they were being fucked. The legs and torso would wander off with the arms, leaving the exophile holding a floating head in his hands while a vagina clung to his penis like a cube of chicken on a shish kebab. However, it was precisely this modularity of parts that Mercury de Sade sought to exploit. Locking himself in Casa de Sade with the two girls, he fondled them roughly, hoping thereby to initiate discontent amongst the components. The royal alien was the first to break down. "I'm a princess," her mouth screamed. "But I'm a whore," her cunt called back. Mercury de Sade hurled her against the wall and she fragmented on impact into a host of frantic little organisms. Her breasts scampered around the room looking for an exit, and her head chased her vagina in circles threatening to bite it. In the meantime, Mercury de Sade shoved himself into the handmaid's ass and pounded her head into the floor, causing her to shatter and leave her rectum wrapped around him.

The room now looked like a henhouse full of headless chickens: the various body parts had run amok, chasing and bumping into each other in a desperate attempt to escape. Mercury de Sade felt something brush his ankle like a cat in the dark, and he looked down to see a head scamper across his foot, trailing its lustrous hair behind it. Using the rectum still snugly attached to his penis, he tried to lure the handmaid's vagina back to him. It had not been on bad terms with the rectum in the first place, but as a virgin it had been frightened by the general melee and had dropped off in a futile attempt to find someplace to hide. Once reunited, however, these two did not want to return to their old torso, so Mercury de Sade trapped the torso of the princess in his hands and threatened it until it agreed to take on the handmaid's vagina and rectum. By way of experiment he coaxed a breast from each woman to attach itself to the torso, but the asymmetry he found displeasing. He knocked the handmaid's breast to the floor and convinced the princess's other breast to join the slowly accumulating female. Of their own accord the vagina and rectum had also won back their old legs, leaving Mercury de Sade holding a new creature who was complete but for a head. However, when he finally went to look for one, he saw that the two heads had engaged in a dogfight in a corner of the room. They were snarling and ripping at each other with their teeth, mutilating what had once been pretty faces. "Well, what do I need heads for anyway?" Mercury de Sade went around the room picking up the remaining orifices, which he threaded onto his fingers with the intention of saving them as replacements. "You wouldn't throw away a spare tire, would you?"

"Are you sure it's ok to give him this address?" asks Mercury de Sade. "Yeah," says Charlotte. "I told him the intersection, not the exact building. He'll think it's just a new friend from school." Together they watch out the front window for Charlotte's father. "That's him," she says, pointing out the window at a big black car. Her flat tone combines resignation and resentment—the weird tone of being angry at someone you're stuck with. It's an awkward moment. How do they say goodbye? They're not exactly lovers, and yet they have attained a certain complicity, the intimacy of thieves. "Before you go," offers Mercury de Sade, "I have a little something for you." Charlotte protests, flattered. "I know it's corny," he says, presenting her with a pink teddy bear, "but I thought maybe you'd like it." Really she loves it, but she hesitates for a second trying to decide what emotion to express. If she shows too much admiration, might he not think she's just a little girl? Then again, he already bought it, so why not love it? "You didn't have to do that," she beams, hugging the bear. "Where did you get it?" she asks. "F.A.O. Schwartz," he lies. Really it came from the spy shop on Madison Avenue. Behind the bear's eyes are little cameras linked to a wireless modem. It's intended for parents who want to keep an eye on their babysitters. Knowledge is power. "Thank you," she gushes. "I love it."

"Look," he says, "you and I are conspirators now." He tries to make "conspirators" sound like "boyfriend and girlfriend." He uses the terminology of crime for the purposes of romance. "I think we should have a code word." Hugging the pink bear, she looks at him with curiosity. When he says "code word," does she hear "nickname" or "pet name" or "diminutive?" She nods, ok, what kind of code word? "Maybe I don't mean a code word," he says, "but an alias. You know, like what if I happen to call and your father picks up the phone? I can't possibly tell him who I am. But if I have an alias, you'll know it was me who called. And vice versa." He gives the appearance of contemplating for a minute. "Ok, I've got it. You'll be Ninfa XIX." She screws up her face. "What's a ninfa?" she asks. He feigns embarrassment, as though it had never occurred to him that he would have to translate for her. "It's Spanish for, let's see, 'sweetheart,'" he explains, lying only slightly. Really it means nymph, nymphet, Lolita. She smiles, pleased. "Why nineteen, then?" she asks. Why nineteen indeed? Certainly he cannot explain to her that there were eighteen other girls before her, girls of various shapes and sizes and ages—or really girls of similar shapes and sizes and ages, since his fetish impels him to repeat himself. "I don't know," he lies, incapable of explaining that his innate sense of order obliges him to name his victims in numerical sequence. "Ninfa XIX just sounds good. It's like James Bond being Agent 007." This answer satisfies her. "And what's your alias?" she asks. "Mercury," he says. "Like the planet," she affirms. "Like the god," he smiles.

Mercury de Sade watches as Ninfa XIX disappears into the passenger door of her father's car, a box-shaped vehicle heavy and rich as a Viennese cake. Inside he can just make out the pink bear in the dark window, and a pair of powerful-looking hands clutching the steering wheel as the car pulls away from the curb. For a moment he tries to imagine the reality behind PacMan, tries to imagine what Charlotte and her father must look like together—but since he has only seen the feet and hands of Mr. Goddard, the image is fragmented, a montage sequence of a girl getting felt up and stomped. Taking a different tact, he tries to project himself into the car as it recedes in the distance, tries to insert himself into the minds of its occupants. "What do we look like when we're fucking?" he asks himself. But rather than envision the tangled bodies of father and daughter, his thoughts turn to outside observers. Exhibitionists would imagine shocked grocery shoppers watching them open their coats, Christians would imagine God watching them commit their peccadilloes, paranoiacs would imagine everyone watching them do nothing at all, but the exophile can only imagine one kind of external observer: the extraterrestrial. What do we look like from space? What do we look like from space when we're fucking? As though receiving a burst of input from a satellite broadcast, Mercury de Sade sees grainy, pixilated video streams of bodies writhing like water snakes. But is that really what aliens would see when we fuck—reptiles? Do we look like Laokoön wrestling the two giant serpents sent to strangle him from the sea? There is only one way to find out, thinks Mercury de Sade, realizing to what good use he can put the SATDATA stolen from Goddard's machine.

Late in life Kant indicated that it was dilemmas or "antinomies" of a basically cosmological nature that inspired what he called his "Copernican revolution" in philosophy: "My starting point was not an investigation into the existence of God, but the antinomy of pure reason: 'The world has a beginning: it has no beginning', etc. down to the fourth... It was these [antinomies] which first stirred me from my dogmatic slumber and drove me to the critique of reason." (Letter to C. Garve, 21 September 1798) However, the cosmos that formed the subject of Kant's cosmology was not uninhabited. No other philosopher of such high caliber wrote as persistently about extraterrestrial life as did Kant. An entire chapter of the early work *Universal Natural History and Theory of the Heavens* (1755) is dedicated to speculations concerning extraterrestrials, which also make their appearance in such fundamental works as the *Critique of Pure Reason* (1781) and the *Critique of Judgment* (1790). In the earlier work, Kant articulated the attitude that he would apparently maintain for the rest of his life: "I am of the opinion that it is not even necessary to assert that all planets must be inhabited, although it would be sheer madness to deny this in respect to all, or even to most of them... At any rate, most planets are certainly inhabited, and those that are not, will be one day." (UNHTH, part III)

If the *vexata quaestio* of his greatest philosophical works concerned the proper limits of reason, from the outset Kant had already begun to probe into the capacities of rational beings, human or otherwise. In *Universal Natural History* Kant tried specifically to work out the cognitive capacities of beings who might inhabit the various planets in the solar system. To this end, he began with the anti-Cartesian argument (not to be fundamentally contradicted by the critiques) that mind is not independent of the body. To the extent that the body is the expression of the chemical constitution of a planet, it follows that the mind and all knowledge is planet-dependent. As empirical evidence, Kant points to the obvious case of man and paints a vivid picture of the terrestriality of his reason. "If one looks for the cause of impediments, which keep human nature in such deep abasement, it will be found in the crudeness of matter into which his spiritual part is sunk... The nerves and fluids of his brain deliver to him only gross and unclear concepts... The sluggishness of his ability to think, which is a consequence of its dependence on gross and rigid matter, is the source not only of depravity but also of error." (UNHTH, part III) If nervous impulses have a finite velocity determined by the conductivity of neuronal cells, then a "cruder" or less conductive substrate will result in slower transmission rates and hence slower or more "sluggish" thoughts. Conversely, the neuronal equivalent of a superconductor—a superneuron?—would result in faster and perhaps qualitatively better thoughts.

The terrestriality of human reason is only one example of the general "planetude" of reason as such. There would also be a "martiality" to the thinking of Martians and a "joviality" to the philosophy of Jovians. It would be possible to speculate on the nature of these intelligences by extrapolating from the physical composition of their respective planets, which determine the body and hence the brain of their inhabitants. In this regard, Kant believed that the further a planet lies from the sun, the cooler, less dense, and hence more ethereal is the matter out of which it is made. If this is true, and if intelligence reflects planetary composition, the necessary conclusion is that cognitive abilities will themselves rarefy—become more ethereal or "spiritual"—with every increase in distance from the sun. On Saturn, the "furthest" planet in the solar system, intelligence would naturally take the most intellectual form. That Voltaire had lampooned the idea of a Saturnian philosopher does not dampen Kant's enthusiasm: "What advances of knowledge should not be achieved by the insight of those happy beings of the uppermost spheres of the heavens!" (UNHTH, part III) Furthermore, to the extent that conduct is guided by reason, not only intelligence but also virtue would be proportional to distance from the sun. The earth, in the "middle" of the solar system, would be caught between vice and virtue—hence all the moral quandaries of man. "Does not a certain middle position between wisdom and unreason belong to the unfortunate faculty of being able to sin? Who knows, are not also the inhabitants of those distant celestial bodies too noble and wise to degrade themselves to [the level of] that stupidity which is inherent in sin, [while] those, however, who inhabit the lower planets are grafted too fast to matter and endowed with all too weak faculties to be obligated to carry the responsibility of their actions before the judgment seat of justice?"

Because the speculations of this early work seem to overstep the "proper" limits of reason, Kant reigned in his later attempts at exophilosophy. No longer did he indulge in exomorphology or the alien equivalent of cognitive science. Rather, Kant's analyses in later works focused on the psychological nature of the human belief in extraterrestrial life. In the *Critique of Pure Reason* Kant succinctly distinguishes between opinion, belief, and knowledge: "Opinion is a consciously insufficient judgment, subjectively as well as objectively. Belief is subjectively sufficient, but is recognized as being objectively insufficient. Knowledge is both subjectively and objectively sufficient." (CPR, "Of Opinion, Knowledge, and Belief") Beliefs are then divided into three kinds: (1) *pragmatical* beliefs employ various means to an end—a doctor believes that a certain cure is best for his patient, although other doctors may not share this belief; (2) *doctrinal* beliefs appear to have no practicable means to determine their end, although in principle such a means may become possible—thus belief in God is doctrinal, insofar as one cannot simply go out and talk to God to verify his existence, but for all that the possibility of revelation is not interdicted a priori; (3) *moral* beliefs require one means to an end—if a man believes that larceny is immoral, then to obtain a good requires that he not-steal. The psychology underlying extraterrestrial life, consequently, is not a matter of opinion or knowledge but of belief—specifically doctrinal belief, insofar as it is empirically possible to verify the existence of planetary inhabitants. In this regard, writes Kant, the hypothetical judgment that aliens exist is analogous to a practical judgment, insofar as it admits in principle of experiential confirmation. And it is this *analogon* "to which the word *belief* may properly be applied, and which we may term *doctrinal belief.* I should not hesitate to stake my all on the truth of the proposition—if there were any possibility of bringing it to the test of experience—that, at least, some one of the planets, which we see, is inhabited. Hence I say that I have not merely the opinion, but the strong belief, on the correctness of which I would stake even many of the advantages of life, that there are inhabitants in other worlds."

This analysis is taken up again in the *Critique of Judgment,* where Kant contrasts belief in extraterrestrial life with belief in "pure embodied thinking spirits." The latter Kant ridicules as "mere romancing," as "what remains over when we take away from a thinking being all that is material and yet let it keep its thought." (CJ, §91, "The Type of Assurance Produced by a Practical Faith") This contrast between the alien and the spirit leads Kant to draw an important distinction between a "fictitious logical entity" (*ens rationis ratiocinantis*) and a rational entity (*ens rationis ratiocinatae*). "With the latter it is anyway possible to substantiate the objective reality of its conception..." The fictitious logical entity is a thing made possible only by language: it is possible to speak of a mind separate from a material body, and yet there is no reason to believe such a thing could exist in a reality that is abundantly, explicitly material. In other words, it is inconceivable that a material human being with senses attuned to material phenomena could experience a "pure thinking spirit." With extraterrestrial life, however, the matter remains open to empirical verification: "for if we could get nearer the planets, which is intrinsically possible, experience would decide whether such inhabitants are there or not."

While this seems like an obvious point, it is more than a matter of reiterating that availability to experience qualifies belief in aliens as doctrinal. The experiential potential of extraterrestrial life ties it directly to the problems of being and knowledge at the core of Kant's philosophy. Kant himself makes this connection: "The objects of experience are not things in themselves, but are given only in experience, and have no existence apart from and independently of experience. That there may be inhabitants in the moon, although no one has ever observed them, must certainly be admitted; but this assertion means only, that we may in the possible progress of experience discover them at some future time. For that which stands in connection with a perception according to the laws of the progress of experience is real. They are therefore really existent, if they stand in empirical connection with my actual or real consciousness, although they are not in themselves real, that is, apart from the progress of experience." (CPR, "Transcendental Idealism as the Key to the Solution of Pure Cosmological Dialectic") In other words, much as Kant's Copernican Revolution asserted that it is not our minds which revolve around objects but rather objects which revolve around our minds, so too does the reality of extraterrestrials hang upon us, upon our experience of them.

One of the arguments against the reality of contact and abduction is as follows: if aliens could be here, they would be here—openly, accessibly, forthrightly, for all to see. Why would aliens come to earth secretively? Why would they slink in and out like men slipping through the revolving door of a porn palace? This argument presumes that aliens have no ulterior motive in coming to earth—but then again, what if they do? Does it not sometimes happen that a visitor desires secrecy in his visits? Mercury de Sade obliged Ninfa XI to urinate into the plastic shell of a computer mouse so that, while sipping it, he might edify her with a little parable: An exophiliac alien wanted to experience human eroticism and thus came to earth in search of authentic terrestrial sex kicks. Much as a traveler in an exotic foreign land might seek to experience indigenous culture, so too did the alien want to experience the affection of a human for another human—it most certainly did not, in other words, want the human to think he was copulating with an extraterrestrial. Consequently, much as a traveler might don local clothing or adapt local custom, so too did the alien guise itself as a human, specifically a female. Entering a hotel bar, it allowed itself to be picked up by a human male. Later, in bed, the man said to the alien (whom he believed was a woman): "I want to fuck you like an animal." The alien was puzzled. "Hunh?" it said in earth slang. "You know," urged the man, "doggy style." This was the last thing the alien wanted. It was seeking authenticity, and if it desired sex in the manner of a dog it would simply take up with a dog. "But I'd rather fuck you like a human," the alien replied. "Hunh?" said the man. "You know," urged the alien, "manny style."

Loitering outside a high school athletic field, Mercury de Sade struggled to keep warm. Although he wore several layers of Thinsulate and Gore-Tex, the deep Mu cold had begun to settle into his bones. He longed for a cup of hot coffee or a bowl of chicken soup—and yet the desire for these remained less than that which compelled him to linger outside in the first place. Though the cold penetrated him like a hypodermic needle injecting ice water into a vein, he knew he would wait until the Mu cheerleaders made their appearance. And when finally they did exit a gym door, hover across a parking lot, and begin to rehearse their routines, a great rush of blood flushed out all traces of the cold with a hot, pulsing, hearty feeling. He could imagine beef stew flowing through his veins as he watched skirts flip in the air, batons twirl, hair fly, breasts bounce. The girls, he saw, resembled humans in the outline of their anatomy, and yet they were gaseous and insubstantial like ghosts. In the crisp cold of the planet, each cheerleader was a kinetic sculpture made of mist or fog or smoke, less a tangible body than an intangible emission, an organic equivalent of the icy haze inside an immense freezer. When one moved, performing a cartwheel or a tumble, it reminded Mercury de Sade of a woman doing the dance of the seven veils: wispy tenuous parts of her body would flow behind her in the air, like a lazy veil hanging on a breeze. Coming to rest, the vapor of an arm or a leg would swirl around the girl the way cigarette smoke sometimes engulfs a smoker's head.

The inhabitants of Mu were made of a substance rarer and finer than their earthly counterparts. Their molecules were less densely packed, so that their flesh was not a solid or liquid but a gas. Of course, this had both advantages and disadvantages. The molecules of their brains were not packed tightly enough to establish good synaptic connections, and thus their thoughts were slower and more sluggish than those of humans. To an earthling, they presented a spaced-out mien, like a hippie or an acid freak. This was an advantage insofar as a fast-thinking exophile could easily rape one before she realized what was going on. On the other hand, their bodies were as rarefied as their minds, and this presented an obvious difficulty: how do you fuck a girl whose flesh has the consistency of cigarette smoke? You could not depend on deriving the usual pleasure of friction from the girls' bodies. When males from their own world embraced them, they copulated the way a low and a high pressure system combine to produce a certain kind of weather. They drifted into each other, pleasure resulting not from friction but from mixing and mingling. But how could Mercury de Sade participate in such an ethereal fuck? His breath might mix with her body, or to be rude he could fart inside her. But aside from the joy of humiliation such an act might procure, how could he obtain physical pleasure for himself? How could the solid matter of his own body enjoy the gaseous matter of theirs?

Dashing out into the midst of the cheerleaders, Mercury de Sade tried to wrap his arms around one—only to end up hugging himself. It was like embracing a mirage. Trying to kiss a girl, he fell face-forward through her body. Resigning himself to the impossibility of physical congress, Mercury de Sade put himself square in the middle of the cheerleaders' gaseous bodies and began to manipulate himself. The girls, whether because of mental turpitude or physical indifference, appeared not to notice him and thus continued their rehearsals, tumbling and gyrating and jumping and cartwheeling around him and over him. Preparing to ejaculate, he aimed at the breasts of one cheerleader, then watched as his heavy fluid tumbled through her vaporous body, descended through her stomach, turned in her pelvis, spiraled downward through her thigh, and finally landed in a white puddle on the frozen ground, where it lay like gum stuck to the underside of a desk. Afterward, Mercury de Sade watched the girls continue their routines. They never even seemed to notice him in their midst. But why should they, he wondered. I did not violate them any more than I would have violated a cloud by ejaculating into it. Their bodies are too rarefied even to perceive mine—which leads me to the conclusion that rape depends on density. Perhaps there is a direct ratio between the density of a body and its ability to be raped: the less dense a body is, the easier material passes through it, and thus the less the body experiences violation. Consequently, human girls are able to be raped only because their bodies are composed primarily of a denser substance, water. But then again, chuckled Mercury de Sade, maybe that's not really rape. Maybe that's just swimming.

Advertisements for automobiles typically show the streamlined vehicle careen-
ing through empty space: a stretch of desert, a coastal highway at night, a lone-
some mountain road with curves. Presumably the idea is to highlight the subject
of the advertisement, and perhaps also to hint that the car in question will fulfill the ideal of driving conditions—the ideal of course being that of the superconductor: rather than fight through snarls of traffic, the driver wants to feel like
an electron moving through a substance with neither friction nor resistance. The
reality of driving, however, is far removed from this ideal. There is always
resistance. Hurtling along the West Side Highway, cell phone cradled in his ear,
Mr. Goddard drives through reality with a technique better suited to the ideal.
He conceives of himself as the only driver on the road. He refuses to view other
vehicles as obstacles. This means that he does not move out of their way, but
rather barrels down on them as though to run them over. Invariably they switch
to the right lane when they see his black warship encroach on their flank. "Crazy
nut," they think as they watch the car shoot past them. They hope to see this
vehicle again—not in their rear-view mirror but on the side of the road, tamed
by an officer of the law, but the truth is that a man with the resources of Mr.
Goddard is no more troubled by the law than he is by morality. He could pay
three speeding tickets a day the way other men pay for chewing gum or cigarettes. And besides, he rarely pays. Why mess with those pesky tickets when
you can keep cops on the payroll?

        Mr. Goddard plows through traffic with one hand guiding the steering
wheel, the other holding a cell phone aloft as though ready to bludgeon someone with it. "I don't care if it can't be done," he barks into the phone. "Do it anyway." His daughter sits in the black leather seat beside him, staring out the window at the reflections of light that play across the Hudson River. "Where'd you
get the goddamned bear?" he glowers. Protectively she hugs it closer to herself.
He can pick on her but not on the bear. "A friend," she asserts. "A friend?" he
repeats. "What kind of friend?" She ignores the question, focusing on the lights
that sparkle on the water. Her father jerks the car to the left, nearly causing her
to fall into his seat. "I said," he says, "what kind of friend? A *boy* friend?"
Inside, Charlotte feels like a cat about to attack a dog. She recognizes that she
is overpowered, and yet she wants to lash out and scratch anyway. Sometimes
it scares the brute off, doesn't it? "It's none of your business what kind of
friend," she almost yells. "I can have friends, can't I?" Mr. Goddard shifts the
bulk of his body in the seat, and Charlotte prepares to be hit. "It's my business,"
he blares, "if it's a boy." The feline coils up inside her, enraged, insulted, so

desirous of striking that she is blind to its consequences. "I tell you," he blusters, slamming the steering wheel with the flat of his hand, "there are days I'm glad your mother died so she doesn't have to see what her baby has become." The wound inflicted by this invocation of her mother is too much to sustain. "Shut up," she screams, and like a knife-thrower she sends her fingernails flying through the air to dig into the back of her father's hand.

In the light of traffic Mr. Goddard is able to observe the three trails of blood on the back of his hand. Far from flying into a rage, he suddenly becomes calm, methodical, consequently more cruel. "Charlotte," he intones, "you know you can't do something like that without being punished... Now I want you to pull down your skirt." A scene of increasing conflict ensues. "But people will see!" she shrieks, looking around at the other vehicles. "It doesn't matter what people see," he commands. "You have to obey your father." She resists. "I won't. I don't care what you do to me. I won't." The car barrels down on a tiny white motorcycle. "I'll run this asshole over if you don't do what I say." The man on the motorcycle turns in fright to look at the crazy car. If it touches his back wheel he'll be thrown against the concrete abutment. He speeds up and swerves lanes like a deer trying to dodge the crosshairs of the hunter. "I will kill this man if you don't take your skirt off," Charlotte's father declares matter-of-factly. In rage and frustration she pulls her skirt down over her thighs and slips her feet out, leaving it on the floor of the car. "And now your panties," he adds. The white cotton briefs from Victoria's Secret tangle in her shoes. "Now I want you to get up on your knees and bend over the back of the seat." She refuses until she sees him accelerate toward the motorcycle. She bends over, her ass facing the windshield for all to see. Do cars even have cigarette lighters anymore? Smoking has been subject to such approbation in recent years that it wouldn't be surprising if cigarette lighters were removed from cars. After all, cars don't come equipped with beer kegs or hypodermic needles. Why should they cater to nicotine addiction? If the lighter remains, it is probably to function as a power supply for portable electronics. Certainly automobile manufacturers would not retain the lighter for its ability to serve as an instrument of sadism—would they? Would they? And yet the orange coil floats across the dark of the car while a chorus of horns celebrates the white buttocks quivering in the windshield.

Although astronomy was an important area of study for Hegel—his dissertation, *De Orbitis Planetarum,* sought philosophical reasons for the sequence and orbits of the planets—he disparaged the stars in general, more than once comparing them to a rash or skin disease. The poet Heinrich Heine recorded in his journal: "One beautiful starry-skyed evening, we two stood next to each other at a window... and I talked of the stars with sentimental enthusiasm and called them the abode of the blessed. The master [Hegel], however, grumbled to himself: 'The stars, hum! hum! the stars are only a gleaming leprosy in the sky.' For God's sake, I shouted, then there is no happy locality up there to reward virtues after death? He, however, staring at me with his pale eyes, said cuttingly: 'So you want to get a tip for having nursed your sick mother and for not having poisoned your dear brother?'" (*Geständnisse,* in *Sämtliche Werke,* XIV) Hegel is not merely scoffing at the ancient idea that after corporeal death the human soul returns to a celestial home. It is the stars themselves that he finds barely worthy of consideration. This outburst to Heine was echoed in the second tome of his *Encyclopedia*: "The tranquility of the stars means more to the heart, for the contemplation of their peace and simplicity calms the passions. Their world is not so interesting from the philosophical point of view as it is to the sentiments however." (*Philosophy of Nature, §268* Addition) Hegel's attitude is clear: the stars are not for philosophers but for sentimentalists, people who "think" with their emotions.

This skepticism toward all things stellar seems to have included extraterrestrial life, although Hegel's arguments to this end are obscure. In the *Encyclopedia* he distinguished four basic "spheres" in the solar system: the cometary, lunar, solar, and planetary. Much as in his dissertation he sought to explain empirical phenomena with recourse to abstract philosophy, so too does he derive vaguely metaphysical qualities from, for example, the rotations of each heavenly body. Of these spheres, however, it is only the planetary that is amenable to life. "It is because planetary nature is the totality, the unity of opposites, while the other spheres, being its inorganic nature, merely exhibit its particular moments, that it is the most perfect to come under consideration here; and this is also true of it as a motion. It is for this reason that living being occurs only on the planets." (*Philosophy of Nature, §270* Addition) Though Hegel mocks the notion that the solar sphere could possess life, a basic ambiguity arises in regard to planets. Does he wish to say that it is the planetary sphere that is conducive to life (insofar as earth is a planet, and earth bears life, the planetary sphere is necessarily conducive to life)? Or does he wish to argue that planets in general are hospitable to life (thus leaving open the prospect of intelligent life on other planets in the solar system)? "Religiosity wants to deck out the sun and moon with people, animals and plants, but only a planet can rise to these things." (*Philosophy of Nature*, §275 Addition) But which planet can rise to life? Mars? Venus? Earth alone?

The determination of this ambiguity resides in the hierarchical schema Hegel so frequently imputes to his subject matter. In the case of cosmology, he argues that the planetary sphere is higher than the other spheres in the solar system—it fosters life because it is the "most perfect"—and that the earth is the highest body in the planetary sphere. "If there is any talk of pride of place, it must be this our earth which we regard as supreme." (*Philosophy of Nature*, §280 Addition) Hegel's reason for regarding earth as the most supreme planet is precisely because it is the origin and dwelling place of that which he elsewhere calls the only reality—Mind or *Geist.* From this it is possible to infer that Hegel must have believed the other planets were uninhabited, at least by intelligent life, since the presence of thinking extraterrestrials would pose a threat to earth's ascendance in the hierarchy of heavenly bodies. Hegel's argument against alien life is thus a new form of anthropocentrism—something like a *noocentrism*: it is not man but Mind that is most important, and insofar as man is the host of Mind, there must be no other intelligent life in the universe. His hypothesis depends on the escalation of an empirical observation (that man possesses intelligence) into a teleological necessity (that man *alone* possesses intelligence). In short, whereas other thinkers find in the solar system no other life and hence no other intelligence, Hegel does the reverse: he argues that there can be no other intelligence in the solar system, hence no other life.

The artist has a studio, the scientist has a laboratory, the intellectual has a study, the writer has a "room of her own." What space is proper to the programmer? When I walk into Casa de Sade I am greeted by the monotonous hum of hard-drive fans and by the red, orange, and green indicator lights that dot the darkness like an electronic constellation. There are cables everywhere, a snake pit of power cords, Ethernet cables, SCSI cables, telephone wire, USB cables, 9-volt adapters, ADB cables, speaker wire, monitor cables, extension cords, serial cables, parallel cables, coaxial cables. Cables crawl up the wall like vines, run along the floor like creepers, tangle in my feet like trip wire. My "machine for living" is becoming a machine pure and simple, and sometimes I feel like I am too. There is an old programmer's slogan that has become part of the general lexicon of banalities: Garbage In, Garbage Out. What this means is that errors almost never derive from computers, which tend to be perfect in their logic, but rather from the errors that humans insert into computers. But if garbage is what a human inserts into a computer, what is it that a computer inserts into a human? Logic. "Listen not to me," the computer would be wont say, "but to the *logos*." A programmer must train himself to think with perfect logic. He cannot allow himself any sloppiness, not even a typo. Philosophers debate whether the computer is not a plausible model for the brain, all the while ignoring the fact that the brain of a programmer slowly *becomes* a computer—perhaps a special type of computer because, unlike the typical desktop variety, the programmer is a computer who can feed himself his own inputs.

Inputs—actually I have something of a fetish for input devices. I must own one example of every input device commercially available: mouse, joystick, trackball, Wacom tablet, handheld pointer, keyboard, microphone (with voice recognition software), digital camera (with image recognition software). Naturally this fetish could be conceived as an extension of a basic fixation with the penis, since the male member is technically an input device. (The cunt is a computer that calculates pleasure and prints it to the face. A scream is the read-out of an ecstatic machine.) However, the mouse should not be reduced to the penis. Each points to its own underlying relation: the mouse connects man and machine, the penis connects man and woman. Perhaps there are only three fundamental relations in life: man/machine, man/woman, man/alien. Interface, intercourse, contact. Manipulate, copulate, communicate. But if this is true, what input device will finally connect man and alien? Spaceships? Radio signals? Prayer? Is the entirety of humanity not guilty of a fetish in regard to this cosmic input device?

We cannot communicate with the alien—nor manipulate nor copulate with the alien—until he makes his presence known. Or perhaps the cause and effect here are backwards: the moment the alien makes his presence known we will be sure both to fuck and manipulate him, ergo it may well be demonstrative of his superior wisdom that he hesitates to introduce himself to mankind. The alien does not want to receive the human input device—at least not in the ass. (Outside this solar system, Greek sex is known as Earth sex.) Conversely, the establishment of contact with extraterrestrial life will not only complete the third relation, that between man and alien, it will also make possible new hybrids. For instance, not only will man be able to treat the alien like a woman—"Take that you fucking bitch," I say, pulling the Martian to the floor by its hair and ripping off its panties to reveal a pert green ass like an upside-down heart—he will also be able to treat the woman like an alien. And if in fact I were to treat a girl as an alien, would she herself eventually come to believe that she is an alien? I might discover something like an extraterrestrial equivalent of the Stockholm Syndrome, in which a kidnap or torture victim comes to identify with her kidnapper or torturer. In the Saturn Syndrome, the subject would come to identify with the extraterrestrial ideology inflicted on her. I would try this with a ninfa, but then again the problem remains—what constitutes extraterrestrial ideology? Would it suffice to glue antennae to her head? Paint her green? Oblige her to reenact scenes from *Alien?*

From the sky, Mercury de Sade gazed out at the various structures that made up the capital of Nu: cathedrals, mortuaries, funeral parlors, cemeteries, elementary schools, playgroups, daycare centers—in short, religious edifices, places of death, and facilities for children. The architecture of the capital expressed, in distant form, the morbid sexuality of the planet, for sex on Nu was tantamount to suicide. Foreplay was self-mutilation—cutting oneself with razor blades or pressing lit cigarettes into the skin—and intercourse itself was death: a Nubian would overdose on sleeping pills to achieve orgasm, or shoot himself in the head and give birth through the gunshot wound. Only the celibate lived long enough to assume positions of leadership, and thus the government of Nu was comprised of alien priests and extraterrestrial rabbis. Moreover, the citizenry of Nu was comprised of that other major group of celibates: children. Some of these would grow up to be new clerics, and the rest of them would sacrifice themselves to species perpetuation by literally fucking themselves to death.

Clearing customs and heading out into the capital, Mercury de Sade set out in search of a junior high school, hoping to locate a sad and therefore horny teenager. On Nu, a deep depression invariably accompanied the onset of puberty. From the vantage point of the species, feelings of self-hatred were necessary for the purposes of reproduction. From the vantage point of the individual, such feelings constituted a vicious circle: the teen feared sex because it was death, and yet he desired death because it was sex. Whereas on earth sex was made up of genital, oral, and anal configurations, all of which were essentially variations on the body and hence on life itself, on Nu all sex consisted of variations on death. A loving couple might play Russian roulette in order to have a baby. An orgy would be a mass suicide à la Jim Jones. And if on earth perversion was defined as sex without reproduction, on Nu perversion was sex without mortality. A normal onanist might bring himself to orgasm by swallowing rat poison, but the perverse one gave himself pleasure drinking milk. A normal exhibitionist would expose himself to others only in freezing cold weather, but a perverse one would expose himself without catching pneumonia. A normal homosexual would fuck other men but make sure to infect himself with AIDS, whereas a perverse one would wear a condom.

Locating the extraterrestrial equivalent of a Catholic school, Mercury de Sade wandered the halls in search of pretty depressives. In a stairwell he saw a teenage boy hang himself with the belt of his uniform. In a lunchroom he saw a girl-next-door type lying on the floor, the post-coital glow of overdose bleaching the life from her features. In a bathroom he saw a young jock submerge his head in a toilet, drowning himself in urine to achieve orgasm death. Finally, in the girls' locker room outside the gym, he came upon a sultry girl about to slit her wrists with an x-acto blade pilfered from art class. Curled up in a corner between lockers, her black skirt wrapped tightly around her contorted hips, she rolled up the white sleeves of her uniform to reveal pale porcelain arms. Moaning through wet lips, she moved the blade across her wrist. A shudder ran through her body, as though the Grim Reaper had pressed his cold lips to the back of her neck, and the girl squeezed her breast with a bloody hand. Aroused, she lay back on the floor and probed between her thighs with red fingers. Mercury de Sade lay on top of her, and she wrapped her arms around his neck. Blood flowed down around his ears, matting his hair, running in red rivulets down his shoulders, dripping back onto the pallid breasts beneath him, forming a red puddle on the floor beneath the weakening buttocks… Afterward, he realized that he wasn't quite sure when the girl had expired. Did I have sex with her, he wondered, or with her corpse? If exophilia is a fetish for aliens, should dead ones count?

Settling himself between two computers, Mercury de Sade uses one to search the internet for information about Arizona. On the other, he aimlessly clicks through various caches of online bestiality. "Sun-swept mountains and valleys, lofty plateaus, narrow canyons, and awesome stretches of desert make Arizona one of the most beautiful states in the nation…" A man guides the piston-like penis of a mule into a woman kneeling on all fours. "Arizona is popularly known as the Grand Canyon State, after its most remarkable physical feature, the Grand Canyon of the Colorado River." A woman with flaring disco hair takes the wet pink member of a Golden Labrador Retriever into her small mouth. "Although the desert landscape looks bleak, it supports a great variety of animal life. A wild pig-like animal, known as the javelina, travels in small herds through the groves of mesquite." A Mexican woman lying on a dirty brown couch holds the corkscrew penis of a pig in her left hand whilst grasping her tit in her right. Mercury de Sade feels a weird boredom, that of a hooker watching television between tricks. Bestiality interests him insofar as it depicts intercourse between species, yet it does not quite suit the stringent requirements of his fetish. After all, man and animal inhabit the same planet. They may be different species, but they're part of the same world. Man is basically a brain on the body of an animal, and thus bestiality isn't even really intercourse between man and animal. "Bestiality" is intercourse between two animals—animal and "manimal." It's no more perverted than two dogs doing it.

After a few hours, he logs off the internet and taps into the pink bear to observe Charlotte moving about her bedroom. The image grows dull after a few minutes so Mercury de Sade sets up a playlist of digital audio files on one computer and fiddles with tests for satellite programming on another. Every few minutes he glances at the video stream to see Charlotte engaged in the banalities of her solitude. But after a while he notices a change. She is speaking heatedly to someone out-of-frame—her father, naturally. If he had audio he would hear the drunken father blare, "I want to see the bull's-eye." Instead he sees one participant in an angry confrontation. She is wearing what looks like a white flannel pajama top with a matching pair of boxer shorts. She gesticulates angrily with her hands. Her fingers curl and claw in the air as though fending off vampire bats. "Keep your electric eye on me, babe," the computer sings. "Put your raygun to my head." The back of her father enters the picture and looms threateningly over Charlotte. Like a crab walking backward she reverses toward the wall behind her bed. In this way the bull's-eye that he wants to see—the concentric rings of a heating coil as burned into the soft white buttocks of a sixteen-year-old—remains safely hidden in the folds of a down comforter. The father lunges onto the bed and grabs at the neck of the pajama top. It tears open and Charlotte slaps at the side of her father's head. "Press your space-face close to mine, love," sings the soundtrack to the world championship wrestling match for the gold belt of incest.

On the nightstand beside Charlotte's bed is a tote-sized can of Static Guard. "Eliminate Static Electricity Instantly." It is a dark blue can with an orange cap, though through the bear's eyes these colors are muted into shades of gray. Static Guard contains Dimethyl Ditallow Ammonium Chloride—a chemical concoction guaranteed to have a harmful effect on the organs of vision. Grasping at it with her hand, Charlotte sprays it across her father's face. "In case of contact with eyes," the can declares, "flush freely with large amounts of water for fifteen minutes. If irritation persists, get medical attention." Wrestling with his daughter, Charlotte's father has no time to rinse his eyes. He paws at her in groping rage, and she fights back, emboldened by his visual impairment. The wrestling match spills off the bed, plows into the dresser and knocks the pink bear onto the floor as well. It lays there on its side recording the blackness beneath Charlotte's bed. Mercury de Sade can no longer see what's happening. Is the father getting the best of her? Pounding her to a pulp? Raping her? He doesn't need eyes to beat her senseless. All he has to do is pin her and bash in her head with a stereo speaker. Or is there some chance that Charlotte is getting the better of him? Would she have the sense to kick him in the nuts? To stab him in the eye with a nail file? "Freak out in a moonage daydream, oh yeah," the soundtrack blares. The phone rings but Mercury de Sade is too engrossed to answer it. "Are you there," a plaintive voice pleads through his answering machine. "It's Ninfa XIX. Are you there? Please be there…"

Schopenhauer did not doubt that physical laws imply the existence of extraterrestrial life. In nature "what is given and consequently is absolutely real" consists "in an immense number of suns floating freely in infinite space and of planets revolving around them," and on the surface of these latter "life has developed which furnishes organic beings of many different degrees." (*Parerga and Paralipomena*, §27) However, while this picture of a plurality of inhabited worlds may have been borrowed from tradition, the rationale for it emerged from the very core of Schopenhauer's philosophy. Schopenhauer believed that will is not only interior to the human subject, but is also found in nature as a force—hence he sought to portray, as the title of his masterwork put it, the world as will. Ultimately it is the exertion of this will that culminates in the creation of life throughout the cosmos. Schopenhauer held an essentially evolutionary view in which the "will-to-live" is objectified in various increasingly complicated forms of matter until it results in the most complex form, the organism. This evolution had already occurred on earth, and Schopenhauer believed that it was only a matter of time before other planets would reach the same stage: "each of the planets that revolve round the innumerable suns in space, although still at the chemical stage where it is the scene of a fearful conflict of the most violent forces or is passing through an interval of peace, nevertheless conceals mysterious forces within its interior. From these there will one day come into existence the plant and animal worlds with all the inexhaustible variety of their forms…. In fact, we can hardly help assuming that what rages in those seas of fire and tempestuous torrents of water and will later endow those flora and fauna with life, is one and the same thing." (*Parerga and Paralipomena*, §85)

Life evolves in stages, according to Schopenhauer, but is this evolution without end? Might there be alien civilizations more advanced than man? Putting a signature twist on the traditional notion of man as the "highest" form of life, Schopenhauer implies that there can be no living creature any more advanced than man: "in my opinion the stage where mankind is reached must be the last because here there has already occurred to man the possibility of denying the will and thus of turning back from all the ways of the world, whereby this *divina commedia* then comes to an end." (*Parerga and Paralipomena*, §85) The world is a form of will, and to the extent that man belongs to the world he too is a form of will. However, whereas in nature the will-force moves steadily forward across inanimate matter, plants, animals, in man it first acquires the ability to turn back on itself. The rock cannot deny itself, the plant cannot defer its desires, the animal does not combat its own instincts, but man is able to wield against himself—and thus against the will-force that traverses him—various forms of self-abnegation, asceticism, suicide. This capacity demonstrates to Schopenhauer that, with man, evolution has reached a different stage. Like a fountain whose waters only reach so high before falling back on themselves, the jet of life reaches its turning point in the stage of development where will ceases to act on matter and begins to react on itself. In this respect man is in fact the "highest" stage of evolution, but he is less a peak than a bend or a warp. Evolution is blunted in man, and in other worlds it must come to a similar conclusion: the extraterrestrial may not resemble man anatomically, but it too will represent a warp in the will-to-live.

Schopenhauer's philosophy is famous less for its ideas than for its tonality—its pessimism—and it is easy to see how this evolutionary schema leads directly to such cynicism and contempt. Man is the "highest" point of evolution, but what is man? An "obvious imperfection and even burlesque distortion," a "bitter indictment against the Creator," and "material for sarcasm." In fact, according to Schopenhauer the best of all possible worlds would have been one in which man had never been created: "it would have been much better if it had been just as impossible for the sun to produce the phenomenon of life on earth as on the moon, and the surface of the earth, like that of the moon, had still been in a crystalline state." (*Parerga and Paralipomena*, §156) Proponents of extraterrestrial life like to contrast the technological, intellectual, and spiritual impoverishment of man with the hypothetical advancements of alien civilization, but for Schopenhauer it's the reverse: it is not extraterrestrial life but extraterrestrial nothingness that is better than man. And since, according to his evolutionary hypothesis, extraterrestrial life could be no more advanced than man, it too is worth less than the "blissful repose" of extraterrestrial nothingness. In short, life on other worlds is as despicable, boring, and inane as that on earth. "We should be driven crazy if we contemplated the lavish and excessive arrangements, the countless flaming fixed stars in infinite space which have nothing to do but illuminate worlds, such being the scene of misery and desolation and, in the luckiest case, yielding nothing but boredom—at any rate to judge from the specimen with which we are familiar." (*Parerga and Paralipomena*, §156) The paradox of Schopenhauer, therefore, is to believe in the existence of extraterrestrial life—but also to believe, because life as such is pointless, that the world would be better without it.

Mercury de Sade could have chosen to live anywhere. He liked the Martian desert of Arizona, the underground urbanism of Montreal, the incipient "future noir" of Los Angeles. Why, then, did he choose Manhattan as the launch pad for his otherworldly fetish? New York could have been, he thought, the exciting futurist city with sliding sidewalks, pedestrian bridges connecting skyscrapers five hundred stories above the ground, aerocars landing on the roofs of towers a mile high. There was a point in time between the two world wars when architects in Manhattan had set about creating the rudiments of this futurist city, traces of which could still be seen in Rockefeller Center, Madison Square, the great skyscrapers of the 1930s, the speculative renderings of Hugh Ferriss. In the main branch of the New York Public Library call slips were still delivered to the stacks by means of pneumatic tubing. Pneumatic tubing—what fantastic, futuristic promise this once held: imagine mail being delivered with a speedy whoosh from the central post office in little bullet-shaped tubes… Even the skyscrapers of the period looked like models for giant rockets. The Chrysler Building pointed into the sky like a study in stone for an Apollo mission, its fabulous crown a prototype nose cone. Rockefeller Center was a model space complex, a Kennedy Space Center right in the middle of Manhattan, complete with its own rocket, the RCA Building. The Empire State Building was not only shaped like a missile or projectile, its spire was originally intended to serve as a landing platform for dirigibles. It was almost as though Manhattan was trying to usher in the space age forty years too soon. Rockets could not yet breach the atmosphere, but building after building in Manhattan temporarily earned the status of tallest in the world, as though one of them would eventually form a concrete bridge with the moon.

But this futurist Manhattan was not to be. What came in its stead, after the war, was the International Style: the Lever House, the Seagram's Building, sleek glass boxes that no longer pointed at the sky but rather filtered out the external world like a pair of sunglasses. Still, if Mercury de Sade perceived the earlier skyscrapers as prototype rockets, these new edifices were the harbingers of architecture for lunar colonies. Their glass skins were trial versions of the domes that science fiction novels erected over lunar outposts in order to allow for the creation of breathable atmospheres. In fact, thought Mercury de Sade, the entirety of Manhattan was a space colony: it was already an island, and he doubted that, if engineers put a bubble around it and filled it with oxygen, anyone would notice—the reason being that, like a lunar colony, Manhattan was already a wholly artificial environment. Underground you could go for miles on the subway and, in the subterranean passages of midtown, for blocks on foot without seeing grass or sunlight or pigeons. Even above ground, these things were less nature than tokens of nature, like pets or houseplants. Parks were reminiscent of the artificial tracts of green that inhabitants of a lunar colony would set up in order to appease their nostalgia for earth—or, more likely, to help oxygenate the atmosphere of their dome. New York may not have become a futurist city, thought Mercury de Sade, and yet there was still less man than moon in Manhattan.

The funeral was being held in a silver metal chapel that looked, to an earthling, like a prototype for a lunar colony. Guests of honor came not by limousine but by hovercraft, and they entered not into stately wooden parlors but into sleek chrome facilities lit by blue lasers like a morbid dance club. Wearing a traditional black suit but also an astronaut's helmet, Mercury de Sade slipped into the rear of a group of mourners. He was able to see the deceased laid out at the front of the room in a coffin made of thick transparent plastic. The cadaver lay nude inside the casket, and Mercury de Sade was able to observe that its anatomy was similar to that of a human in all respects but one: in the middle of the deceased's face, right where an earthling would expect to see a nose, there was in fact a rectal orifice. On Xi, blowing the nose and wiping the ass were the same. A sniffle did not indicate the beginning of a cold but the end of a flatulence-inducing meal. Stepping to the podium, an extraterrestrial cleric began his funeral oration, and Mercury de Sade turned his gaze to the assembled mourners. It might have been a funeral on earth, he thought, noting many accoutrements familiar to a human: the males wore somber black suits, the females black dresses which reached to the floor. However, many of the males sported obvious erections under their mourning outfits. As the cleric spoke, the males would reach inside their black trousers and squeeze their erections with blatant excitement, their gaze directed toward the daughter of the deceased. For her part, the daughter wore a combination of garments belonging in part to the mourner and in part to the hooker. Though a black veil covered her face, there was very little at all to cover her breast or thigh.

On Planet Xi, contraception was unknown. Homosexuality was inconceivable. Masturbation was unimaginable. Only genital sex was acceptable, and every sexual act resulted in impregnation of the Xi female. And while this may have been a tremendous boon in the early development of the planet, such that its inhabitants were never in danger of dying out, at the same time it inevitably culminated in overpopulation. Because a single planet can sustain only a finite number of inhabitants, terrible wars raged over the allocation of resources. Eventually the most militant creatures battled their way to power and recognized that, to retain both the health of their planet and the ascendancy of their leadership, it would be necessary to limit population growth. Consequently, they issued a Draconian edict asserting that for every creature born another must die. Plainly there were two ways to accommodate such a ruling. Some aliens, brutes by nature, would kill someone in order to rape the victim's wife, sister, or daughter. Not being so vicious, however, most aliens abided by a different method of compliance whereby females would have sex only when a member of their family died of natural causes. (Incapable of becoming pregnant, males were not obliged to await the deaths of their own relatives.) Because this inevitably meant that sexual relations were practiced during periods of mourning, there gradually occurred a strange convergence of bereavement and titillation. Feelings of lust and loss were inextricably mixed. Cadavers caused cocks to swell and cunts to moisten. Trappings of grief became indistinguishable from symbols of sex. Black veils acquired the allure of lingerie, and females frequently dressed like groupies and sluts at the death rites of their loved ones.

Mercury de Sade recognized that, immediately following the funeral oration, a fracas would ensue as males vied for the right to fertilize the daughter of the deceased. In frenzied frustration they would fight and hurl each other to the ground—and so much the better if anybody was killed, because it would immediately make the victim's wife or date or family legally available for rape and pillage. Although he considered entering into this orgiastic riot, Mercury de Sade was aware that his chances for success were statistically slim. However, he did have one undisputed advantage over the locals. Non-reproductive sexual practices were repugnant to the men of Xi: oral and anal sex both required the male to insert himself into the face of his partner, and it was as inconceivable to them as fucking an ear or a nose would be to a human. Mercury de Sade, however, was very easily able to conceive of such an act, and to this end he sidestepped the fracas that began upon completion of the oration. The daughter bent over the coffin weeping hot tears while the males of Xi battled for the right to dog her from behind. Meanwhile Mercury de Sade climbed up on the casket and positioned himself in front of her. Lifting the veil of mourning from her face, he saw that her rectum was lubricated with tears. She reached up to daub at it with a tissue, but he pushed her hand away. Grabbing her by the hair, he pulled her head down over his penis, then instructed her to lick his balls as he ass-fucked her in the face.

Mercury de Sade climbs out of the subway at the 72nd Street station and walks the few blocks to Charlotte's brownstone, which is situated on a quiet residential street lined with trees. The trick here is not to transform the people he passes into witnesses. Right now they're just ordinary, unobservant people: an immigrant worker perched on a green milk crate in front of a deli, a man walking a white dog so old and decrepit that it looks like it's been boiled, a couple in professional attire groping each other in the doorway of a basement apartment. It's like walking along a path with a low wire strung across it: if you stumble on the wire, you trip the alarm, the signal goes up, a floodlight bears down on you, suddenly you're on stage, a performer playing to an audience full of damaging testimony. Finally Mercury de Sade locates Charlotte's building and slithers up the steps into the vestibule. Inside, he reluctantly withdraws his cell phone and dials her number. This, he recognizes, is sheer idiocy. The call will be a matter of record, and even their words might be captured by some surveillance device that records cell phone conversations the way a camera in a bank records every customer. "Ninfa XIX," he says, "it's Mercury. I'm at your front door." In a voice that sounds lethargic or drunk, she mumbles the numeric code for the electronic lock. He presses the combination and enters a corridor lit only by the spectral yellow glow of a streetlight. Still holding the cell phone to his ear, she guides him through dark rooms to a steep wooden staircase. Mounting the steps, he approaches the third floor, where she has locked herself into a bathroom.

Because the bathroom adjoins her bedroom, it is necessary to pass by the body of her father in order to retrieve her. "I think... I... killed him," Charlotte slurs, her voice distant, weird, zomboid. "Jesus, don't say that into the phone," he hisses. "Look, I'm right outside the bathroom now. I'm going to hang up and... Just stay inside there until I knock three times, ok?" Leaning over the body, he looks for signs of life. The face around the eyes is puffy as though stung by a bee, but there's a pulse, deep breathing. The man is not dead. He is in some comatose state that lies halfway between drunken sleep and the unconsciousness of having been walloped in the head with a blunt instrument. He will wake up in a few hours with a vicious headache and stinging eyes. This is not good. This is a problem. Mercury de Sade stands up and looks around the room. The pink bear lies on the floor beside the bed. On a dresser is a mirrored tray with makeup and cosmetics. Taped to the wall is a picture of the film actor Johnny Depp. Across from the bed is a portable television set. Mercury de Sade takes it and sets it on the floor, positioning the screen in front of her father's face. Behind the man's head is a wall. Gaining leverage by balancing his arms against the wall, Mercury de Sade kicks the television with all his might. It explodes in glass and sparks, engulfing the face. The body twitches and paws at the air. An arm wraps itself around Mercury de Sade's left calf. With his other leg he kicks at the television again, then works at it with his foot so that the shards of glass still attached to the television push into the flesh of the face.

After a few moments the body lies still, crumpled against the wall with the television attached to its face, a freaky prosthetic. Mercury de Sade moves backward to extract his leg, but the arm is slow to detach itself. The body rolls over, then the arm drops to the floor. Mercury de Sade wipes his shoe on a pillow then raps on the bathroom door. Hearing nothing, he tries the doorknob. "Ninfa XIX," he hisses, "it's me." It's an old lock on the door, so finally he is able to slip it open with the edge of an ATM card. Charlotte is sitting with her arms hunched over her knees in the bathtub, rocking slightly as though trying to put herself to sleep. She gives the appearance of somnambulism. She does not look at Mercury de Sade when he enters. Her eyes focus on the drain of the tub. Regardless how much one loves/hates a parent, the reality of parricide is over-whelming. How can a person cope with the knowledge—or in Charlotte's case, the mistaken belief—that she killed a parent, even if the act was one of self-defense? The irony is that she kills the parent to save herself, and yet the self she saves becomes loathsome. She repudiates it—repudiates a self capable of such selfish murder, and so the drain at the bottom of the bathtub becomes attractive. She wants to leak out through it, turn on the water, melt away like dirt, form a lumpy, skin-colored fluid that drops down into the sewer and loses itself in the viscous brown streams of urban waste—the shit of niggers and Muslims and Chinese day laborers.

Arguments for the existence of extraterrestrial life are frequently based on analogy. But what exactly is the logical basis of an analogy? Much as Kant turned from astronomical or cosmological considerations in order to analyze the nature of belief in extraterrestrial life, so too does Mill eschew the empirical in order to probe the logic of the extraterrestrial hypothesis. If an analogy is essentially an inference from one resemblance to another—for example, earth and Mars resemble one another in being planets, so perhaps they also resemble in being inhabited—what is to distinguish such an inference from a proper induction? "The difference is, that in the case of a complete induction it has been previously shown, by due comparison of instances, that there is an invariable conjunction between the former property or properties and the latter property"— say, between the fact of being a planet and the possibility of being inhabited— "but in what is called analogical reasoning, no such conjunction has been made out." (*System of Logic*, III:xx, §2) An induction, in other words, draws an explicit causal relation between two resemblances, whereas an analogy only suggests such a relation. If the fact of being a planet were shown to cause life to develop, the extraterrestrial hypothesis would depend on an induction. But since it only vaguely suggests such a relation, it remains an analogy.

Mill makes a further distinction between the kinds of properties in which two things may resemble one another. There are *ultimate* and *derivative* properties, the latter being obtained from the former. In this regard, Mill compares the earth and moon: "I might infer that there are probably inhabitants in the moon, because there are inhabitants on the earth, in the sea, and in the air: and this is the evidence of analogy." He assumes that the property of being inhabited is derivative: "The circumstances of having inhabitants is here assumed not to be an ultimate property, but (as is reasonable to suppose) a consequence of other properties." Life does not appear *sui generis,* but rather derives from other ultimate properties: availability of carbon, presence of liquid water, and so on. In any reasoning by analogy, therefore, it is not simply a matter of identifying points of resemblance, but rather of distinguishing between eight different kinds of relation based on ultimate and derivative resemblances and differences. (There are four relations of resemblance—ultimate-ultimate, derivative-derivative, ultimate-derivative, derivative-ultimate—and four corresponding relations of difference.) Obviously, for example, to compare an ultimate to a derivative property severely weakens an analogy. Or if an analogy is strengthened by every point of resemblance, it is also generally weakened by every point of difference.

From this Mill draws a shocking conclusion. In the case of extraterrestrial life, the resemblance between derivative properties (having life) may actually indicate a deeper *dissimilarity* between ultimate properties. In such a case, far from strengthening the analogy, surface resemblances only weaken it. "But considering that some of the circumstances which are wanting on the moon are among those which, on the earth, are found to be indispensable conditions of animal life, we may conclude that if that phenomenon does exist in the moon... it must be as an effect of causes totally different from those on which it depends here; as a consequence, therefore, of the moon's differences from the earth, not of the points of agreement. Viewed in this light, all the resemblances which exist become presumptions against, not in favor of, the moon's being inhabited. Since life cannot exist there in the manner in which it exists here, the greater the resemblance of the lunar world to the terrestrial in other respects, the less reason we have to believe that it can sustain life." For example, because the moon has no significant liquid water, life there would have to develop in some other medium—say, in a certain kind of mineral dust (since the entire surface of the moon is covered with a pulverized rock dust not unlike the sand on a beach.) If this life form depended on dust, water would clearly be inimical to it. Consequently, if the moon agreed with earth in the presence of the ultimate property necessary for terrestrial life (water), this resemblance would actually result in a logical "counter-probability" for the presence of lunar life.

The irony of an extraterrestrial sex fetish is that the distinctions between man and alien, terrestrial and extraterrestrial, are far from rigorous. In the first place, how do you define man exactly? Certainly many thinkers have tried to define him: homo sapiens, homo faber, homo ludens, homo rationalis, etc. The fact that none of these are definitive already indicates the difficulty in characterizing man as such. And if man cannot describe himself with any certainty, how can that which is non-man or alien be defined? The irony is that it is possible to suffer an extraterrestrial sex fetish without knowing exactly what it is you lust for. Not only are you ignorant of the multiplicity and variety of individual alien beings, you do not even know what an alien as such must be. Is an alien a little green man? Or a sexless gray being with an ovoid head and black almond-shaped eyes? The typical alienologist equates human with terrestrial and alien with extraterrestrial, but certainly this equation is doomed to collapse with the advent of interplanetary communication and travel. If a man is born on Mars, is he to be considered a terrestrial? This would make a mockery of the term itself. A terrestrial is clearly a being of earth. Consequently, a human born on Mars is an extraterrestrial, and by the same logic an alien born on earth is a terrestrial. In this light, it is not paradoxical for an exophile to entertain a fetish for an extraterrestrial being who is a human in every respect except that of planetary origin. An extraterrestrial sex fetish could be satisfied with a sixteen-year-old virgin from Mars. Conversely, a pedophile could pay an interloper to arrange a sexual encounter with a sixteen year-old virgin in some third-world nation of earth—and find that the sixteen year old has a blue head with sixteen eyes. Why? Because in the space age, the terrestriality of a creature will not be identical to its humanity. And vice versa.

   If the terms man and terrestrial, alien and extraterrestrial, are not strictly identifiable, they still might be used in conjunction. For instance, one could speak of terrestrial men and terrestrial aliens, extraterrestrial men and extraterrestrial aliens. Similarly, were the implicit terrestrialism or earth bias replaced with that of another planet or star—as would happen, say, if earth were to become uninhabitable and the center of human affairs transferred to Mars—one could still speak of Martian men and Martian aliens, extramartian men and extramartian aliens. However, even such precise distinctions as these might be undermined by other advances in scientific knowledge—for example, were the panspermia theory to prove true. This theory holds that life did not originate on earth but was rather transferred to it from the stars. The scientist's version of the theory argues that basic forms of early life such as bacteria may have ridden to earth aboard comets or meteorites. The fanatic's version argues that intelligent space-faring alien beings left some of their own kind here as colonists. In either case, panspermia might severely undermine simplistic distinctions between man and alien, terrestrial and extraterrestrial. Suppose a man born on earth meets an alien born anywhere besides earth—in other words, suppose a terrestrial human encounters an extraterrestrial alien—and further suppose that, by virtue of panspermia, the alien is an exact replica or reflection or imitation of the human. They have the same anatomy, the same DNA, and they stand there facing each other like a single entity in front of a mirror. Were they to engage in sexual relations, would it be an act between different species, a type of cosmic bestiality? Or would it be a cosmic homosexuality? Does the act occur between a man and an alien? Between a man and another man? Between an alien and another alien? And if they were to have a mutual orgasm, would it be panspermia all over again?

Mercury de Sade paused at a corner beneath the elevated rocket rail. Decrepit arc lamps punctuated the dark, which had a grimy feel as though somebody had stamped out the sun with a muddy boot. The street was desolate and empty until a rocket shrieked by overhead: in the scalding orange glow he was able to make out a homeless alien curled up in a dirty Tyvek blanket. On any other planet the alien would be drunk on cheap wine, thought Mercury de Sade, but on this one he has probably had the very soul sucked out of him. The Omicron spaceport was notorious for the illicit pleasures it offered, as also for the risks incurred by those who furnished both the supply and demand. Sometimes a man came here looking for his grail and was subject to a sudden, brutal act of violence before ever laying eyes on it. He was raided by exotic pirates, cheated by whores from Uranus, snuffed out by bounty hunters from another world, robbed by pickpockets with multiple arms like Hindu gods. At other times a man came here and lived to seize on his grail—only to discover that this was worse than being killed in the pursuit. He would ingest a drug thought to give eternal life, learning too late that its equally eternal side effect was a loud, ceaseless buzzing in the brain. Or he would sodomize a young boy, but during the act the golden youth would turn into a Martian insect and eat him alive. It was only one man out of a thousand who came to Omicron and walked away happy, but for the obsessed and the possessed these were odds good enough.

Mercury de Sade put a coin into the payphone and dialed a numerical formula. A voice synthesizer answered, and Mercury de Sade punched in another series of numbers. While the computer processed the input, he inspected the inscrutable graffiti written on the grubby wall behind the phone: *fuck you* in a thousand weird tongues, dirty limericks in the idioms of Sirius and Rigel, contact information for whorehouses in the asteroid belt. The computer came back online and announced a nearby address. Mercury de Sade turned warily down the street, watching for any sign that might indicate a trap or a setup. Finally he reached the rendezvous. He had been instructed to knock rather than use the intercom, so he raised his fist and pounded on the green metallic door. A red beam like a laser pointer whisked by, outlining his features from behind, and he realized that someone in the building across the street must have scanned him. The door opened, and Mercury de Sade was only momentarily surprised to see a familiar face greet him. That's not really *her,* he thought. They've already digitized my memory. This realization did not prevent him from admiring the consummate skill with which they reproduced every detail: how her eyes sparkled, how her hands moved, how she smelled like vanilla extract. Mercury de Sade was intrigued by the perfection of the replica and beguiled by the memories associated with it—or rather by the memories from which it was hewn. But that's not why I'm here, he reminded himself. I'm not one to fuck my own memories.

The most exotic, most dangerous kick on planet Omicron was not simply to make love to an alien. It was to visit a time whore. Here a man could indulge in perversities that were no longer bodily and hence spatial. On Omicron there were temporal perversities. A man could have sex with his own memory, or even run the entire fuck film backwards: his penis erects quickly, sucks in a geyser of its own ejaculate, pumps in and out of his partner until the man finds himself putting on his clothes during a purely cerebral climax of fore-play and kisses. Some libertines came to Omicron for the time travel equivalent of sexual tourism: they wanted to go back to the nineteenth century and live out a Toulouse-Lautrec fantasy, they wanted to go back to ancient Greece to indulge burning pederastic longings, some even wanted to venture far back into the evolution of man so that they could come home to their depraved friends and brag of having raped the missing link. The most dangerous fetish of all, however, was to fuck back into time itself. This ran the risk of changing the order of events in a man's life. Every old time whore could tell a story about some adventurer in orgasm who fucked himself into non-existence by diddling around with his past: perhaps his death ended up at the beginning of his life, or his birth ended up at the end, so that either way there was a short circuit between existence and non-existence—in which case the life fuse would invariably blow, resulting in complete personal blackout.

Mercury de Sade did not travel to Omicron for past kicks, however. What he wanted was to fuck the future—to experience the last possible moment in the evolution of sex before the universe explodes or collapses or exhausts itself. He explained to the time whore what he was after, and did not haggle when she named an exorbitant amount. She led him by the hand into a private cubicle. She removed her clothes, and to maintain the right mood for the encounter he asked her to cease replicating a female body from his past. Accommodating him, she took on a vague, idealistic form intended to excite him without reminding him of anyone particular. They lay down together on a clean, white bunk, and he inserted himself inside her. When he approached climax, neutron stars exploded beneath his eyelids. Animals began to look like plants, and plants like rocks. Nipples became stalactites and brains hardened like minerals. He felt as though he had added himself to a great copulation already in progress: flora fornicated fauna, germs ejaculated forces into the sky, sub-atomic particles clutched in amorous embraces on orders too microscopic to perceive, and Mercury de Sade had only to press himself into these copulating congeries like a peanut into balls of caramel corn. However, this gave him no direct, personal pleasure. He sensed, rather, that his presence increased the general orgasmic index of the entire humping manifold, which then flowed back down to him in the form of electro-genital streamings that coursed through his body. I have wings, a carapace, a skin, he thought. I am everywhere, in everything. I mingle with smells, grow with plants, flow with water, vibrate with sound, shine with light. I penetrate each atom. Perhaps I am no longer even a man, he exulted, but rather a simple molecule of fuck.

The current estimate is that, in the future, all household appliances will be connected to computer networks. If this is true, however, then the appliances in the kitchen of Mercury de Sade would be like empty hard drives or blank web pages. The refrigerator is bare. The oven has never been used. Nevertheless, Mercury de Sade collects the few things that are in his cupboards—coffee, peanut butter, cereal—and carries them down to the street in a garbage bag. Forced "fasting," as cults know, is an effective tool in the breakdown of a personality. When he returns to Casa de Sade, Charlotte remains slumped in a chair hugging her pink bear. She is stuck in a repeat loop that executes no instructions. "Ninfa XIX," he prods her, "can you hear me? Can you understand what I'm saying?" Charlotte is an unplugged television set, neither emitting nor receiving signals. "I'm going out," he says. "I want to make sure no one is on to us. While I'm gone, make sure you don't answer the door or the phone or go out or anything, all right? It could very well be the police." Standing up, he looks down at her in the chair. At least zombies raise mindless hell and scare the natives. Charlotte is less than a zombie. She is blank, wiped clean, reformatted without an operating system. He turns to leave, but then from the corner of his eye he sees that she makes a small movement. "Beep?" she moans, looking up at him. "What?" he asks. "Beep," she mumbles, a lethargic arm holding out the stolen beeper. "Yes, of course," lies Mercury de Sade, turning for the door, "I'll beep you."

Leaving the apartment, he feels his sexuality rise up in him like an urge to vomit. He has to find something to puke in—if not an alien, a girl. But can this possibly satisfy him? A fetishist is, to use a term from nineteenth-century psychology, a monomaniac. He wants only one thing. It is the very nature of a fetish to be singular. The shoe fetishist wants shoes—not hair or faces or legs leading up to musty mounds of flesh. He just wants shoes. Lots of shoes. Shoes galore. This is to say that he wants something both singular and repetitive. He doesn't want one shoe for all eternity, he wants a series of shoes. Or various series of shoes: red shoes, leather shoes, shoes with high heels, shoes that smell like powder and sweat. Fetishism can be analyzed in the terms of set theory. It's all about sequences and series of repeating elements. Everything else—everything that falls outside the definition of the fetishist's set—is pure distraction. The shoe fetishist would spurn the naked supermodel. In his thoughts he would not lust after the naked body, but would wonder how he could scam the shoes she must have left somewhere. That's the way it is with a fetish. You really can't help yourself. You spend a lot of time scheming. How can I get Cindy out of the room so I can sneak into her closet? Would she notice if I hid a pair of patent-leather pumps in the pocket of my khakis? But if you think this sounds like a tough life, imagine the predicament of a man with a fetish for extraterrestrial sexuality. It's an itch you can't scratch. You sit there in a room with a pretty and increasingly vulnerable sixteen-year-old girl and all you can think about is how you can make her over into something that you've never even seen before. If I put a white T-shirt on her and pour lime Gatorade all over her body, will that do it? Should I get her to reenact scenes from *ET the Extraterrestrial?*

In an effort to appease the insatiable demands of his fetish, Mercury de Sade sets out for Times Square, where hookers and tourists and drag queens and bums wander through the magma of pink neon like survivors of a sexual cataclysm. Lights flash and blink as though to announce air raids from defunct Communist powers, and mounted police make sudden appearances like horsemen of the apocalypse. Although the porn emporia are being replaced by megastores and cineplexes, sex still rattles its chains in Times Square like the ghost of a transvestite hooker shaking her anal beads, and soon Mercury de Sade finds himself in a sex shop. Entering a "buddy booth," he tries to jerk off staring at the flabby tits of a Hispanic crack addict. Uninspired, he watches the girl shake her brown ass at him through a Plexiglas divider, and for no particularly logical reason the incisive phrase "All sex is nostalgia for sex" floats through his mind. Isn't that perhaps the very formula for human sexuality? After all, if one is nostalgic in sex, this nostalgia must take humanity as its object—that is, proper exophilia having yet to transpire, all sex is necessarily nostalgia for sex with humans. Conversely, if exophilia has never transpired in the past, must sex with aliens not be an act of the future? And if it is of the future, thinks Mercury de Sade, might it not be of *my* future? Incapable of climax, he returns to the street in search of—well, there are plenty of freaks but no aliens in Times Square. How is he to get off?

Kierkegaard stakes his position with regard to extraterrestrial life in the course of a polemic with one of his contemporaries, a well-known professor and man of letters by the name of Johan Ludvig Heiberg. In a review of Kierkegaard's pseudonymous work *Repetition,* Heiberg remarked that its author had failed to distinguish sufficiently between natural and spiritual repetition: "The author presumably has had the natural category in view, and perhaps without knowing it has stretched the validity of the concept beyond its proper limits." This observation deeply offended Kierkegaard, who promptly launched a string of attacks in which serious elucidations of the concept of repetition alternated with *ad hominem* mockery of the offending party. Because Heiberg, in addition to his other accomplishments, was an amateur astronomer who had publicly speculated about extraterrestrial life, Kierkegaard's mockery came to bear on the professor's belief in aliens. "But in these latter days," Kierkegaard writes, Heiberg "turns his gaze upward to celestial things, where he studies the orbits of the stars, and replies to him who in concern asks him about the conclusion that there is nothing to preclude imagining that on other planets there are human beings with wings. And insofar as he turns his gaze for a moment toward earth, he contemplates not countries, not individuals, not the continents, but the whole terrestrial globe, and from such an evanescent standpoint that it takes great soul to have courage enough to grasp comfort in the statement 'that also in an astronomical sense the earth takes a highly respectable place in the heavens.'" ("A Little Contribution by Constantine Constantantius, Author of Repetition," *Repetition*)

Certainly this ridicule expresses a deep skepticism on Kierkegaard's part. Because he tended to write about ideas not abstractly but as they were embodied in living subjects—in *Repetition* Kierkegaard claimed to "let the concept come into being in the individual"—an *ad hominem* attack also serves for him as an intellectual refutation. If Heiberg stands for extraterrestrial life, then to disparage Heiberg is to repudiate extraterrestrial life. However, why would Kierkegaard object so vehemently to the possibility of life in other worlds? In large measure, this vehemence expressed the deeper conflict with Heiberg about the nature of repetition. Kierkegaard had taken great pains to articulate different kinds of repetition. His primary distinction, as Heiberg had correctly perceived, was between the repetition of nature (the recurrence of seasons or the revolutions of the sun) and the repetition of spirit. This latter, however, is more difficult to define, for spiritual repetition itself consists of three levels. The first involves a simple repetition of pleasures: connoisseurship, intoxication, sexuality. This soon gives way to boredom and thus to a second level of repetition: one adjusts to the idea that repetition is inevitable by seeking to extract change or novelty from repetition itself. This, however, is a doomed strategy, and thus at the end there emerges the third level of repetition, which is spiritual repetition proper. "Freedom itself is now repetition... So then what freedom now fears is not repetition but change, what it wills is not change but repetition." (*Repetition*, Part First) In other words, at this third level one no longer strives to force repetition to conform to the exigencies of novelty. Rather, one comes to will repetition itself. Purity of heart is to will one thing—over and over and over.

But what does it mean to will repetition? In art, for example, a painter who repeats the works of others is a mere copyist, while one who makes everything entirely new would have no recognizable style whatsoever. "Indeed, if there were no repetition, what then would life be? Who would wish to be a tablet upon which time writes every instant a new inscription? or to be a mere memorial of the past?" (*Repetition*, Part First) The great artist, then, is precisely he who wills repetition—specifically an internal or "spiritual" kind of repetition that defines his individual style (these strokes of the brush, those colors...). Individuality is thus created by repetition, for without repetition individual style either dissolves into chaos or devolves into imitation. Consequently, if individuality as such—in life as much as in art—depends upon repetition, the depth of the misunderstanding between Heiberg and Kierkegaard becomes apparent. Heiberg plainly sides with the very first kind of repetition, the natural. The existence of extraterrestrial life would itself demonstrate a great, cosmic repetition, the recurrence of life throughout the universe. The question "Is the universe inhabited?" also means "Does life repeat?" And "Is man alone?" means "Does life fail to repeat?"

Kierkegaard, conversely, does not deny that nature repeats, nor strictly speaking that extraterrestrial life may exist. His criticism is simply that the proponents of extraterrestrial life prefer natural to spiritual repetition, that they accord higher worth to a hypothetical alien than to the immediate reality of an individual with spirit: "as soon as one, like a psychologist, turns one's mind away from all this great and high-sounding talk about the heavens and world history to the smaller, to the inexhaustible and blessed object of concern, to individuals—then what meaning does repetition have in the domain of the spirit, for indeed, every individual, just in being an individual, is qualified as spirit." ("Open Letter to Professor Heiberg, Knight of Danebrog, From Constantine Constantantius," *Repetition*) Kierkegaard thus subjects Heiberg to a double judgment: intellectually, exophilosophy is misguided insofar as it turns its back on the all-important category of the individual; existentially (or even morally), the individual commits an error in judgment insofar as he pursues exophilosophy and thereby fails to confront the problems of individuality. In short, Kierkegaard criticizes not only exophilosophy, but the individual who chooses exophilosophy. He who "fixes his eyes on heavenly things, counts the stars, reckons their courses, and watches for the heavenly inhabitants of those distant planets, forgetting the earth and earthly life, states, kingdoms, lands, associations, and individuals" is like the man who cannot find his hat when it is on his head. ("Preface IV," *Prefaces*) He looks for life elsewhere when really he himself is all the life that matters.

What exactly is obsession? An *idée fixe,* a singular goal that takes over the mind and gains control of it from without like a homing beam. The Latin root of the verb "to obsess" means *to sit before.* An obsession is an object that sits before the mind, filling up its field of view so that the mind is incapable of perceiving anything outside the obsession. In this sense, it is to be distinguished from the long-term Pavlovian conditioning characteristic of cults and religions. Whereas obsession attaches itself to an object, conditioning infiltrates the subject. It is a kind of "subsession" or *sitting beneath.* Conditioning sits at the bottom of the mind, pushing and guiding it from the subconscious. It is not the field of view that is blocked, but rather the viewer who is trained to block out elements of the field. Obsession takes over the mind of an individual, subsession spreads like a virus across the minds of a group. Accordingly, obsession is an extreme form of the subject-object relation. It is the form of the subject-object relation in which the obsessive cannot see the relation, only the object. Conversely, subsession is primarily an intersubjective phenomenon: the "subsessive" is already in communication with other subjects acting from within. Subsession is the form of the intersubjective relation in which the subsessive cannot divest himself of unconscious relations with other subjects: when he finally sees the object, he does so only through the relation.

Clearly Mercury de Sade does not show evidence of subsession. It would be wrong to construe his extraterrestrial sex fetish as the expression of an intersubjective status quo. In this sense, Mercury de Sade is to be strictly distinguished from alienologists of the cult type such as Do, leader of the Heaven's Gate cult. That Do sought to form a community of believers around his extraterrestrial fetish, and that he even sought to prolong this community into death, indicates the subsessive nature of his enterprise. Ironically, although celibacy may be construed as an imposition of distance between individuals, Do even sought to utilize celibacy as a means to bring his followers closer together "spiritually" or communally. In contrast, Mercury de Sade utilizes sexuality—which might be construed as a means of uniting individuals—as a way of cutting himself off from people. That his victims are conflated with machines, both physically and symbolically, points to an effort to identify them with something non-human and therefore objective. Sadism further objectifies his victims, and thus every act of sexual sadism is simultaneously an attack on an implicit collective: to degrade a girl is to insult humanity. This also emerges in the extraterrestrial sex fetish itself. Mercury de Sade turns that which is most uniquely human—the impulse to join with other humans in procreation—toward a union which can result only in the gratification of a personal obsession. In short, to fuck—or most especially, to impregnate—a woman is to love mankind, but to fuck an alien is to love no one but oneself.

Astrology wars had decimated earth. A Capricorn seized power under a waxing Mars and declared a jihad on what were called parasites in the bloodstream of the Zodiac. "When half of them are niggers and Jews," he said, "twelve signs are too many." Congress passed a bill authorizing the cleansing of the Zodiac, which was to be achieved by the forced extinction of people born in certain designated months. Gangs of young thugs, dressed like state police in khaki uniforms and squeaky black boots, roamed the streets performing surprise inspections of horoscopes. Leos were frequently cudgeled to death with billy clubs, and screaming Virgos were dragged away by the hair to be deterred in constellation camps. There they were raped by guards and herded into "black holes," immense ovens where they were burned like trash. Everywhere the niggers and kikes of the Zodiac were being flushed out and subject to astrocide. Like all regimes of terror, however, this astrological class war caused the underworld to thrive: ingenious counterfeiters manufactured fraudulent birth certificates that drained many a family of heirlooms and savings, unscrupulous traders grew fabulously rich selling black market horoscopes to desperate Gemini, and free-wheeling smugglers concealed frightened Cancers in the fuel tanks of their spaceships in order to sneak them into interplanetary safe zones.

For his part, Mercury de Sade would sweep into a constellation camp and make off with tearful Virgos, who were grateful to be saved from the descent to non-being in black holes. Rather than take them to an interplanetary safe zone, however, Mercury de Sade would transport his Virgo booty to Pi, where the girls were to participate in the communications infrastructure of that planet. On Pi, a female was simultaneously a sexual and a semantic object. Each woman stood for something, like a letter in an alphabet or a symbol in a lexicon. When a male wanted to communicate, he would fuck the appropriate series of symbols in front of his peers, and they would respond by fucking yet another series. In this way, a simple statement such as "hello" or "goodbye" required at least a threesome, and heated arguments would culminate in orgies that bordered on senseless babbling. The males of Pi were thus inspired to be very garrulous, although they faced one constant struggle: because every word, symbol, and concept was grounded in a corresponding body, it was plainly necessary to avail oneself of a new body in order to coin a word, introduce a concept, or sometimes even to further a discussion at all. But where were new bodies to come from? This was not a problem solved by reproduction, which only resulted in more of the same. Instead, exophiles would bring females from a plurality of worlds and donate them to the vocabulary of the planet. In return, they would be granted permission to take part in the furthest reaches of speculative discourse—which was rewarding for an exophile, insofar as metaphysical propositions were formulated through acts of creative sodomy and abstruse areas of aesthetics were illumined by variations in the sadistic treatment of nubile alien girls.

The Virgo had not existed in the alphabet of Pi until Mercury de Sade brought his first stowaway, a young girl with flashing eyes and thick hair that gave off a golden shine like urine with glitter in it. The Pi beings adored her, quickly transforming her into the fuckable equivalent of a buzzword. She was only one lone girl, however, and although she was rich in semantic potential her physical endurance had its limits. The Pis essentially fucked her to death, and without her body to express themselves they were left struggling even to make vague references to her by means of other sex objects. Thus began Mercury de Sade's Virgo enterprise, smuggling girls from the constellation camps of earth and injecting them into the lexicon of Pi. New heights of discourse quickly became possible on that world, but one problem remained: as the Pis grew aware of the increasing greatness of their thoughts and interactions, they also realized that they had no means of preserving them. How could they progress culturally and intellectually when every thought had the life span of an orgasm? Through a complex series of sex acts, Mercury de Sade tried to show them the concepts of art and literature. Once they managed to understand, the Pis initiated a program whereby they embalmed girls of every type in all known positions of sexual submission. The idea was that these frozen figures would form the elements of a lexicon more enduring than the ephemeral sex acts of communication. To preserve a great thought, it was only necessary to arrange the embalmed bodies of so many females in a proper semantic sequence.

Entering a "goth" bar, the music and smoke hit Mercury de Sade in the face like a bucket of dirty water. Standing at the counter, he orders seltzer water and scrutinizes the crowd. A man with black clothes and skin the color of a jellyfish puffs on a clove cigarette and tries to initiate a conversation over the medieval blare of a cathedral-like anthem. Ignoring him, Mercury de Sade observes a girl seated alone at a table. She has unnatural copper-red hair, an oval face, small red mouth, bad skin, brown eyes, funny nose, long black legs, black leather boots that reach to her knees, black tights, purple sweater, black leather jacket. She sits, a cell phone placed conspicuously on the table, reading the bathing suit issue of a magazine called *Maxim*. Girls with bad skin frequently dye their hair this unnatural red color—perhaps because the red hair diminishes the visual impact of red skin (acne or scrubbing or rashes). Normally red is a warning signal, the color of a flare in the sky, and thus when it appears on the human face it serves not to attract but to warn and hence to repel. To dye the hair red thus appropriates the color of warning, makes it part of a deliberate appearance, as though the message is no longer "Warning!" but rather "Fashion statement!" Initiating a close encounter, Mercury de Sade buys the fashion statement a drink. "My name is Nancy," she smiles, "you know, like Sid and Nancy." She notes his sensitive eyes and gentle voice. She likes how his appearance combines what she perceives to be goth (the neatly shaved head) with preppy or casual (crewneck sweater, cotton trousers, black leather wingtips with a shoelace stained by blood). He looks like an Ivy League version of Anton LaVey, she thinks, recalling the famous satanist.

Walking up Broadway, Nancy cups her arm through Mercury de Sade's elbow like a finger through the handle of a teacup. She smiles brightly and her teeth, reflecting the neon haze of Times Square, are red. Entering her hotel, they pass through a forbidding "lobby" that looks like a concrete car park. Once inside, they mount escalators lined with glowing yellow bulbs and ascend to the real lobby, which is located on the eighth floor. "It's a beautiful hotel, isn't it?" she remarks. "It reminds me of the architecture in *Blade Runner*." Stepping off the escalators, they see the tower of the hotel shoot upwards above them, an internal vault that could house an Apollo rocket. A tremendous column runs up the center of the vault, and small lozenge-like elevators glide up and down in the flutes of the column. Around the perimeter, dark plants dangle from the white terraced floors where the rooms are located, giving the impression of a hanging garden that has been vertically elevated to the height of a skyscraper. "You know what I like about *Blade Runner?*" opines Mercury de Sade, rolling the film in his head. "That scene where Harrison Ford gets the replicant chick to have sex with him. He shoves her against the wall and says, 'Tell me to put my hands on you.' She obeys and says, 'Put your hands on me.' She repeats what he instructs her to say and then, like an artificial intelligence program, picks up on the idea and does it on her own. It's basically the way you program a computer." Soon they enter Nancy's room and, beneath the glowing jungle of logos and jingles and taglines and advertisements—Virgin, Jell-O, eTrade—that push at the window from outside, she says "Put your hands on me."

They fuck in the bathroom. "Sex is a creative flow," writes D.H. Lawrence, but "the excrementory flow is toward dissolution, decreation, if we may use such a word… This is the secret of really vulgar and of pornographical people: the sex flow and the excrement flow is the same thing to them… Then sex is dirt and dirt is sex." Goth girls, corporate girls, Ivory girls, "it" girls, arty girls, schoolgirls, salesgirls, preppies, cheerleaders, waitresses, southern belles, tennis players, groupies, nurses, Eurotrash, models, nuns, female wrestlers, fashion heads, biker chicks, Madonna wannabes, babysitters, nieces, daughters, sisters, wives, mistresses—they all comprise a system of curves, tubes, holes, the ejaculate equivalent of sewers and gutters that run through the bodies of a thousand million girls. The collective body of the women of humankind is a waste processing plant for the jism of man. Fucking a girl is like humping a dumpster. It's just throwing sperm in the trash. How could Mercury de Sade not grow sick of these heaps of humanity? "You're such a clichéd goth bitch," he snarls, whacking Nancy in the face with his laptop computer. She falls backward off the toilet and lands in the bathtub. The keyboard shatters and letters fly off like popcorn. Blood streams from her mouth. A look of astonishment dissolves into pain and fear. Fragments of teeth mingle with broken keys spelling chaotic fragments of language across her exposed breasts—roots that never evolved into words, acronyms that do not break down into meaningful phrases, anagrams that cannot be reorganized into properly syntactical units. He picks five keys out of the tub—fortunately there are no repeating letters, since he only has one key for each letter—and presses them into her forehead, spelling out "a-l-i-e-n."

The rise of meta-analysis—inquiry into the nature of belief in extraterrestrial life and into the logical infrastructure of pro-life argumentation—in nineteenth-century exophilosophy continued in the works of C.S. Peirce. Following Mill, Peirce recognized the analogical basis of the typical argument for extraterrestrial life. "*Analogy* is the inference that a not very large collection of objects which agree in various respects may very likely agree in another respect. For instance, the earth and Mars agree in so many respects that it seems not unlikely they may agree in being inhabited." ("Kinds of Reasoning," *Lessons from the History of Science*) However, if analogy makes extraterrestrial life plausible by yoking together planetary conditions, probability ties extraterrestrial life to another eventuality—ironically, one in which the very plausibility of alien existence comes at the expense of human life. "We may take it as certain," writes Peirce, "that the human race will ultimately be extirpated; because there is a certain chance of it every year, and in an indefinitely long time the chance of survival compounds itself nearer and nearer to zero. But, on the other hand, we may take it as certain that other intellectual races exist on other planets,—if not of our solar system, then of others; and also that innumerable new intellectual races have yet to be developed; so that on the whole, it may be regarded as most certain that intellectual life in the universe will never finally cease." ("An American Plato," *Writings of C.S. Peirce*, vol. V)

But why is Peirce so certain of these outcomes? What are his criteria for such certainty? In general Peirce held that certitude was the effect of a cumulative process of agreement. The greater the number of minds that study a question over a longer and longer period of time, the more probable or descriptive of reality will opinion become. Today the certainty that the earth revolves around the sun is greater than five hundred years ago. Such epistemological progress indicates, for Peirce, that certainty is similar to a limit function in mathematics: opinion and belief may never quite attain certainty, but they approach it so closely that for all intents and purposes they function as certainties (without actually becoming them). It is in this respect that Peirce is able to consider the end of human life and the existence of alien life as certainties. Not only do we know more and more about real possibilities for global destruction (such as the sun dying or an asteroid colliding with earth), we also create more possibilities technologically (nuclear bombs, chemical and biological weapons) and foster more possibilities socially (economic inequities, religious strife, terrorism). Given all the apocalyptic possibilities and an indefinite amount of time, is it not likely that man will finally cease to keep his balance on the tightrope of existence? Such a pessimistic prospect is complemented, however, by an optimistic one. It is near certain, according to Peirce, that intelligent life exists elsewhere in the universe. Although he fails to articulate the reasoning that causes this opinion to approach certainty, presumably it was his evolutionary cosmology that led Peirce to believe in a standard pro-life argument: if conditions for intelligent life on earth are typical of the universe as a whole, then in an indefinitely long period of time it is probable that other life forms will evolve.

It is at this juncture that Peirce's two certitudes—the extirpation of human life and the existence of extraterrestrial life—point to a conclusion the philosopher himself seems hesitant to avow. The practical solubility of the question "Does extraterrestrial life exist?" depends simply on whether human life is sufficiently prolonged to answer it: either we live long enough to undergo a close encounter, or long enough to inspect the entire universe and thereby ascertain that it is devoid of life (although to inspect the entire universe would imply that we would ourselves have traversed it enough to sow it with life—human life). Consequently, this thought is inevitable: if only we live long enough, we will answer the question of extraterrestrial life; odds are, however, that human life will not last very long; therefore odds are that we will not live to answer the question of extraterrestrial life. In short, extraterrestrial life may well exist, but it is equally probable that we will never know anything about it.

Returning to the anonymous crowds of the Gotham evening, I pick out random faces and imagine them graced with filaments of sperm. Men and women, black and white, old and young, ugly and pretty—each face receives the cum shot it deserves, wetting the eyelash of a red-haired girl coming out of the Warner Brothers store with a Marvin the Martian doll, or clotting like snot beneath the nose of a Hispanic man wearing a yellow sweatshirt and blue jeans. Have you ever seen how cum can fly through the air? I take myself for a perverted Johnny Appleseed walking along with a bucket of jism, scooping out handfuls and tossing cream pies of cum into the faces I meet. I see ejaculate everywhere: rivers of cum in the gutters, men using buckets of cum rather than wheat paste to smear posters to the boarded walls of construction sites, Times Square on New Year's Eve—the ball drops and unleashes a torrent of cum across the revelers. (Images of victims of mudslides in Venezuela, mud transmuted into ejaculate— and me standing on top of the mountain like a Rain God, spraying cum down on the terrified villagers as they are washed away into a heaving sea of goo.) Why do I imagine this? Why does the entire world deliquesce into seminal fluid? Is it some graffiti impulse, as though I tag the faces of humanity with my sperm? (I train an army of children to scamper up fire escapes and drop balloons filled with cum on the heads of the baton twirlers taking part in a victory parade.) Is it some ontological vision that thrusts itself at me? Philosophy began with Thales, who hypothesized that the entire world was made of water. Might philosophy not also arrive someday at a man who conceives of the entire world as seminal fluid? (Christians at a soup kitchen, scooping out ladles of ejaculate—mixed with orange carrots, like a stew—to the needy.)

If these thoughts transpire in my head—the head of a mere pedestrian, so far as others are concerned—I wonder how many other heads are filled with how many other visions. No doubt there are frustrated men who imagine blowing everyone away with a machine gun. Some guys want to stage a one-man commando raid on a McDonald's—I envision something similar, except substituting my penis for the gun. (A woman lying on the floor amid smashed Happy Meal boxes, my sperm on her french fries…) No doubt many men also perform mental rapes on various passersby. However, do these merely remain compensatory dreams of random heterosexual intercourse? Or do they ever attain the ontological grandiosity of a pathological Thales? Do men look at me and see me drowned in the shower of their own ejaculate? Do they envision themselves smearing their jism into my bald head? Probably they do. I cannot say what visions transpire in other heads, but I can say that this is what I see…

Scene from the movie *ET the Extraterrestrial:* in an image that consciously evokes the Sistine Chapel (God extending his finger toward Adam), ET stretches his finger out toward that of Gertie (played by a young Drew Barrymore). Certainly the director and producers intended this as a symbol of "contact," but when I see it all of a sudden their fingers deliquesce, melt off into streams of ejaculate that run down Gertie's arm into her armpit, run down the little ribcage inside her dress, form a puddle on the floor, so that both Gertie and alien melt like wax figures under a heat lamp. People—or rather, creatures—are nothing but temporary coagulations of ejaculate. (This is solipsism without the mind-body dichotomy. Rather than believe that people are projections of my mind, I believe that they are projections of my body—which implies that human beings, including the actress Drew Barrymore, are essentially cum shots.)

If the entire universe were comprised of semen (rather than, say, water or fundamental particles), this would have decisive consequences for extraterrestrial life. For example, human beings might originate in my left nut, whilst aliens come from my right. "Contact" occurs when the two are commingled in an act of ejaculation. Depending on circumstances, "contact" might thus amount to nothing—suppose man meets alien in a "pearl necklace" (a cum shot around the neck): both would expire as they dry to the surface of the neck in question. (It's like old Elmer's Glue when it dries.) However, suppose that the contact ejaculation occurs in a shot placed directly into the vagina. Rather than suffer the languishing death of desiccation, the alien and human separate back out into individual sperms—and consequently a race for the egg ensues. Who will reach it first? Will the owner of the vagina give birth to man or alien? Some would place their bets on the human sperm: after all, the human sperm has been running in this race for many centuries now, and so it's basically competing on home turf. (Cilia, longtime fans of the sperm home team, do the "wave" in a fallopian tube.) On the other hand, the alien sperms may be endowed with a superior technology that will enable them to swim through the cervix at astounding speeds. It is also possible that the teams arrive at the egg at the same time, in which case an intergalactic battle occurs right there in the reproductive tract. Endometriosis may really be the scarred landscape left behind after alien and human sperm have engaged in battle. Then again, it is also possible that the alien sperm, being not only technologically superior but also wiser than the human, would abstain from combat altogether. Why should it want to impregnate a human? Humans don't use dogs as surrogate mothers.

Owing to the quantitative increase of sexual activity during weekend hours, the futuristic skyscrapers and lights of Rho had been obscured by a veritable smog. It was like London on a foggy night, except that the fog was composed of sperm gas. All across the city men lay in the beds of wives, girlfriends, dates, hookers, leaking semen into the atmosphere. To Mercury de Sade the thick smell was wretched, but on the streets lone females could be seen drifting along, reproductive snouts in the air, soaking up secondhand smoke in a mood of subdued satiation. Some even clustered in front of hotels and massage parlors, where the seminal smog was thick enough to make itself felt on the skin, like humidity on a hot summer day. Hiding in doorways little boys lit cigarettes and squeezed them between their thighs like smoking penises. Girl children with underdeveloped snouts played games, waving their arms in the air like vaginas, breathing rapidly and hyperventilating in simulation of ecstasies which they were not yet mature enough to enjoy. Donning a gas mask, Mercury de Sade made his way down the street past men who looked like candidates for spontaneous combustion and women groping the air with their vaginas like elephants feeling for peanuts with their trunks.

Setting aside the rare, exotic types hypothesized by physicists, matter takes one of three basic forms: solid, liquid, gas. And while on earth semen invariably takes the form of a liquid, on other planets the alien equivalent of seminal fluid may come in other forms. For example, there are aliens who ejaculate a fertile substance in solid blocks the size of sugar cubes. The blocks drop out of their penises in little piles like packages at the end of an assembly line. The female of the species then inserts a block of sperm into her reproductive orifice and, with the relish of a girl holding a sugar cube against her tongue, melts it with mucus and sucking. On other planets, conversely, seminal matter comes in the form of a gas. On Rho, there were creatures who developed bulbous erections that deflated like balloons when they ejaculated. Out the tip of these erections floated a heavy and, to an earthling, foul-smelling gas that hung in the air like smog. The males would crumple to the floor in pleasure, a seminal smoke leaking out of them with the lazy persistence of a smoldering fire. Naturally the females of Rho were anatomically equipped to capture this smoke. They possessed long, tube-like vaginas similar to the snout of the aardvark. After a male had blown his seminal gas into the atmosphere, the prehensile orifice of the female could be seen writhing in the air like a charmed snake in an ecstatic effort to breathe the spermy gas. Orgasm for the female was indistinguishable from hyperventilation, and reproduction did not occur, as for the human, after the ingestion of a lone, fertilizing particle. Rather, it was a process more like the one by means of which a smoker acquires cancer: the female had to expose herself to clouds of sperm regularly and for long periods of time in order to contract a fetus.

Curiously, earthlings were themselves viewed as sexual delights on Rho. The men of earth possessed an ability to satisfy the female of Rho in a way that the males of the planet could only envy. Consequently, it was very easy for Mercury de Sade to arrange a rendezvous with a comely Rho. Arriving at his appointment, Mercury de Sade found his partner to be a tall, lean female. While dormant, the long tube of flesh attached to her crotch curled around her neck like a boa. As they began to fondle one another, the vagina uncurled and sniffed around him with the shamelessness of a dog, probing into ass and armpit. Soon they had assumed the close encounter equivalent of the sixty-nine sexual position. While he licked at her ass, her mouth enclosed his penis like an airlock, and he felt a funny sensation in his legs like a diver getting the bends. He was underwater, holding his breath. To break through the surface would be climactic. In his mind's eye he looked up and saw bubbles of air speeding away from him toward the surface. He pushed with his intestines and a pocket of gas exploded inside him, shooting out of his body and directly into the vagina that had latched onto his ass like a vacuum cleaner. With every fart, the female Rho quivered in orgasm and responded by squeezing out a turd that Mercury de Sade gobbled up. They had formed a complete circuit of the three forms of matter: solid shit dropped from her ass to his mouth, liquid semen streamed from his penis to her mouth, and gaseous farts blew like wind from his bowels to her vagina. When they were done, however, and lay there in exhaustion, Mercury de Sade had already begun to think of new varieties of pleasure. After all, why set aside those rare, exotic types of matter? What would he have to do to ejaculate a quantum foam?

To the side of the eighth-floor lobby at the hotel there are payphones that allow computer hookups. Mercury de Sade plugs his abused laptop into one of the phones and, manipulating the little rods that stick out where the keys used to be, taps into the surveillance camera clutched to Charlotte's chest. The image of Casa de Sade comes in, fuzzy and gray as an old snapshot. At the bottom edge of the image he can make out Charlotte's knees. Apparently she is sitting in the chair, or has never left the chair, or has returned to the chair. This is good, insofar as it indicates that no police have burst into Casa de Sade with a search warrant. It is puzzling, insofar as Mercury de Sade is not quite sure what to make of Charlotte. Has she flipped her lid? At this juncture he would have expected crying, hysteria, fear, melodrama. Instead, she appears to suffer some form of shock. Will she come out of it? How should he handle the situation? He loiters on the street in front of Casa de Sade for a while before feeling certain no police have staked him out. Finally he enters the building and, proceeding up the stairs to his apartment, finds Charlotte still slumped in the chair. Moving with hydraulic slowness, her head cranes itself in his direction. "Beep," she moans. "I'm sorry," he lies, "that I didn't beep you. I was afraid it would let the cops know you were here." The explanation doesn't seem to register. She repeats "beep" several times with distant abjection, a computer sounding the increasingly weak warning of a failing power supply.

Leaning over her, Mercury de Sade lifts her arm and lets it drop—or rather, she lets it drop—or rather, she seems to lack all will, animation, motivation, and so her arm drops with the same easy motion as an object drifting in space. It's not her body that's in free fall, but free fall that's in her body. Because of this, the scene that ensues entirely lacks tension. For Mercury de Sade, it's like waking up and finding the world has become pliant to his touch. It's the ideal of driving, the superconductor ideal, applied to sex. Everything is smooth, frictionless flow. He could ram a videocassette into her asshole and Charlotte would no offer resistance. Moreover, this lack of resistance gives the whole scene a dream-like quality. When a man fantasizes, why should he include the thousand real impediments to his satisfaction? The waking wet dream is the sexual superconductor. Nothing intervenes between the desire and its fulfillment. An exophile longs to see a Little Green Man remove his panties and offer his ass for intercourse, and in the fantasy it happens without the intervention of countless unpredictable obstructions: Alien Interest Groups picketing for extraterrestrials' right to sexual self-determination, the Society for the Prevention of Cruelty to Aliens protesting the exploitation of Little Green Men by sadistic computer programmers… Reality becomes dreamy to the precise extent that Mercury de Sade can now do precisely what he wants to Ninfa XIX. Or can he? This is what he can do: molest her, rape her, kill her—or, should he desire, he can also be nice to her, buy her candy and fancy clothes. But this is what he cannot do: transform her by a simple fiat into a creature from beyond earth. And ironically, this is exactly what he wants to do. He can do anything, in short, except that which he most wants to do, and for this reason he does that which the frustrated always do: hurt other people.

"I'll bet you must be starving," he says, standing up. "Would you like something to eat?" Taking Charlotte by the hand and pulling her up from the chair, he leads her to the bank of computer equipment that lines an entire wall. Beneath and behind the computers is a snake pit of wires, cables, phone lines, power cords, surge protectors. Cupping the back of her head in his hand, he guides her face down into the gray balls of dust that lie like tumbleweed among the cables. "Stick out your tongue, Charlotte," he says. Although physically pliant, she does not seem to hear his words, so he opens her mouth with his fingers and yanks on her tongue. Guiding her head to the back of a computer, he drags her tongue along the SCSI connector that attaches a cable to the CPU. Against the silvery metal her pink tongue looks incongruously animalistic, like a tropical fish plucked from its tank and dropped into the back of a transistor radio. Having encircled the connector, she works her way down the gray cable. Near the floor, she begins to pick up dust, which turns from gray to black as it is moistened by the saliva on her tongue. "Good, good," he says, intending not simply to degrade her by obliging her to lick his SCSI cables, but to program in her a tolerance for degradation itself. It's the same principle as a vaccination or inoculation: by commencing with a small dose of humiliation, he can gradually increase the dosage and thereby lead her into extremes of new behavior. Man, said Dostoievski, is the animal that can adapt to anything—and with a little prodding, adds Mercury de Sade to himself, there's no reason woman can't adapt to this.

Whereas many philosophers approach the subject of extraterrestrial life indirectly, as a consequence of entirely other concerns, for Bergson it emerges from a doctrine central to his entire philosophy, the *élan vital*. Born in the year that Darwin published the *Origin of Species*, Bergson accepted the theory of evolution in outline but felt that the prevailing mechanistic interpretation of it failed to explain reality sufficiently. Behind the movement of a human body there lay willpower, and behind the movement of a heavenly body there lay gravitational force, so should there not also be a force or impulse interior to the movement of evolution? The external, mechanical aspect of evolution consisted of interaction between organisms and their environment, but the internal aspect of evolution was this inner impulsion, an *élan vital*. It had first passed into inert matter as an originary impulse or *élan original de la vie* and over the course of generations differentiated matter into the forms most efficient for its own perpetuation. In a certain respect, it is therefore improper even to say that "life evolved," since it is not the vital impetus itself that changes but rather the form and matter of the organisms that it traverses. On earth, for example, this "creative evolution" resulted in two forms of life: plants, whose essence is to extract energy from sunlight and store it in organic molecules, and animals, who steal sustenance from plants and from other animals in order to disburse it in energetically prodigal expenditures such as walking and running.

For Bergson, then, evolution is not merely adaptation of organism to environment. The vital impetus also exerts itself from within the organism in order to exploit matter to its own ends—hence its "creativity." However, if the signs of this process are apparent on earth, what of other worlds? "If [life's] essential aim is to catch up usable energy in order to expend it in explosive actions, it probably chooses, in each solar system and on each planet, as it does on the earth, the fittest means to get this result in the circumstances with which it is confronted. That is at least what reasoning by analogy leads to, and we use analogy the wrong way when we declare life to be impossible wherever the circumstances with which it is confronted are other than those on the earth. The truth is that life is possible wherever energy descends the incline indicated by Carnot's law and where a cause of inverse direction can retard the descent—that is to say, probably, in all the worlds suspended from all the stars." (*Creative Evolution*, ch. III) In other words, analogy fails when it is used to transfer terrestrial conditions to extraterrestrial worlds. Why would life on other worlds depend on a contingency such as the planetary conditions specific to earth?

However, this does not mean that the *élan vital* fails to inspire life in other worlds. On earth the vital impetus seizes hold of matter and differentiates it into flora and fauna. On other worlds, it might simply take a different course. "If the element characteristic of the substances that supply energy to the organism had been other than carbon, the element characteristic of the plastic substances would probably have been other than nitrogen, and the chemistry of living bodies would then have been radically different from what it is. The result would have been living forms without analogy to those we know, whose anatomy would have been different, whose physiology would also have been different... It is therefore probable that life goes on in other planets, in other solar systems also, under forms of which we have no idea, in physical conditions to which it seems to us, from the point of view of our physiology, to be absolutely opposed." This basic argument had already been put forward by previous thinkers, most especially by Kant: local conditions determine the morphology of a planet's inhabitants. Kant's proto-evolutionary view, however, remained too passive and mechanical. It portrays a unidirectional flow of influence from the environment to the organism, without allowing for the reverse.

In the terms of an active, creative evolution, it is not only the planet that shapes the evolution of its inhabitants, it is the vital impetus that shapes organisms and at the limit even their planets. It may even be possible for the vital impetus to bypass organisms as such and operate directly on the planetary environment: "it is not even necessary that life should be concentrated and determined in organisms properly so called, that is, in definite bodies presenting to the flow of energy ready-made elastic canals. It can be conceived (although it can hardly be imagined) that energy might be saved up, and then expended on varying lines running across a matter not yet solidified. Every essential of life would still be there, since there would still be slow accumulation of energy and sudden release." Bergson thus arrives philosophically at a possibility of life other thinkers only reach by way of literature and wild speculation. The *élan vital* may animate something like the "living" ocean of Stanislaw Lem's *Solaris*. It may resemble the Jovian clouds imagined by Carl Sagan—city-sized "floaters" that "eat" pre-formed organic molecules or synthesize their own by ingesting solar energy. Or it may appear as the congelations of magnetized interstellar gas dreamed up by physicst Fred Hoyle—"black clouds" that channel ions and electrons through flux tubes traversing a "body" made solely of magnetic fields. These extravagant life forms are all members of a category first invented by Bergson: living entities formed not as reactions to planetary features but rather planetary (or even universal) features that are themselves taken up and possessed by the vital impetus. In short, the *élan vital* leads Bergson directly to the discovery of a new possibility of existence: not only extraterrestrial but *extra-organismal* life.

The question "What kinds of sex do aliens have?" can be approached through analogy with the question "What kinds of sex do humans have in space?" Although limited by the configuration of earthly anatomy, sexual relations between humans under actual extraterrestrial conditions can provide important insights into the potentials of alien sexuality. To this end, while NASA publication 14-307-1792, "Experiment 8 Postflight Summary," avows that the "sensitive nature of the videotapes and first-hand observations precludes a public release of the raw data," its sanitized overview of sexual experiments conducted aboard a space shuttle mission is nevertheless the most informative and perhaps the only empirical document published to date. According to the document, two astronauts—a male and female referred to as the "co-investigators"— erected a "pneumatic sound deadening barrier between the lower deck and the flight deck" of the space shuttle and performed a series of ten experiments designed to evaluate sexual positions under zero-gravity conditions. Because the "conventional approach to marital relationships (sometimes described as the missionary approach) is highly dependent on gravity to keep the partners together," the co-investigators tried three basic approaches: (1) elastic belts to bind the astronauts during relations: with the belt around the waist or the thighs, the "partners faced each other in the standard or missionary posture"; (2) an "inflatable tunnel" designed to wrap the astronauts together: the "partners faced each other in the standard missionary posture. The tunnel enclosed the partners roughly from the knees to waist and pressed them together"; (3) "natural" or "unassisted" methods in which the partners clung to each other with hands, thighs, and toes: for example, the "standard missionary posture, augmented by having the female hook her legs around the male's thighs and both partners hug each other."

According to admittedly subjective criteria, none of these approaches was satisfactory. The elastic belts "reminded the partners of practices sometimes associated with bondage, a subject that neither found particularly appealing." The inflatable tunnel "tended to get sticky with sweat and other discharges." The unassisted approaches were physically too difficult to maintain: "as the runs approached their climaxes, an unexpected problem arose. One or the other partner tended to let go." Although these may seem like failed experiments, in fact they point toward important conclusions. Most significantly, the extreme difficulty of simulating the "conventional approach to marital relationships" in space confirms a direct relation of dependence between the missionary position and the earth's gravitational field. This means that, though the G spot may or may not be a myth, G-forces are in fact a sexual reality. Furthermore, because the quantity and quality of terrestrial gravity is unique in the solar system and uncommon in deep space, the missionary position itself is necessarily a "provincial" proclivity. In fact, it will be difficult for puritans to portray the missionary position as the only "civilized" sexual comportment when there are other civilizations whose sexualities have adapted to other gravitational fields. It would stand to reason that on planets of lesser gravity, sexual partners may float into their relations like clouds, while on planets of greater gravity they may press down into each other in prolonged bouts of copulation that resemble geological processes of sedimentation. The missionary position may well prove to be taboo in the Crab nebula, and perversion may therefore be less a psychological disorder than a geographical mistake, a matter of being born in the purlieus of earth with the sexuality of Altair.

However, if these sexual experiments comprise a process of elimination, drastically decreasing the probability that the missionary position will play a significant role in extraterrestrial sexuality, is it not still possible to utilize human subjects to infer something positive about the nature of alien lust? After all, human sexuality far exceeds the "conventional approach to marital relationships." To this end, the space shuttle astronauts did perform one experiment "involving non-procreative marital relations." This experiment utilized the zero gravity equivalent of the position known popularly as "sixty-nine," with each astronaut "gripping the other's head between their thighs and hugging the other's hips with their arms." Significantly, not only did the astronauts judge this position "most satisfactory," they even deemed it "more rewarding than analogous postures used in a gravitational field." In plain language, while the missionary position suffered from absence of gravity, the sixty-nine—perhaps henceforth to be known as the "spiral galaxy?"—gained in presumably inverse relationship (that is, the lesser the gravity, the greater the pleasure). Clearly this is an important discovery, insofar as it implies that the sexuality proper to outer space is non-reproductive in nature. If true, this would make it difficult for human beings to explore and colonize the cosmos, since they will lose the urge to procreate as they leave the planet. In this light, it is significant that NASA publication 14-307-1792 is supplemented by a contractor report giving oblique details of a "manipulator" device whose purpose clearly seems to be masturbatory: "the use of the redundant manipulator allowed for single subject use of the system as a unisexual device. We believe that this could be of great importance for long duration flights where the subject can not find a suitable partner."

Combining the results of the space shuttle experiments, it is possible to infer that optimal sexuality under extraterrestrial conditions is (1) non-procreative, (2) suggestive of bondage, and (3) needful of technological assistance.

In short, sex without gravity is sadomasochistic sodomy with gadgets. This implies that any beings currently capable of sexually sustaining the rigors of interstellar travel are essentially ET S&M freaks. If the reports of tabloid newspapers have any substance, when aliens kidnap a human it is not "medical" or scientific investigations they commit on his or her body, but rather some kind of kinky sadism from Polaris. Furthermore, if man wishes to participate in the cosmic community of beings, it is imperative he understand that *this is what he will become.* Consequently, astronauts preparing for prolonged flight missions should undergo training with sadists and dominatrixes. In this way, bondage in the command module can be accomplished with no more psychodrama than is wanted. In addition, scientists who believe that the only way to explore space is through "generational" endeavors must develop ways to ensure that astronauts do in fact procreate. For example, the female body might be re-engineered, reversing the positions of the mouth and vagina so that relations of sodomy can lead to the reproductive effects of the "conventional approach to marital relationships." For those female astronauts disinclined to undergo such invasive procedures, it would do well to remember that under such conditions sexuality will require individual sacrifice in order to assure the progress of humankind. When Buck Rogers is done fucking her in the mouth, she can proudly remind herself that one small *shtup* for man is in fact one great *shtup* for mankind.

Sigma was not a planet but a flotilla of spaceships. The actual planet from which this convoy of rockets originated was no longer even known. Plainly some government or corporation or enterprise had wanted to explore deep space. To this end, the Sigma ships were set up—physically, politically, scientifically—utilizing what could be called the generational principle of space travel: because no mortal individual can live long enough to traverse the incredible distances of interstellar space, the ships were to maintain their crew and their population using controlled reproduction techniques. The first cosmonauts would never reach a new star system but their children or, more likely, their children's children, would see fantastic unknown suns. It was a logical plan for coping with interstellar distances, and its proponents could not have foreseen how it came to fail. First, the spaceships drifted so long that the descendants no longer even knew where they were from or why they had been set adrift. Essentially they conceived of their ships as their "earth," and only the occasional Existentialist ever wondered about the why or the wherefore of their voyage—since, in fact, it no longer seemed to be a voyage to most of the voyagers. Second, it took very few generations of population control before the reproductive policies governing the ship came to seem oppressive. "Why should our sexual desires be channeled into the narrow straits of reproduction?" cried the inciters and provocateurs. Soon sons rebelled against fathers in the outer space equivalent of the sexual revolution of the earthly 1960s. Henceforth, there was to be free love, reproductive choice, individual freedom.

Like many rebellions, however, this one ceased to liberate people from the old values and quickly began to terrorize them with the new. If the old regime insisted on reproduction, then the new one held up its opposite as the law of the land. Genital sex was outlawed since it was an "anachronism belonging to the former tyranny of species perpetuation." Stormtroopers burst into the bedrooms of married couples looking for violations such as the missionary position. In the stead of genitalia, the ass was to become the "pleasure of the people." Revolutionaries took control of the fertility laboratories and utilized the equipment to explore ways of enhancing anal sex. At first scientists hoped to develop an anal clitoris, so that pleasure and not police would guarantee compliance with the Greek Sex Code. However, this modest effort gave way to a full-blown attempt to breed an entirely new rectum. Various mutations were tried on political prisoners until finally a fantastic new sexual organ was invented: the all-purpose reversible anus. When excited, this anus would reverse itself like the finger of a dish glove filled with air and protrude from the backside, taking on the bizarre appearance of a rectal penis. The now temporarily "male" alien could thrust this slimy pseudo-penis deep into the corresponding anus of his partner. When he was done, the partners could reverse positions—and in this way social and sexual equality were guaranteed. Gender no longer sundered the populace. The penis slowly became a useless appendage, shriveling up like an old pepper in the sun. The vagina all but closed up, like an old wound. Breasts began to disappear, getting smaller with every generation. Fully developed college-age aliens possessed the bodies of twelve-year-old girls.

Having successfully insinuated himself into the Sigma spaceships, Mercury de Sade knew to be cautious in any sexual encounter. Although there were probably dissidents who would have cherished the seminal fluid he was capable of delivering, at the same time he had to remain leery of spies, agents, snitches. Any sexual partner might really be a stool pigeon ready to inform the police that this infiltrator did not comply with the laws prohibiting the transmission of fertility substances. Consequently, when finally he undertook to fuck a Sigma, he had to proceed with extreme caution. "Let me fuck you," said the Sigma, its rectal penis protruding in anticipation. "No," said Mercury de Sade. "Let me do you." The Sigma lay down on its stomach and, behind its back, Mercury de Sade surreptitiously swallowed a small tab of chocolate laxative. The rectal penis of the alien had deflated somewhat and lay lazily across its left buttock, so Mercury de Sade pushed it back in with his finger to form an orifice. However, grasping the back of the Sigma's shoulders, he soon reached a dilemma. For him, the cum shot was like branding a cow or writing "Kilroy was here" on a bathroom wall. Mercury de Sade felt a compulsion to climax on the surface of the alien, and yet, on Sigma, to "frost the cake" could only incriminate him. Careful to dissimulate the signs of his passion, Mercury de Sade thus concealed the evidence of his infiltration deep inside the body beneath him. Then, squatting over it, he released what the laxative had wrought inside him, intending to fool the alien with the normal product of a rectal penis: a cum shit.

Now Charlotte is basically a pliant body—human, of course, but... Is this inevitable? Does she have to be human? Does Mercury de Sade not intend to make an alien out of her somehow? Well, but how? Where do you begin? You can't saw her hands off and replace them with tentacles—or rather, you could, but she wouldn't be able to wiggle them or wrap them around your penis. Anyway, how do you know aliens have tentacles? If you attach tentacles to her arms, might you not just succeed in making her an octopus? Isn't there a tremendous failure of imagination here? After all, *tentacles*—this is just transferring the strangeness of an earthly sea creature to a human. A really alien creature, a girl even, would certainly differ in a much wilder way. If humans and animals have evolved different anatomies in response to what is essentially the same environment (i.e. earth), would vastly dissimilar environments not result in anatomies far more different than those of the human and the octopus? To change Charlotte it would therefore be necessary to change her environment. And yet, if her environment is to be alien, plainly it would also be necessary for Mercury de Sade to become alien, because he is himself part of her environment. But how can he possibly do this?

Frustrated, Mercury de Sade sits ruminating in his desk chair. Above the computers is a shelf lined with DVDs. Taking down the disk of the film *Alien,* he inserts it into a computer and jumps forward to the end of the story. Ripley, played by the actress Sigourney Weaver, blows up her mother ship to kill a menacing alien and escapes in a space capsule. To while away the long hours of space flight, she then prepares to enter a cryogenic chamber. She removes her clothes, revealing a taut thin body in clinging white underwear. Her dark nipples peer through a cut-off T-shirt, and when she bends over an instrument panel the crack of her ass emerges from her panties. Suddenly the menacing alien reappears—it too has stowed away on the space capsule. Ripley retreats in fear, backing into a closet where she stands quivering, sweaty, frightened. The camera pans down her body as she slips into a white padded spacesuit: it points directly into her crotch as she lifts her leg, then turns upward to emphasize her panting chest. It's a classic damsel-in-distress situation: before the giant reptilian alien, she seems especially vulnerable in her underwear. Naturally, though, Hollywood likes its happy ending, and so she goes on to kill the hideous slithering extraterrestrial. But what of a more realistic ending? Is it not likely the menacing beast would have raped and ravaged the girl? "Maybe we should reenact this scene," Mercury de Sade suggests to his nearly comatose companion. "I'll be the alien. You be Ripley."

Dressing Ninfa XIX in white panties and T-shirt, Mercury de Sade illuminates her with halogen bulbs to mimic the spectral light of the space capsule, then mists her with water to make her look sweaty—and also to make her underwear transparent. Stepping through the video frame by frame, he compels Ninfa XIX to follow the exact movements of Ripley. When Ripley bends over the instrument panel, Ninfa XIX bends over a computer—but then rather than proceed directly to the next scene, Mercury de Sade pauses the video, presses his face against her ass, drags his tongue along the crack above her panties. As Ripley moves to the closet, Ninfa XIX imitates her and Mercury de Sade imitates the camera. He crawls on the floor to emulate the low vantage point of the crotch shot as Ripley dons the space suit, then drags his tongue up her body in simulation of the camera's upward pan. When he reaches her navel, the street buzzer suddenly rings, blaring out through Casa de Sade like a police siren. "Shit," he exclaims. He peers into the viewcam that monitors the vestibule. There are two detectives in brown suits and Florsheim shoes. He presses the listen button on the intercom. "You ever notice how there are no niggers on the *Jetsons?*" says the one. "No," says the other. "Well, I guess the future looks bright!" says the first, laughing. Mercury de Sade releases the button, strategizes for a moment, then presses the speak button. "Hello? Can I help you?" he calls out. The detectives hurriedly compose their faces into masks of intimidation and raise their badges to the camera mounted in a high corner of the vestibule. "Just give me one minute to throw some clothes on," says Mercury de Sade, buzzing them into the building. He is not undressed but he turns to Charlotte, who is half-naked. In a loft apartment consisting of one large room and a lot of computer equipment, where could he possibly hide her?

Husserl uses the example of extraterrestrial life to probe the problem at the very core of his philosophy. That is, if philosophy is to begin with an examination of individual consciousness, how is it possible to assert the existence of anything lying outside that consciousness? To tackle the question, Husserl distinguishes between worlds possible in principle and in fact. "The hypothetical assumption of something real outside this world is, of course, 'logically' possible," he writes. (*Ideas* I, §48, "The Logical Possibility and the Material Countersense of a World Outside Ours") The actuality of these possible worlds depends on their availability to conscious experience: "something transcendent necessarily must be experienceable not merely by an Ego conceived as an empty logical possibility but by any *actual* Ego." However, to prevent anyone from arguing that there exists a plurality of mutually external worlds (because every consciousness experiences its own world), Husserl reasons that whatever is "cognizable by one ego must of *essential necessity*, be cognizable by *any* Ego. Even though it is not *in fact* the case that each stands, or can stand, in a relationship of 'empathy,' of mutual understanding with every other, as, e.g., not having such relationship to mental lives on the planets of the remotest stars, nevertheless there exist, eidetically regarded, *essential possibilities of effecting a mutual understanding* and therefore possibilities also that the worlds of experience separated in fact become joined by concatenation of actual experience to make up the one intersubjective world, the correlate of the unitary world of mental lives."

To clarify, Husserl argues first that worlds possible in principle are reduced to unity by the actual experience of egos. However, the cogency of this argument depends on the unification of these egos (else a plurality of egos might lead back to a plurality of worlds). But is it possible to speak of a unification of actual egos? Husserl argues that any mutual understanding or "empathy" unrealized in actuality is still attainable in principle and therefore points to precisely such a unification, what he calls a "unitary world of mental lives." In consequence, not only are mental lives—whether human or from the "planets of the remotest stars"—brought together, but so also are the "worlds" that they experience. In this regard, all possible worlds become "one intersubjective world." Why, then, is the philosopher able to be certain that there is an objective world beyond the limits of his own subjectivity? Because this intersubjective world serves as the "correlate" of the mental one. The reduction of possible worlds leaves, like the remainder of a mathematical operation, the assertion of a necessary world defined as the only field available for conscious experience. Extraterrestrials could not inhabit other worlds, because these "other" worlds are phantoms of logical possibility. In actuality, whether a being hails from earth, Mars, or Polaris, he belongs to a single world. Husserl even conflates this singular world with earth. "This world is," he writes, "as the *life-world* for a human community capable of mutual understanding, *our earth*, which includes within itself all these different environing worlds with their modifications and their pasts—the more so since we have no knowledge of other heavenly bodies as environing worlds for possible human habitation." (*Experience and Judgment*, "The Necessary Connection, on the Basis of Time as the Form of Sensibility, between the Intentional Objects of All Perceptions and Positional Presentifications of an Ego and a Community of Egos") But does this mean that the world is limited to planet earth?

If there are no other planets suitable for life, then the world seems to contract to earth. However, if there are other planets suitable for life, Husserl's statement leaves open the possibility that these would still be part of a singular world, an expanded "earth." That Husserl did understand "earth" in this manner is clear from an important text in which he investigates the phenomenological origin of spatiality. Arguing that spatiality is grounded in the planet earth as "basis-body," he considers the possibility of "new" earths. "But what do two earths mean?" he asks. "Two pieces of one earth with a humanity. Together, they would become one basis." ("Foundational Investigations of the Phenomenological Origin of the Spatiality of Nature") Going on to speculate about what has since become a platitude of science fiction—that of generations of people born on spaceships—he concludes that, for their inhabitants, these spaceships would also "be my 'earth,' my primitive home." Even the moon comes to be "earth" in this sense: "Why should I not think of the moon as something like an earth, as therefore something like a dwelling place of living beings?... Certainly, I can conceive of human beings and brutes already being there... Indeed, a fragment of the earth (like an ice floe) may have become detached.... [but] there is only one humanity and one earth—all fragments belong to it which are or have been detached from it." When two earths, numerous spaceships, and one moon can be "earth," the world is clearly not confined to a planet. Rather, earth itself is as large as the world, and in this sense it is not only humans but also aliens who inhabit earth. "The totality of the We, of human beings or 'animate beings,' is in this sense earthly—and immediately has no contrary in the nonearthly."

To describe Casa de Sade is to analyze the influence of computer technology on architecture—or more precisely, the influence of the computer on the design of habitable space. In this respect, it should be clarified that there are qualitatively different levels of influence. The average user who owns only one computer simply positions it on his desk, and in this circumstance the computer physically affects living space little more than a typewriter. The domestic space of the user who owns only one laptop machine is affected even less, since in this case the laptop adapts itself to the environment: it can be used in bed, on the couch, at the kitchen table, etc. However, these basic influences are not true of Casa de Sade for the simple reason that its inhabitant is not an average user. Rather, Mercury de Sade is a member of the new class of computer professionals for whom living and working space are the two "sides" of a Möbius strip—which is to say that the two kinds of space are mapped onto one another. Casa de Sade is comprised of one large, loft-like space in which there are no dividing walls save those for the bathroom. Rather than physically distinct rooms there are functionally defined areas or zones: an eating area, a sleeping area, and so on. The computer, however, encroaches on these zones like an uncontainable growth. Not only are there a multiplicity of CPUs, there are a host of supporting devices: wires, cables, cords, storage media, input devices, burners, hubs. Even the bathroom serves as a storage area for a stack of old monitors. It is as though an internal conflict has arisen in the "machine for living." The machine has launched an attack against the living, has increasingly come to occupy the space and colonize it with wires and gizmos.

Simultaneously, while the computer extends its copper tentacles and fiber-optic feelers into space, it also consumes the accoutrements of external reality. The physical desktop belonging to a piece of furniture becomes the software desktop displayed by most operating systems. The windows and the trash become Windows and its "recycling bin." The machine for living usurps the identity of the life space and thereby becomes a living machine. In this respect its architectural influence has been much more profound than that of its forebear, the television. It is well-known how the television altered domestic space: couches and chairs that used to face each other were turned toward the box, so that interaction with other humans was replaced by mutual absorption of the centralized broadcast. However, while the television may have had a deleterious influence on intersubjective relations, it did not strip the good life from the machine for living. The Lazy Boy, a big comfortable chair poised in front of the television, symbolized the fact that domestic space under the conditions of television remained a haven from work. With the computer, however, the Lazy Boy is replaced by the office chair with castors on the bottom. In this, one no longer relaxes but becomes an attendant of the computers, rolling from machine to machine like a little robot on wheels. If domestic space becomes a living machine, its occupant becomes a mechanic—or perhaps even mechanical. In this sense, the computer exerts an influence on Casa de Sade comparable to that which the frequently extravagant appliances of sadism exert on architectural space. The gadgets of S&M cause a room to forcibly polarize its occupants. In the dungeon, you are on one side of pain or the other—either its purveyor or its victim. So too in Casa de Sade: you are on one side of technology or the other—either its purveyor or its victim.

The neoclassical headquarters of the university had been constructed using a shiny, chrome-like metal of intergalactic origin. Standing at the foot of the grand staircase leading up to its front, Mercury de Sade watched the metallic façade reflect the green light of the Tau sun. The building, he thought, was appropriately monumental for an intergalactic institute of higher learning: it was the New York Public Library made of metal. Here aliens from a thousand cultures came to study with a stellar faculty, and Mercury de Sade watched as sophomores from Saturn and grad students from the Crab nebula wandered down the stairs, groping each other and talking of Michelangelo. Mounting the staircase, he paused to admire an enormous sculpture of Ludwig Wittgenstein masturbating. An inscription on the base of the statue quoted from the *Tractatus Logico-Philosophicus:* "A thought contains the possibility of the situation of which it is the thought. What is thinkable is possible too." It was an epigram appropriate for a civilization that had overcome the mind-body dichotomy, thought Mercury de Sade. After all, if the gap between body and mind disappears, does it not mean that the creations of the mind acquire the potential to become very real?

On Tau the dichotomy of mind and body had been resolved by sexuality. There was a direct relation between the activities of the body and the abilities of the mind. Sex increased intelligence. Nymphomaniacs became geniuses, and the greatest advances of society depended on the promiscuity of its most talented minds. The Marie Curie of Tau was a slut and a whore, and its Einstein a star of pornography. In the throes of orgasm two creatures of Tau would shout out the formulae of quantum physics. The cries of climax would be interspersed with abstruse theories of metaphysics and commentaries on an extraterrestrial Kant. Conversely, the celibate—clergymen, for example—were idiots. Virgins were dumb as dogs. To educate them it was necessary to molest them, and thus did elementary schools compete to hire pedophiles. Scholarship funds sponsored gangbangs. Students crammed for exams by pulling all-nighters in massage parlors. The Tau equivalent of the NAACP took out ads placing the caption "A mind is a terrible thing to waste" beneath the image of a black girl being raped. Ivy League universities sponsored colloquia on neurology that included group-gropes as a matter of course. Scientists revealed the fruits of their research in pornographic magazines. Esoteric propositions of ontology were adumbrated in centerfold layouts. Striptease was utilized to explain Brownian motion, and deep throat used as a model for the mathematics of black holes.

Having passed the entrance examinations, Mercury de Sade began to attend classes in exophilosophy. The professor was a transvestite braineater from a star located in Virgo. Whenever there was a question, she would push her strap-on into the student's anus in parody of the maieutic method. "I'll ruin your ass with the thesis," she would snarl. "Then I'll rape your mouth for the antithesis and your cunt for the synthesis." Revelations were accompanied by wild orgasms. "I understand," the student would scream, quivering like jelly and, in the case of men, spurting semen across the course textbook. Sometimes these revelations would be shared by the entire student body and an orgy of class consciousness would break out. Male creatures would form a major premise and females a minor premise in a great syllogism of fuck that would conclude in a climax of enlightenment. "I get it," all would scream in ecstatic comprehension. However, group sex was forbidden during exams, so students would sit masturbating at their desks while filling in their answers with a pencil. Term papers read like a pastiche of philosophical speculation and X-rated fantasy. In his paper, Mercury de Sade explored the following hypothesis: if we get smarter by fucking, do we get hornier by philosophizing? And if so, does it not stand to reason that ultimately the two converge (such that thought and sex become indistinguishable)?

Who are the detectives? Roger Smith is forty-three, salt and pepper hair, slightly portly. His gun gives him a rash under his armpit so he keeps a felt pad hooked to the underside of his shoulder holster with Velcro. He has a square head like a cement block but a face that crumples easily into hilarity. He likes to laugh, although there is a certain lurid quality to his jocularity, like a man who is able to appreciate the humor in raping a nun or defacing a synagogue. Wherever he goes the smell of after-shave precedes him—it comes from a little green bottle which he pours into his hand and slaps into his cheeks as though punishing himself. His partner Roger Wesson is a bachelor. Wesson lives in a small house that is really a beach bungalow. He jogs every morning before breakfast, which consists of an omelet of egg whites, toast, and tea. Tall, broad, with angular features, he looks like a pug-nosed Mikhail Baryshnikov. When he was younger, women found his tough good looks irresistible, and this has left him with a diligent concern for his health and appearance. Although he is aging well and will be capable of football until he's sixty, at the same time the angles of his face lose their attractiveness with age and start to frighten. He's naturally intimidating. He has a face that could slice through you. It's hard to bullshit the man. For this reason the two make good partners: one is jocular and the other severe.

When Mercury de Sade opens the door of his apartment they scan him with lie-detector eyes. They have no time for a joker like Mercury de Sade. To them he looks like some kind of fag or maybe artist—same thing. Shaved head, broad shoulders, but there's something feminine about him. His eyes are too wet and his voice too appeasing. He's just the kind of queer to pick up with a teenager. He's not man enough to ball a woman of experience. It's too bad the Goddard girl is only sixteen—if she were younger they could at least book him with statutory rape. If they're lucky, maybe they can find evidence of a prior relationship and get him anyway. Letters can be very incriminating. Make a note to check if they have email accounts. Get a log from their ISPs. Check phone records. "What can I do for you, officers?" asks Mercury de Sade. Twenty years on the force and this prig kid calls me an officer. "*Detective* Smith and I would like to ask you a few questions," states Wesson. There has been a murder. A man has been pummeled to death and his daughter is missing. "Kidnapped?" asks Mercury de Sade. There's no note. Maybe she committed the murder. Maybe she ran away with a lover boy who committed the murder. "But we don't speculate," says Wesson, "we investigate." Mercury de Sade is deferential. "Anyway," he demurs, "what does this have to do with me? Was it one of my neighbors?" The subject in question is Charlotte Goddard. Mercury de Sade fakes astonishment. Records show two phone calls around the time of the murder. "I did speak to her," admits Mercury de Sade. "She was very upset... Her father had been abusing her, you know."

"Mind if we look around a bit?" Big white loft, clean, windows facing the street, a wall of computers, electrical cables running everywhere along the floor, a stack of maybe fifteen monitors piled inside the bathroom. "You making a pyramid or something?" Charlotte is buried in this pile of monitors. The whole shithouse could explode: one of her pathetic little beeps, the cops look significantly at each other and start dismantling the pile. "I recycle computers," says Mercury de Sade, verbose in an effort to distract them. "I can't stand to see them in the trash. To me it's like seeing human limbs thrown in a dumpster. You know, someday computers will outlive people—not because they'll be made with better parts, but because they'll be able to repair themselves—and then we probably will begin to find human limbs or even entire humans in the trash. The computers won't have any use for us. Why should they? Motherboards may break and hard drives may go bad, but unlike the internal organs of people they don't *rot*." Something ain't right about this guy. Can't say whether he's guilty or hiding anything necessarily, but there's something off about him. "You sure got a lot of computers," says Wesson. "That's my field," says Mercury de Sade. "I'm in computers." Wesson looks hard at him, performing a lobotomy with his eyes. "Yeah, well, we're in perpetrators." The vibe is ominous for a moment. "Then I guess we don't have much in common," says Mercury de Sade. "You should hope not," states Wesson. They give him their cards and exit, leaving a smell of after-shave hanging in the air, the weird chemical odor of Big Brother. Peering out through the front windows, Mercury de Sade watches them climb into a black box-shaped vehicle heavy and rich as a Viennese cake. Just visible inside the car is a big head swathed in white like the invisible man wrapped in bandages.

The notion of a plurality of worlds had been entertained by philosophers for over two thousand years without the definition of "world" having been taken into rigorous account. Generally speaking a "world" was equated to one of the known planets, sometimes to a distant star, particularly if either of these was thought to be inhabited. "World" was thus defined roughly as "planet with life." However, with the advent of the twentieth century the definition of "world" would come to be probed by an entire series of philosophers, perhaps the first of which was Ludwig Wittgenstein. In the *Tractatus Logico-Philosophicus*, Wittgenstein argued that a world was coextensive with a language: "*The limits of my language* mean the limits of my world." (*Tractatus Logico-Philosophicus*, §5.6) While in principle this left open the possibility of a plurality of worlds—insofar as there could be a plurality of languages to constitute them—it implied that none of them could ever be known: a world that lay beyond the limits of my language could not be cognized. However, this basically solipsistic view was turned on its head by Wittgenstein's later work: if in the *Tractatus* it was language that defined the limits of a world, with the *Philosophical Investigations* it is a world that comes to define the limits of a language. Language is no longer a purely logical system of semantic relations but rather a *Sprachspiel,* a "language-game" in which meaning is derived in counterpoint to action, gesture, and life: "the term 'language-game' is meant to bring into prominence the fact that the *speaking* of language is part of an activity, or of a form of life." (*Philosophical Investigations*, §23)

It is at this juncture that the Martian enters into the philosophy of Wittgenstein (a fact emphasized by the alien interlocutor in Derek Jarman's artful film of the philosopher). "If you came to a foreign tribe, whose language you didn't know at all and you wished to know what words corresponded to 'good,' 'fine,' etc., what would you look for? You would look for smiles, gestures, food, toys… If you went to Mars and men were spheres with sticks coming out, you wouldn't know what to look for… Certainly we must interpret the gestures of the tribe on the analogy of ours… We don't start from certain words, but from certain occasions or activities." (*Lectures and Conversations*, §6) No Martian language could be understood as a self-contained system of logical relationships. To understand Martian language requires reference to Martian forms of life. French can be translated into Russian because each language still refers to fundamentally human forms of life: smiles, gestures, food, toys. But what if Martians play with their food and nourish themselves on toys? What if their smile consists of sliding, like a bead on an abacus, one of their spheres from one side to the other of a stick? The problem of translation is not simply that two languages encounter one another, but that two forms of life must interpenetrate. "I see a picture," wrote Wittgenstein. "It represents an old man walking up a steep path leaning on a stick.—How? Might it not have looked just the same if he had been sliding downhill in that position? Perhaps a Martian would describe the picture so. I do not need to explain why *we* do not describe it so." (*Philosophical Investigations,* §139b) Why do we—we earthlings—not describe it so? Because we understand the form of life associated with the picture: gravity acts in such a way on a human body struggling uphill, a person sliding backward would not have the poise of a person walking forward, an old man needs a cane, etc. "What belongs to a language game," wrote Wittgenstein, "is a whole culture." (*Lectures and Conversations,* §26) And for this reason, man and alien may well be incapable of understanding one another: even if they speak the same language, they play fundamentally different games.

To err is human
To be true is the opposite of to err
To be true is the opposite of human (C1)

Humanity is terrestrial
The opposite of terrestrial is extraterrestrial
The opposite of human is extraterrestrial (C2)

To be true is the opposite of human (C1)
The opposite of human is extraterrestrial (C2)
To be true is extraterrestrial (C3)

Philosophy is a love of wisdom
Wisdom is inherently true
Philosophy is a love of truth (C4)

To be true is extraterrestrial (C3)
Philosophy is a love of truth (C4)
Philosophy is a love of the extraterrestrial (C5)

Philosophy is a love of the extraterrestrial (C5)
To love the extraterrestrial is exophilia
Philosophy is exophilia (C6)

Philosophy is exophilia (C6)
Exophilosophy is a type of philosophy
Exophilosophy is exophilia (C7)

Although planet Upsilon, like Saturn, was encircled by rings, these were never regarded as desirable real estate until population pressure intensified the need for habitable space. Consequently, what had formerly been a mere belt of debris floating in a black vacuum was transformed through one of the greatest projects of civil engineering in the history of the cosmos. The entire ring was encased in a great plastic donut, the floating debris making it up was artificially stabilized, and a breathable atmosphere was created by means of tremendous air purifiers. Before long, the more successful parts of the new circle had become the extra-terrestrial equivalent of New York's Fifth Avenue, Paris's Champs Elysées, or Vienna's Ringstrasse. Glamorous shops offering the latest in haute couture, expensive restaurants serving seafood from Uranus, exclusive galleries showing the latest sculptures from the Crab nebula—all these attracted a well-to-do clientele, who strutted along the moving sidewalks like runway models. Conversely, if parts of Upsilon's ring became a parade ground for the jet setters of Mars and the celebrities of Polaris, other parts were naturally less desirable. Leaks in the tube or irregularities in the debris caused developers to shun certain areas. These naturally became the extraterrestrial equivalent of New York's Times Square, Paris's Pigalle, or Vienna's Ringstrasse. Porn emporia showing the latest in hardcore, illicit brothels serving seedy tourists from Uranus, topless bars offering the hottest strippers from the Crab nebula—all these attracted a disreputable clientele, who shuffled along the moving sidewalks like furtive runaways.

Upon arrival at Upsilon, Mercury de Sade took a room in a shabby hotel in the red light district. Depositing his things in his room, he could hear the throes of fucking next door—an osmotic sound, like someone slurping up a milkshake. After freshening up, he hid his valuables in the room and headed down to the street. Wandering under the plastic porticoes of the ring dome, past neon signs promising adult pleasures, Mercury de Sade watched as face after face passed him by—always the same face, except when it belonged to an "alien" or non-Upsilonian such as himself. But even these alien faces, he knew, were subject to become the same as the others. A native rapist might assault a woman on business from Betelgeuse, and rather than leave her lying in the gutter, battered and bruised, he would leave behind an exact replica of himself, an Upsilonian—or rather, *the* Upsilonian, for on this planet the law of convergence had made all sexuality recede, like parallel train tracks merging on the horizon, to a single vanishing point. Reproduction on Upsilon did not occur through any of the usual means familiar to an earthling. Upsilonians did not have babies, but rather imposed a new form—their own—on their sexual partners. Copulation served as a hostile takeover of atoms and molecules belonging to the weaker partner. When a man laid down with a woman, he rose up again from a man—from himself. Whereas on earth cloning served as an asexual means of reproduction, on Upsilon it was the opposite: to fuck another was to clone oneself. Naturally, in a closed society such a sexuality could function for only so long: eventually the entire planet was populated by a single individual repeated numerous times, the Upsilonian.

Entering into the dimly lit corridor of a whorehouse, Mercury de Sade paused. Was he sure he wanted to go through with this? After all, to fuck an Upsilonian was to risk the loss of his own personal identity. But then again, he thought, Upsilonians are the only creatures in the cosmos to be exophiliac by nature. Because they are all iterations of one creature, sex between themselves is essentially masturbation—not sex between but with themselves. Therefore they prefer to do it with outsiders, aliens. I'm an exophile by design, they're exophiles by nature. Does it matter what body we use to fuck other creatures of the cosmos? Bracing himself with the thought, Mercury de Sade completed a transaction and soon found himself fucking the Upsilonian. The physical act was accompanied by weird vibes of empathy and communion. It was almost love-like, except that there was something invasive about it. He felt a total identification with the creature. Weirdly, he even began to pick up on the Upsilonian's sexual fantasies. It wasn't just fucking him, it was fantasizing about other creatures at the same time. Mercury de Sade was able to observe as a procession of earthlings passed through its head in positions of sexual submission. Having himself dreamed of nothing but aliens, the vision of human sex objects sent a shudder through him. Is this what it means to become an extraterrestrial? he wondered. I'd spend my time fantasizing about human beings? If that's the case, he thought, I'd rather remain a man.

"You think he believed you were cops?" Mr. Goddard sits in the back of his own car as the detectives chauffeur him away from Casa de Sade. His entire head is wrapped in gauze bandages. Little dark stains in the gauze indicate where the slashes and gashes in his face still ooze. Peering out from narrow slits, his eyes resemble these stains, as though they too leak an evil, malodorous pus. When the car pauses at a red light, Mr. Goddard turns his glance to a young gay man waiting to cross the street, and without quite knowing why the man begins to wonder if he is HIV positive. "We *are* cops," retorts Wesson, steering the vehicle through traffic. "You know what I mean, idiot," barks Mr. Goddard. "Did he believe you were there on official business?" Wesson chafes beneath the mean tone of Mr. Goddard, so Smith, who is naturally diplomatic, tries to answer for him. "He didn't seem surprised to see us," says Smith. "Then the little fucker's guilty," Mr. Goddard spits out. "Guilty of what?" asks Smith. "Guilty of Charlotte," Mr. Goddard hollers like a wrestling coach shouting through a megaphone. "That girl deserves *punishment*. She needs to be *disciplined…*" While the head inside the gauze rants on like an angry fist inside a hand puppet, Smith and Wesson exchange that look of telepathy that comes from years of partnership. He's bonkers, they agree, but what can they do about it?

"And what about the camera?" demands Mr. Goddard. "Did you idiots plant it?" Wesson describes how he concealed a surveillance camera the size of a postage stamp inside the apartment. "So how do we see it?" Mr. Goddard barks. Wesson explains that the video camera transmits to channel 59 of any UHF-enabled monitor or television for a radius of up to two hundred feet. "Two hundred feet?" screams Mr. Goddard. "Two hundred feet? If it only transmits for two hundred feet, then what the fuck are we doing two miles away?" He leans forward and slaps Wesson on the back of the head. The effect is decidedly not comparable to that of the three stooges slapping each other around. There is nothing funny about it. Wesson can barely stand it, he'd gladly shoot Mr. Goddard in the mouth with his pistol, but he can't. "Turn this fucking vehicle around, you moron!" yells Mr. Goddard. Wesson makes a U-turn in the middle of a busy street and speeds back toward Casa de Sade. Mr. Goddard flicks on the monitor in the back seat of the car. It emits nothing but static until the vehicle approaches its destination. Wesson parks by the curb and a fragmented image comes in: Charlotte standing half-naked in the loft with a computer monitor over her head. "You've heard of the man in the iron mask," Mercury de Sade can be heard to say, "now you can be the girl with the monitor head."

They watch as Mercury de Sade removes the monitor and struggles to fit a newer one over her head without removing the cathode-ray tube inside. "What the hell is he doing?" asks Smith, puzzled. Once the monitor is in place, Mercury de Sade hooks it to a laptop and places it inside a backpack, which he slings over her shoulders. "Now that's what I call portable," he can be heard to say. "Beep," moans Charlotte. She stands holding the pink bear clutched to her chest, and the image of Casa de Sade—from the apparent vantage point of the bear—projects across her face in blurry grayscale video. "That's that stuffed animal," blusters Mr. Goddard, recognizing the bear. "There must be a surveillance camera inside it." He almost feels a new respect for Mercury de Sade, the way a duelist appreciates an equally accomplished opponent. He watches as Mercury de Sade unbuttons Charlotte's blouse and holds her arms out in front of her, so that the bear stares back at her chest. Her breasts, pushed together between her biceps, project across the screen of the monitor on her head. Like a third nipple behind the ghostly breasts, her nose pushes against the glass of the monitor and gives the appearance of a weird alien anatomy, part sex and part sensory organ. "What do you want us to do?" asks Smith. "Maybe we can get him to punish her for us," intones Mr. Goddard, the smile on his face contracting cheek muscles in such a way as to cause a drop of pus to seep out through the gauze.

With their allegiance to Karl Marx and their pursuit of sociological and psychological analyses, the Frankfurt School theoreticians did not emphasize the contrived nature of belief in extraterrestrial life without also demonstrating the cultural context in which this belief was able to flourish. Specifically, this context was one dominated by post-industrial capitalism and its "culture industry." Walter Benjamin (1892-1940) described how a cartoon by the nineteenth-century satirist Grandville indicated that the extraterrestrial had become less an astronomical speculation than a commodity fetish. "Grandville's fantasies extend the character of a commodity to the universe. They modernize it. Saturn's ring becomes a cast-iron balcony on which the inhabitants of the planet take the air in the evening." ("Paris, Capital of the Nineteenth Century") In a letter to Benjamin discussing the 1935 text, Theodor Adorno (1903-1969) argued that the "Saturn ring should not become a cast-iron balcony, but the balcony should become the real Saturn ring." In other words, this industrial modernization of the universe ought not occur without exerting an equally dialectical influence on the inhabitants of earth. Consequently, in a 1939 French redaction of the text, Benjamin added: "Saturn's ring becomes a cast-iron balcony on which the inhabitants of the planet take the air in the evening. In the same manner a cast-iron balcony would become... the ring of Saturn and those who traversed it would see themselves caught up in a phantasmagoria wherein they would be transformed into inhabitants of Saturn." ("Paris, capitale de la dix-neuvième siècle") In short, under the conditions of capitalism extraterrestrial life was to be found not in the stars but the sideshow, where the alienation of industrial life was sublimated into the cheap thrill of becoming an "alien."

It is precisely this vicarious element of the commodity fetish that serves as the basis for a theory later put forward by Adorno. The whole panoply of paranormal phenomena—occultism, telepathy, astrology, demonology, extraterrestrial life—acquires an entirely new character under capitalism. Formerly, "superstition was an attempt, however awkward, to cope with problems for which no better or more rational means were available." (*The Stars Down to Earth*) In modernity, however, superstition is blatantly incompatible with rational knowledge and yet acquires an alluring veneer of pseudo-rationality through its objectification in mass media. Adorno calls this *secondary superstition:* "people responding to the stimuli we are here investigating seem in a way 'alien' to the experience on which they claim their decisions are based. They participate in them largely through the mediations of magazines and newspapers... and frequently accept such information as reliable sources of advice rather than pretend to have any personal basis for their belief." In other words, the strength of belief in paranormal phenomena derives not from empirical experience—people do not themselves see ghosts or claim powers of telekinesis—but from vicarious consumption of the world of weirdness reified by newspapers, movies, television, the internet. Such a pseudo-rationalization of the irrational reinforces the economic and social inequities embedded in capitalism. In astrology, for example, "in as much as the social system is the 'fate' of most individuals independent of their will and interest, it is projected upon the stars in order thus to obtain a degree of dignity and justification" for what is essentially a state of subjugation.

Although Adorno's analyses bear primarily on astrology and occultism, he specifies that extraterrestrial life is also a form of secondary superstition. "Thus, the term 'another world' which once had a metaphysical meaning, is here brought down to the level of astronomy and obtains an empirical ring. Ghosts and horrible threats often reviving repulsive freakish entities of olden times, are treated as natural and scientific objects coming out of space from another star and preferably from another galaxy." And though Adorno decries the manner in which such irrational fears are given rational semblances, an alienist might well object: Is it really so irrational to fear that aliens might invade earth? Might horrible monsters from Mars not annihilate the globe with cosmic death rays? Here Adorno indicates that reason—specifically in the form of modern science—constrains the wilder speculations of exomorphology: "to the best of today's scientific knowledge the 'law of convergence' would probably lead even on distant stars to developments much more similar to those on earth than it appears in the secularizations of demonology enjoyed by the science fiction reader." In other words, Adorno assumes that the conditions necessary to create life on earth would resemble the conditions necessary to create life on any planet. Consequently, alien life forms would resemble earthly life forms to a relatively high degree. The implication is that there is nothing to fear from creatures resembling men, hence the fear of alien invasion is irrational. However, this does leave one further possibility by means of which this fear could regain its reasonableness: perhaps it is precisely because aliens will resemble men that their arrival ought to terrify.

Extraterrestrial beings are widely thought to be more intelligent than man. Contactees often claim that aliens have imparted to them messages of profound philosophical significance. Some even think that alien beings have undertaken a tremendous educational initiative here on earth: each abduction is an attempt to prepare man for intelligent participation in intergalactic culture. If this is true, however, then man is a patently lazy pupil, for the philosophical annunciations of alien beings have never been collected and analyzed in their entirety. Currently they lie scattered in the confessions of contactees in much the same way that the philosophy of the ancients lay mutilated in the texts of Roman and medieval writers until nineteenth-century scholars began to assemble them. Would posterity know anything of Anaximander or Heraclitus if not for the efforts of these diligent philologists? Are we not perhaps ignorant of an extraterrestrial Anaximander only because we have been too lazy to extract his utterances from the abduction accounts in which they lie embedded? Have we turned a deaf ear to a Heraclitus from Mars? To find out, philosophical statements or *philosophemes* from a number of leading abduction accounts have been compiled, analyzed, and categorized. Precise guidelines for the selection of philosophemes were developed, such that only those statements directly attributed to an extraterrestrial intelligence were considered. Contactee reflections on the meaning of the abduction experience, hypothetical reasons for alien visitations to earth, possible methods of interstellar space travel, and so on, were expressly excluded in favor of more properly philosophical pronouncements. Many possible alien amanuenses were eliminated on the basis of these criteria, leaving four who seemed richest in extraterrestrial philosophemes:

George Adamski, the founder of a cult called the Royal Order of Tibet, claimed to have been abducted in a California desert in November 1952. In his book *Inside the Spaceships,* Adamski describes an entire series of encounters with a Venusian named Orthon and other aliens who take him aboard their spaceship seemingly for the sole purpose of philosophical discussion. Although topics range from telepathy to the meaning of life, the primary theme is that of man's self-destructiveness. "My son," says the alien, "our main purpose in coming to you at this time is to warn you of the grave danger which threatens men of earth today." This grave danger is of course the atomic bomb. The aliens explain to Adamski that the destruction of planet earth by nuclear weaponry would upset a cosmic balance. The aliens are thus obliged to interfere with the natural evolution of mankind, and have begun a series of contacts in order to effectuate their peaceable mission.

Betty Andreasson was a typical housewife until she was abducted in January 1967. Her subsequent account, much of which emerged under hypnosis, set the pattern for later abduction scenarios: four aliens entered her house, communicated with her via telepathy, escorted her to a spaceship, submitted her to a violating medical examination, and finally introduced her to their leader, Quazgaa. Philosophically, though her account includes mysterious alien formulae and pseudo-Heraclitean utterances, thinly veiled religious truisms reflecting Andreasson's unabashed Christian fundamentalism predominate. The aliens "love the human race. They have come to help the human race. And, unless man will accept, he will not be saved, he will not live." Although the cold war paranoia of Adamski is translated in Andreasson into the language of religious salvation, the underlying ethical question remains that of human self-destruction— and the answer remains that of alien rescue.

John Mack is the only one of the extraterrestrial amanuenses not to have claimed—at least publicly—to have been abducted by aliens. A psychiatrist on the faculty of Harvard University, Mack has earned tremendous notoriety by taking the claims of abductees seriously, not only as a psychological but as a social phenomenon. His authority as an Ivy League thinker is severely undercut by the loose, credulous, unmethodical approach of his writing, and yet the accounts collected in his book *Abduction* abound in alien philosophemes. Many of these demonstrate Mack's own concern with ecological issues and non-Western modes of thought. "It would appear from the information that abductees receive," he writes, "that the earth has value or importance in a larger, interrelated cosmic system that mirrors the interconnectedness of life on earth. The alien abduction phenomenon represents, then, some sort of corrective initiative." It is immediately apparent that this ecological awareness scarcely differs from Adamski's atomic paranoia, and thus Mack too emphasizes one central theme: human salvation.

Marshall Applewhite, a.k.a. "Do," was a handsome music teacher deeply conflicted about his homosexuality until he met Bonnie Lu Nettles in a mental hospital in Texas. Together the two founded an ascetic cult that eventually came to be known as Heaven's Gate. Although Nettles died of cancer some years before, the mass suicide of the thirty-nine cult members (including Applewhite) in March 1997 brought the cult's philosophical and theological ideas to international attention. For Applewhite, religious transcendence represents an evolutionary possibility—one has to "overcome" the human body. Because the human body is a mere "vehicle" for a soul, this evolutionary process is not physical but spiritual in nature (sex is to be avoided, drink eschewed, addictions overcome). Only select human beings complete this evolutionary process and thereby attain to something called the Next Level Above Human. This is less a "level" properly speaking than an extraterrestrial locale from which alien beings periodically come to save the chosen. These beings, "representatives" of the Kingdom of God, come to earth on flying saucers in order to catalyze the spiritual evolution of the chosen, whose souls will be "disconnected" from their physical vehicles in order to be transported to the Next Level Above Human.

These primary sources indicate that the fundamental concern of alienosophy is ethics. Aliens seem particularly devoted to the "love thy neighbor" principle: according to Adamski, the aliens would rather destroy themselves than allow harm to come to mankind. That cold war paranoia and ecological awareness are inextricably bound up with the rhetoric of salvation only demonstrates the naturally keen awareness which an intergalactic space traveler would possess of the close relation between a life form and its host environment: while to save the planet is not necessarily to save man, to destroy the planet is almost certainly to destroy him. In this regard, "Sara" (a patient of Mack) explains that her alien encounter caused her to understand how people "have to redefine philosophically what they mean by environment. People think, 'Oh, my environment.' But, it's like environment is [complete]... environment is... infinite. And it has an infinite number of characteristics, and they extend from physical to emotional-psychic to interplanor and cross-sectional... You are your environment." Ontologically, the identification of individual and environment results in absurdities such as the syllogism latent in Sara's statement: environment is infinite, she says, and yet you are your environment, so the necessary conclusion must be that *you are infinite*. This is an oxymoron insofar as it equates the finite—the individual—with the infinite. How can a creature limited in space and time be infinite?

"You are your environment" must thus be intended as an ethical principle meaning roughly "Your actions affect everything else, and conversely." Another of Mack's patients, "Joe," explains that there "is a golden thread that connects all life together." From such statements it is possible to infer that whenever extraterrestrial thinkers approach mierology (the study of part/whole relations), it is always from the vantage point of morality. Although the technology of aliens must be very advanced for them to travel to earth, their philosophical musings do not revolve around sophisticated part/whole conundrums (such as the perplexity in set theory that an infinite set can be a member of itself) but rather on the practical ramifications of mierology for life and living.

Notably absent from these ethical philosophemes, however, are indications of how such "interconnection awareness" influences alien culture itself. How, for example, are aliens capable of creating advanced technological devices without exploiting or exhausting natural resources? Aliens seem very concerned to steer man away from anthropocentric habits of thought—they inform "Scott" that "success on earth would take an incredible shift, a shift from ego gratification to aspiring to achieve"—and yet they themselves demonstrate only an undue concern with man. Do they love their neighbor more than they love themselves? If it is "bad" for man to think of himself first, why is it "good" for the aliens to think first of man?

Is it because aliens are superior in intelligence? "Each of us," Orthon tells Adamski, "recognizes himself as the intelligence and not the body." The implication is that aliens have mastered a dilemma which has long haunted philosophy: mind-body duality. How is it that an immaterial "thing" such as the mind or soul can communicate with a material body? Alienosophy doesn't say, although it does go far in elaborating the consequences of this split. Reincarnation, for example, ensues from the notion that the mind or soul can be separated from the body. Adamski's aliens affirm that "through rebirth, we receive a new body." Adamski asks whether memory accumulates and persists from reincarnation to reincarnation, and Orthon replies: "Eternal man forgets nothing. But the memory of things learned in a former body seldom manifests as more than an instinctive knowledge of, or gravitation toward, certain familiar things." Applewhite puts it another way: "The soul has its own 'brain' or 'hard drive' that accumulates only information of the Next Level—mundane as well as theoretical or philosophical." The soul as epistemological organ—is this not identical to Plato's theory of anamnesis? Plato holds that the soul acquires nearly absolute knowledge by virtue of being eternal. This knowledge, though, is lost or forgotten at the moment of birth. Learning is therefore a process of causing the human brain to recollect the knowledge of the soul. Perhaps this is what aliens mean when they tell Andreasson that "knowledge is sought out through the spirit." Or perhaps "Jerry" (a patient of Mack) realizes this when she writes that "technical data does not lead to the discovery of other beings. Spiritual data does."

But are humans capable of understanding "spiritual" data? Are human cognitive faculties able to comprehend alien data? By all accounts the human brain is an astonishing organ: into the space of a quart of milk it folds a hundred billion neurons and a hundred trillion synaptic connections capable of performing calculations at speeds thousands of times faster than the desktop computer. But is it not just possible that the extraterrestrial brain is even better? "Scott" claims that aliens "think much faster than we do... It's confusing when they talk to us with their minds. Too much information. Our minds are not used to such contact. It's sensory overload." Barring the fact that the mind cannot have "sensory" overload, Scott may well be right. General nervous impulses travel at about eighty meters per second, and a typical layer-to-layer communication in the brain requires a mere ten milliseconds. If alien beings are made of substances more conductive than neural cells, they would exceed these speeds and thereby think faster than humans. Certainly this would lead to dire philosophical consequences. For example, there is a direct ratio between the complexity of a thought and the base speed at which a brain is able to operate. Computers have helped to make this apparent: supercomputers have produced mathematical proofs that no human has ever verified for the simple reason that a lifetime would not suffice to duplicate all the necessary calculations. So too might it be with the wisdom of aliens: if they think faster, their superior wisdom would be so intricate that a human could not grok it in a lifetime. An alien might process in a second a syllogism that man could only follow in a year or a decade.

Any further comparison of alien and human cognitive abilities seems impossible, since extraterrestrials have yet to offer themselves for neurocognitive testing. Or rather, if abductee accounts are any indication, further comparison is impossible for us but not for aliens, since they already seem to have undertaken in-depth research into human abilities. When an interviewer asks Andreasson to define man's "true nature," she responds (speaking for the aliens): "Man seeks to destroy himself. Greed, greed, greed, greed. And because of greed, it draws all foul things. Everything has been provided for man. Simple things. He could be advanced so far, but greed gets in the way." This definition of man as a greedy, self-destructive creature is echoed in many accounts, but is it true? The definition implies that greed leads to self-destruction, but this is by no means an accepted hypothesis. A biologist might argue that greed is a virtue from the vantage point of evolution, insofar as to hoard resources is to optimize prospects for long-term survival, and even an ethical egoist might assert that local greed promotes global welfare (for example, maximum personal consumption might contribute to a bustling economy). Dropping the implied causal chain between greed and self-destruction, the definition still deviates from the testimony of history. Statistically suicide and mass suicide are aberrations. World population rates continue to escalate exponentially. If aliens believe that the true nature of man lies in self-destruction, this can only serve as proof of their alienation—for it is apparent that they do not know man at all.

The nefarious purpose of the alien sex offensive was to utilize human females for alien reproduction. Because a viral epidemic had previously killed the entire population of Phi females, the necessity for self-reproduction had caused the surviving males to develop a technological, warlike method of species perpetuation unlike any other in the universe. After selecting a target planet, the Phis would abduct a small cadre of its inhabitants, depersonalize and retrain them as FTs—Fertility Terrorists, who would be returned to their original planet with instructions to infiltrate transportation hubs, food gathering areas, educational institutions. In such heavily trafficked social centers the FTs were to dispatch SSBs—Seminal Sticky Bombs, baseball-sized sacs of Phi seed mixed with liquid explosive—by approaching a target female with pickpocket stealth and slapping an SSB onto her body. Rather than burst upon impact, however, the bomb would attach itself by means of tiny spines with in-curving hooks that were not only difficult but painful to remove. In humans a slight bleeding accompanied the attachment process, but once in place the spines clawed so stubbornly into the body that attempts to detach them could rip and tear steak-sized chunks of flesh.

Following attachment, the FT would have approximately ten seconds to make his escape. Mercury de Sade kept this clearly in mind as he sought for his first target at the airport. Finally he spotted a brunette stewardess, perhaps in her mid-twenties, wearing a blue uniform with cream-colored stockings. He watched her purchase a frappuccino and a non-fat lemon poppy seed muffin at the airport espresso bar, and then trailed her to a newsstand. While she browsed through fashion magazines, he crept alongside her nonchalantly. He picked up a tabloid and used it to cover his movements as he withdrew an SSB. When the stewardess bent over to pick up another magazine, he reached out and slapped the SSB to her shoulder. It was like hitting someone with a water balloon, he thought, slipping away hurriedly. Once at a safe remove, he turned and watched. In a frantic effort to pry the SSB from her body, the stewardess screamed and a young boy with Tourette's Syndrome screamed back in retarded parody. A businessman dropped his briefcase and spilled pornographic magazines on the floor. A black woman buying a hot dog squirted mustard on her hand. A ticket agent fell unconscious onto the luggage conveyor belt behind her. An airplane crashed in the distance, and a spot of blood appeared on the cream-colored blouse of the stewardess's uniform. The SSB exploded: a mushroom cloud of blood momentarily enshrouded his victim, and then her arm could be seen dangling six inches below her shoulder on a piece of shredded muscle. Coating the wound was the unmistakable clear gelatinous slime of Phi seminal fluid, which immediately began to leech into severed veins and truncated arteries.

Viewed under a microscope, Phi semen teemed with slippery black tadpoles of lethal fertility, and it was these that Mercury de Sade, as he turned to complete his escape, observed in his mind's eye. They would rampage through the body looking for any organ that could be transformed into a womb. In humans they usually commandeered the heart, since its four chambers could be easily utilized for the purposes of incubation. Although a victim of Phi insemination would normally recuperate from the effects of the SSB explosion, after several months—really a gestation period—she would begin to feel congestion or constriction in the chest. This would naturally be mistaken for incipient cardiac failure, until the Phi fetus would burst through the heart and move into the left breast in search of food. Subsequently, the victim would experience massive internal hemorrhaging as the fetus consumed the rich nutritional resources found in the adipose tissue of the breast. This feeding process would cause the breast to distend unnaturally, and the movements of the fetus inside the breast would give the overall appearance of a gerbil wriggling in a sock. Not infrequently a woman would lie motionless on the floor as she bled to death, but her breast would continue to jiggle on its own as though the ghost of a stripper were utilizing her body to convey a message from the afterworld.

As citizens of earth realized that the breasts of their women were the point of entry for hostile aliens intent on hybridization, they scrambled to implement defensive procedures. Decoys were planted at strategic locations. Strutting about supermarkets and train stations with large round breasts, these decoys would attract FTs anxious to find good breeding grounds for the Phis. The effects of the SSB explosion would be minimized by protective girdles and undergarments, and if fertilization were to occur a second-line defense was already in place: each woman had breast implants made of boric acid, which poisoned any fetus eating its way through the breast. Another defensive procedure utilized random sampling to sift out Phi carriers. Operatives specially trained in obscure forms of medical terrorism would infiltrate schoolyards, burger joints, subway stations. At random they would run up to a female and jab a hypodermic needle into her left breast, injecting it with a vaccine that would force miscarriage of any incumbent fetus. And while miscarriage within the breast was an excruciatingly painful procedure for the victim—to the point where it was not uncommon for a woman to bite off her own nipple and strive to extract the hemorrhaging mutant from her body by probing into her flesh with a fingernail—nevertheless it was a necessary sacrifice for the greater good of mankind.

The stewardess stands in the aisle of the airplane performing the choreography of safety to the tune of a recorded voice. She shows how to buckle the seat belt and how to put on the yellow oxygen mask. The programmer in Mercury de Sade watches this performance with interest. Is there not something robotic about her routine? The voice says "seat cushion may be used as a flotation device," and right on cue she demonstrates how to use the blue cushion. The extent to which the stewardess is robotic may be judged by the ease with which she could be replaced by an automaton. For example, it is difficult to replace a sales clerk with a robot, because a sales clerk performs a very subtle and qualitative job, responding to the nuances and flattering the insecurities of the customer. A stewardess, however, has a job that is repetitive and hence simple to automate: convey safety regulations, check seat belts, distribute food. Who needs her? Probably it is an occupation that fails to be automated only because the bulk of travelers are businessmen who like to look at the white stockings and hourglass silhouettes of the women of the air. When a stewardess reaches into the overhead compartment in order to jam a piece of obese luggage into place, it nicely reveals the slope of her breast and the curve of her ass. Why give that up to automation? Then again, robots do not have to be designed without the attributes of gender—do silicon breast implants not already point the way toward the automation of cleavage? It may well be that men of the future will nurture latent obsessions for the sexuality of robots.

Naturally Mercury de Sade and Ninfa XIX cannot sit around New York waiting for the police to make a case. It's not so awkward to explain a phone call, but what about the videotape of them in her father's office? What about the blood on his shoe? What about microscopic bits of evidence that he may have shed at the crime scene? Might the fingernails of the male victim not contain incriminating bits of fabric or flakes of skin? Landing in Flagstaff in the late afternoon, Mercury de Sade picks up a rental car, a small silver import that gives the appearance of a lunar landing vehicle. Checking into a shabby motel across from some train tracks, he deposits Charlotte in a room, then returns to his car. Since he is in Flagstaff, he wants to visit the Lowell Observatory. Finding the turn-off for Mars Hill Road, he climbs the side of the hill to the observatory. A parking lot and low-lying brick building that turns out to be the visitors' center comes into view. He buys a ticket and wanders through the Tools of the Astronomer exhibit hall. Although there are no outright weapons among the tools, he amuses himself imagining how astronomical instruments could be diverted from their original purposes. What sadistic use might one make of a spectrograph? Although it would certainly be possible to dismantle a spectrograph and poke at a girl with its metallic parts, he tries to figure out exactly how one could use the device's inherent metrical properties for the purposes of sexual cruelty. Since a spectrograph disperses electromagnetic radiation into a measurable spectrum, it is apparent that the girl would first have to be irradiated. You'd have to wear a lead condom to fuck her.

Leaving the exhibit, Mercury de Sade joins a guided tour that leads up the Pluto Walk—a path that forms a scale model of the solar system, so that in walking one acquires a sense of the immense distance between the sun and various planets. At the end of the path is the dome in which Clyde Tombaugh worked to discover Pluto. While the guide describes the rustic origins of the astronomer, who began watching stars in the cornfields of his parents' farm, Mercury de Sade imagines the long, lonely nights he must have passed in the observatory. What kind of weird star fetish causes a man to sit in the cold darkness staring at the sky for months on end? Perhaps it was really just a mask for some other fetish. He imagines Tombaugh crossed with Vlad the Impaler: an observatory dome dedicated to the purposes of a bizarre sexual obsession, a woman impaled on a large brass telescope, the astronomer standing with his head between her legs, cranking her clitoris when the telescope is out of focus— "I can see Uranus, but where is Planet X?" he asks, thrusting the scope deeper inside. "It's right beside Planet G spot," she moans. Leaving the dome, Mercury de Sade climbs a small hill to join a line of people waiting to take a turn at a large telescope ensconced in another dome. As the night air grows cold, he observes Saturn through the giant telescope. Astronomy and pornography have been the two greatest enterprises of looking in human history, and it is in the mind of Mercury de Sade that they finally converge. Saturn becomes the locus of an astronomical sexuality, its bands a form of cosmic bondage. *120 Days of Saturn:* astronauts in an isolated planetary outpost reenact the classic work of the divine marquis on a series of extraterrestrial beings, torturing and fucking them to death.

For Karl Popper, the question was not "Do aliens exist?" but rather "What criteria must a hypothesis about aliens satisfy in order to be legitimate or credible?" In every scientific endeavor, Popper distinguished between an *explicandum* or state of affairs to be explained and its *explicans* or explanation. For example, the relation of the sun and the earth is an explicandum: "the sun revolves around the earth" and "the earth revolves around the sun" are each a possible explicans. Both the explicandum and the explicans must satisfy certain conditions for scientific legitimacy. In the former case, it may be taken "as a rule, that the explicandum is more or less well known to be true, or assumed to be so known. For there is little point in asking for an explanation of a state of affairs which may turn out to be entirely imaginary." Extraterrestrial life, however, is just one such peculiar state of affairs: "Flying saucers may represent such a case: the explanation needed may not be one of flying saucers, but of the reports of flying saucers; yet should flying saucers exist, then no further explanation of the *reports* would be required." ("The Aim of Science," *Realism and the Aim of Science*) But if UFOs are possibly an "imaginary" explicandum, how is the reality of the explicandum to be ascertained? Which is the real explicandum—flying saucers, or the reports of flying saucers? As an object of scientific inquiry, the UFO thus occupies a strange position. When studying the relation between the earth and the sun, the researcher may not know which is the best explanation, but at least he is certain of his explicandum. In the case of the flying saucer, however, he must not only seek a probable explicans but, in the first place, determine the truth or reality of the explicandum.

This problem is tantamount to determining the truth or reality of any given state of affairs. But isn't this an ultimate question of the sort that is never finally answered? What is reality? Although Popper lists the conditions that an explanation must satisfy in order to be credible, he does not give similar conditions for the reality of a state of affairs. Consequently, to reach the reality of the explicandum it is necessary to traverse the pathway of the explicans. What constitutes a good explanation? Popper rejected the common theory that the legitimacy of an explanation rests in its empirical verifiability. If it is possible to "verify" with one's own two eyes that the sun revolves around the earth, then verifiability must err in its basic premise, which is that a confirming instance is tantamount to proof. In contrast, Popper argues that the legitimacy of a scientific explanation is established by its *falsifiability*. Whereas verifiability seeks empirical confirmation, falsifiability consists of deducing testable or "falsifiable" corollaries from the explanation. The legitimacy of an explanation therefore emerges from its overall ability to produce deductions that are not confuted. For example, when considering the earth and sun, verifiability produces a false positive (the eye confirms that the sun orbits the earth). Falsifiability examines the matter differently. From the proposition that the sun rotates around the earth, it deduces testable propositions: the earth should be stationary in space, the sun should move in an ellipse, the earth should be the center of the solar system. Because all of these propositions are able to be disproved, the theory that gives rise to them is deemed false. Conversely, the thesis that the earth rotates around the sun gives rise to testable propositions—the earth should move in space, should show an elliptical orbit, should possess a velocity, etc.— which are unable to be disproved, and therefore the thesis is shown to be tenable.

How does this help to ascertain the reality of flying saucers as explicandum? Because if UFOs and not the reports of UFOs constitute a genuine or real explicandum, they must meet two criteria: first, they must be capable of generating falsifiable propositions; second, these propositions must withstand confutation. As an explicandum, flying saucers do in fact fulfill the first condition, giving rise to a series of testable hypotheses: they may originate from foreign nations, they may be secret experiments conducted by military organizations, they may hail from Mars or other planets in the solar system, they may come from other stars or galaxies. However, none of these propositions is incapable of being disproved: the collapse of the Soviet Union revealed no evidence of a technological capacity to produce flying saucers; the American government has declassified its research into flying saucers; space probes have shown the solar system to be uninhabited by intelligent life; the theory of relativity indicates almost insurmountable difficulties in intergalactic travel. Consequently, the fact that none of these propositions survives falsifiability suggests that flying saucers are merely an "imaginary" explicandum. Popper thus implies a new formula for determining the reality of a state of affairs: an explicandum, all of whose explicans are falsifiable, is probably not a "real" or "true" explicandum. In plain language: if every conceivable explanation for a state of affairs is untrue, then that state of affairs itself must be called into question. This harks back to an old principle in philosophy which states that an effect can possess only as much reality as its cause. Consequently, if its potential causes are unreal, as appears to be the case in flying saucers, how can its effect not be imaginary?

If, in its effort to define man, alienosophy really holds that man is nothing more than a greedy suicide, it would most certainly seem to err. Not only does "man is a greedy suicide" fail to square with the empirical evidence of human history, it also falls short of the many productive definitions of man already offered by human philosophy: homo sapiens, homo religiosus, homo faber, homo ludens, "man is a featherless biped," "man is the measure of all things," "man is a rational animal," "man is the animal that can adapt to anything." Human philosophy so excels the alien on this point that it calls into question the value of alienosophy, the superiority of extraterrestrial intelligence, and the intentionality of the philosophemes identified in abductee accounts. Scientists know to be wary of *experimenter effects* (which occur when the experimenter does not allow the data to speak for themselves but rather extracts his expectations from them)—must the philosopher not also be chary of conceptualizer effects? Might the entirety of alienosophy not result from the hope that, scattered in the philosophical *objets trouvés* of abduction accounts, there lie genuine remnants of an extraterrestrial intelligence? Is it not less an expression of logic than of longing to extract philosophemes from alien hearsay without first defining the minimal criteria for a *philosophical* concept or idea?

What is a philosophical concept? To define it by means of the philosopheme begs the question, since this already presumes an intrinsic philosophicality. How, then, does something become philosophy? How does a concept work in such a manner that it becomes philosophical? *First*, a concept must have a handle by means of which it can be called or instantiated. Essentially this is the concept's proper name: apeiron, cogito, monad, will to power, dasein. *Second*, a concept must declare the values of its properties. For instance, each concept interprets ontology and epistemology in its own way: the *cogito ergo sum* of Descartes sets ontology to "I" (being in the first person: being is my being) and epistemology to "think" (knowledge is through reason), whereas the *esse est percipi* of Berkeley sets ontology to "all" (being in the infinitive: being is being as such) and epistemology to "perception" (knowledge is through perception). *Third,* the concept must declare the relation of its properties. These consist not only of internal relations between properties but also external relations between other concepts. In turn, these external relations may take two forms. Horizontally, the concept enters into relation with the various concepts of its progenitor (in Descartes, the relation of cogito, God, and extension) and with those of contemporaries (Descartes' extension, Leibniz's monad, Spinoza's substance). Vertically, the concept enters into relation with other concepts in the history of thought (Anaximander's apeiron, Spinoza's substance, Gauss's finite but unbounded surfaces). In short, it is a matter of specifying either the concept's *lateral resonance* or its *vertical inheritance.*

This last function of the concept points the way toward a definition of the *philosophical* concept—is the line traced from concept to concept not philosophy as such? Does the set of all such concepts in their mutual resonance and inheritance not comprise the history of philosophy? Although it may at first appear tautologous to characterize philosophy as the set of all philosophical concepts, from an operational standpoint it is much more productive than defining philosophy as the study of "ultimate questions." The inscrutable question "what is a philosophical concept?" can be replaced with a much more scientific one: how does a concept enter into the total set of philosophical concepts? Here the plethora of trajectories can be disentangled in order to trace the genealogy of each individual concept in itself. One concept may be pushed in by the hubris of its creator, another is copied into the philosophy set from a religious or scientific set, a third staggers in after life-threatening exposure to the desert conditions of obscurity. However, if this overall genealogy is traced back to its logical limit, is there not the danger of falling into an infinite regress? If philosophy is the set of philosophical concepts, how did the first concept enter into a set that did not yet exist?

In this regard the origins of philosophy in ancient Greece are revelatory. Among the pre-Socratic thinkers proto-philosophical concepts emerged before there was a proper philosophical set, thus forcing many philosophies to make their appearance on earth masquerading as a member of some other established set: engineering, in the case of Thales, or religion, in the case of Pythagoras. However, as a resonance began to emerge between concepts that were initially appropriated by other sets, the set of philosophical concepts gradually self-organized. This process was not a mysterious philosophical animism: the tradition of masters and disciples already constituted a mechanism for set formation, so that when Pythagoras formed a "brotherhood" and Plato founded an academy, these were merely further elaborations in a legacy of self-organization. Philosophy thus began as the set of concepts espoused by the set of Pythagoreans or the set of Platonicians, and as the resonances between these sets magnified, the set of philosophical concepts was formed. As a result, philosophy need no longer be defined tautologously as the set of philosophical concepts, since a more specific definition can now be achieved: *philosophy is the set of concepts initialized by Thales.*

Once the set is declared it proliferates through the spawning of subsets and supersets, through the fusion of unions and the fission of intersections. At times thinkers try to squeeze the essence out of philosophy in order to discover its superset: this is not a qualitatively "best" set but rather the most abstract one, the ancestor of every set and every member, of the concept of dog as well as that of incest or number. The superset might look something like {being, knowledge}, as when Spinoza reduces the world to the attributes of extension and mind. At other times philosophy works in the interstice between this superset and the lowest subsets: when a meditation on the concept of being takes as its example the concept of a table or a dog sleeping beneath it, philosophy essentially forms a *daemonic* set, mediating between the high and low. At still other times, philosophy copies members from entirely separate sets into itself: "I is an other" is generated in an epistolary set by the poet Rimbaud, is gradually taken up by a literary set and then copied into the set of philosophical concepts. Consequently, not only does the concept replicate itself in sets for which it was never intended, its series of replications comes to form another set in itself: {epistolary: "I is an other", literary: "I is an other", philosophical: "I is an other"}. This occurs to philosophical concepts as well, as they are displaced from their host sets and carried across strange new contexts: the cogito begins in a traditional philosophical set, evolves within the set to form a basis for the ruminations of existentialism, then suddenly leaps out into popular culture to give bastardizations such as "I shop therefore I am."

This set-theoretical formulation of philosophy makes it possible to evaluate the appearance of putatively philosophical concepts in the midst of alien discourse. If a baby were to form the syllables *cogito ergo sum,* it would be a marvel but one of no philosophical significance: {gaga, googoo, cogito} belongs to a pre-linguistic set and thus its "cogito" member has no more conceptual meaning than "gaga" or "googoo." Whenever a "philosophical" concept makes its appearance in a set of aphilosophical members, its philosophicality is immediately compromised. For example, "Eva" (a patient of Mack) summarizes the ideas conveyed to her by aliens by stating that "You either perceive it and it exists, or you don't perceive it and, therefore, it does not exist." This is of course a near paraphrase of Berkeley's *to be is to be perceived.* But why does Berkeley's idea deserve the estimation it receives while Eva's deserves nothing at all? Because the normal set of concepts running through Eva's brain is something like {food, sex, makeup, clothes}, and when *esse est percipi* is appended to the end of the set, obviously it is an aberration. Likewise, when Betty Andreasson intones that "within fire are many answers," she reveals no secret Heraclitean alliance. To the contrary, her pseudo-Ephesian mumblings are appended to a set of obvious religiosity—something like {father, son, holy ghost, ecpyrosis}—and thus are to be construed less as concepts than as articles or perhaps even artifices of faith.

Certainly aberrations sometimes appear in philosophical sets as well:

Plato's transmigration of souls, Descartes' pineal gland, Berkeley's tar water, Nietzsche's eternal return. But just as these are eventually pruned from the set by philosophers of the future, so too must philosophical intrusions into the sets of everyday life be weeded out from the alienosophical set in formation. But if this fledgling set were pruned in such a manner, would anything at all remain of alienosophy? Are the ethical platitudes and epistemological clichés extracted from abductee accounts not the stuff and substance of alienosophy to date? To be fair, it is ex post facto and in discursive fashion that abductees relate the concepts revealed to them by aliens. Their intention is not to formulate cogent logical arguments. If Immanuel Kant abducted someone, dictated his philosophy to him and then released him, would a similar trivialization of the conceptual content not occur? "Kant said that reason had to seek out its own limits, and that people should treat each other not as means but as ends." Nevertheless, the alleged superiority of extraterrestrial intelligence requires that their philosophy be more intelligent than that of man—and this, with its trite reflections of human minds, it plainly fails to be. The claim that "aliens are more intelligent than man" is thus soundly confuted by analysis of philosophical claims attributed to aliens. One of two conclusions must necessarily ensue. Either aliens must be less intelligent than man, which is difficult to believe, or man must be fabricating his own aliens—dumb ones at that. And is there any difficulty in believing that man is capable of deferring to the intellectual superiority of aliens who are not only dumb but nonexistent?

Docking at port Chi, Mercury de Sade slid into the special armor he had commissioned for the planet. It had been molded from a sleek synthetic metal laced with diamond dust, which made it not only extremely hard but sparkly. I look like a medieval knight who's gone in for glam rock, he thought. Triggering switches in the fingertips of his titanium gloves, he checked his crotch gear: protruding from his pelvis like the mouth of a dustbuster was a retractable vent, whose purpose was not only to protect but to destroy. Utilizing semen compressed into a reaction chamber, the vent could shoot a pressurized stream of ejaculate with a force of impact sufficient to throw a grown man off his feet. "Here I cum," he laughed, deactivating the laser shield and descending into the port. Immediately he felt a kick to his ribs as a fracas of aliens punched and wrestled past. It was like walking into the middle of a hotly contested football game. The entire port seemed to have broken out in a brawl. Wanting to conserve himself for the parthenomachy, he ignored a sharp blow to the head, withdrew a plain metal baseball bat, and began to beat his way through the rioting aliens. Over and over he felt the bat make contact: it would glance off a shoulder blade or land with a fleshy thud on a pelvic muscle, and each time he heard a grunt or growl of orgasmic glee. Once a huge gush of white fluid splattered across his visor, and when he had wiped it off he was able to see the perpetrator lying on the ground in abused bliss, a look of satisfaction peering up through the welts on his purple face, which was soft as an old teabag from years of orgiastic battering.

On earth the abusive nature of sexuality had been hidden and disguised by evolutionary developments that blinded man to the intrinsic violence of sex. If a female earthling were to grab the arm of a man and yank it repetitively, he would experience discomfort or pain—and yet the same motion applied to a penis would result in pleasure. If a male earthling were to stick a finger in the eye of a woman, she would experience pain—and yet the same finger pushed into a cunt would result in pleasure. On Chi, however, no specialized organs had evolved to transmute abuse into ecstasy. Rather, the violence of sexuality was expressed through full-body combat, total warfare of the senses. To woo a girl, a man would punch her in the face. To fuck her, he might whack her with a tire iron. A monogamous couple was one in which each partner tortured the other exclusively. An open relationship resembled a barroom brawl with fucking. Women would beat the sperm out of men with clubs and sticks, and men would kick women with their boots until their ribs broke in ecstasy. Businessmen with split lips and sprained arms would ejaculate from bleeding penises, and housewives with black eyes and broken noses would climax from ruptured G spots. Nipples might be twisted off with pliers in riots of lust, and a hand might be jammed so roughly into a rectum that the fingers would break and swell up inside, giving prostate pleasure. Chi was the planet whose inhabitants literally beat the fuck out of each other.

In such an atmosphere it was impossible to distinguish rape from consensus. A vicious assault might really be an expression of affection on the part of a solicitous boyfriend. An apparently random attack could be the culmination of prolonged consensual foreplay. However, the one class of alien exempted from these acts of violence were virgins. Children could not be battered by adults for the obvious reason that not enough would survive in order to perpetuate the species. Consequently, it evolved that children were strictly safeguarded from sexual abuse until puberty, when they were formally inducted into combat. Each month a municipality would hold its own parthenomachy, an open event at which regional virgins were exhibited in a coliseum and released into battle. Naturally the brawling at such events was intense, since everyone—Mercury de Sade included—wanted to be the first to box a virgin on the ears. With the other combatants he waited on the coliseum floor until the virgins were released. All of a sudden it was as though a great wind traversed the stadium, picking bodies up into the air and smashing them into one another. Mercury de Sade swung boldly and deliberately with his baseball bat, causing orgasm and unconsciousness in all directions. With his bare hands he strangled and pummeled a virgin alien, causing her vagina to moisten with anticipation before rupturing her hymen with repeated punching. Finally he pointed his mechanized crotch at her, throwing her thirty feet in the air with a blast of pressurized semen. "How's that," called Mercury de Sade, watching her fall to the ground in a concussion of delight, "for your first wargasm?"

The motel is a shabby white building with a red neon sign that makes a buzzing sound like a mosquito zapper. Entering the motel office, Smith and Wesson ring the metal bell on the front desk. A timid man in a green plaid flannel shirt emerges. "Can I help you gentlemen?" Smith and Wesson show him their badges, but the man fails to question whether their New York credentials carry any authority in Arizona. In response to their inquiries, he explains that Mercury de Sade checked in, deposited the "purdy girl" traveling with him, and left again in a silver rental car. "So the girl is here right now, but the man isn't?" they ask. "That's right," says the clerk, proud to contribute an important clue to the solution of a great crime. "May we have the room key?" asks Smith. The clerk steps in front of the counter, anxious to lead the detectives to the room in question, but Wesson puts a bracing hand across the front of his chest. "That's all right," Wesson says, his tone falling on the man like a billy club. "If we need your help, we'll ask for it. Just give us the key." The clerk, who strikes them as a bit slow or dim-witted, is embarrassed. "Well, all right," he says, handing over the white plastic fob attached to the key. "I'll wait right here in case you fellers need any assistance." As the detectives exit the office, he expects them to walk straight along the corridor leading to the room in question, but instead they return to their vehicle. He watches as they help another person emerge from the back seat. It must be the victim of the crime, he thinks, seeing the gauze bandages that encircle the head of Mr. Goddard. "That poor man," he sighs, watching as the detectives transfer him to a wheelchair.

Withdrawing their weapons from their holsters, Smith and Wesson lead the approach to the motel room. Mr. Goddard follows behind them, a watchdog on wheels. A window looking into the room shows the blue-gray glow of a television monitor. They peer in, listen against the door, satisfy themselves that there is no one but Charlotte inside, then insert the key into the lock. The door opens and they step in, guns drawn. Charlotte is lying curled on the bed in a fetal position. Her eyes are fixed on the television, which is tuned to static. While Smith quickly inspects the rest of the room, Wesson stands beside her with his gun still drawn. She must be on some drug, he thinks, trying to make out whether her eyes are dilated. Maybe a sedative or even heroin. She's like a zombie. After assuring himself that the rest of the room is empty, Smith steps outside to fetch Mr. Goddard. He wheels him into the room, then steps back outside to stand watch for the return of Mercury de Sade. "Charlotte," calls Mr. Goddard, drawing out the syllables in a mocking but almost grandmotherly tone. "Charlotte, it's your father." Turning to Wesson, he barks through the gauze binding his head: "Wheel me closer, you stupid ape." Wesson positions the wheelchair right beside the bed. This is a weird scene, he thinks, unsure what Mr. Goddard intends to do.

When Charlotte fails to respond to her father in any way, when her eyes fail even to flicker away from the static on the television, Mr. Goddard turns to Wesson. "What's the matter with her?" he hollers. "I think she must be drugged," Wesson replies. "She probably doesn't even hear you." Mr. Goddard grunts and sits looking at her for a moment, contemplating. Really it's an ethical issue. Can you punish someone if she is not aware enough to understand that she is being punished? Suddenly Mr. Goddard spasms in his wheelchair, as though seized by decision. "Pin her," he yells at Wesson. "Pin her?" repeats the detective. "Can't you hear?" yells Mr. Goddard. "I said *pin her.*" Moving to the bed, Wesson rolls Charlotte from her side to her back. Leaning forward in his wheelchair, Mr. Goddard reaches up under her skirt and yanks down her white panties. Leaning back, he then retrieves a small electronic device from his pocket. "What is that?" asks Wesson. "A satellite tracking device," says Mr. Goddard with a rhetorical flourish, a triumphal note, a brass band inside his voice box. "And what are you going to do with it?" the detective asks. "This," hisses Mr. Goddard, suddenly shoving his hand up Charlotte's skirt. Wesson watches as the hand bulges and moves beneath the fabric of the skirt. "You value your car enough to put a LoJack in it," squeals Mr. Goddard, referring to the small transmitter used to protect against car theft. "Should I not value my daughter as much as my car?"

The philosophy of Jean-Paul Sartre would seem to merit not even the slightest mention in the history of exophilosophy. Concerned as the philosopher was with the existence of man, the question of extraterrestrial life scarcely occurs in his voluminous works. Even an occasional reference, as in his article analyzing the concept of genocide in the context of the Vietnam War, bespeaks a contempt for the issue: "The peasants," he wrote, "get ready to harvest the rice south of the 17th parallel. American soldiers come and burn their houses and want to transfer them to a strategic hamlet. The peasants protest. What else can they do bare-handed against these Martians?" ("On Genocide") To equate soldiers with Martians is to imply two things. First, it suggests that the American soldiers are as superior to the Vietnamese peasants technologically as Martians would pre-sumably be to earthlings. Second, it suggests that the myth of Martian or extra-terrestrial life is already identified with the complex of violence, technology, and imperialism that the "politicized" Sartre of the decades following World War II sought to oppose through an increasing commitment to Marxism. Moreover, if this is true—that Sartre viewed extraterrestrial life from a basical-ly "radical" and Marxist vantage point—then his conception of alien life would be easy enough to reconstruct even without more detailed references. From the Marxist standpoint, extraterrestrial life is essentially a myth fed to the people by the media, which serves as the propaganda apparatus of an exploitative elite; like religion, the myth of alien life thus serves as a kind of "opium of the mass-es," diverting class consciousness from oppressive conditions of existence and inducing it to embrace violence and technology by cloaking it in glorified bat-tles between flying saucers.

If this reconstruction of Sartre's view of extraterrestrial life is accu-rate, certainly it aligns a major philosopher with the "existentialist" tradition, reaching back to Kierkegaard, that emphasizes the importance of man at the expense of speculations extraterrestrial. However, of far greater significance to exophilosophy is another Sartrean notion that would at first appear to have lit-tle to do with extraterrestrial life. That is, in the classic, pre-Marxist works of existentialism for which he became famous, Sartre elaborated a view of exis-tence that stressed its contingency, randomness, and superfluity. In the novel *Nausea*, Sartre wrote: "We were a heap of living creatures, irritated, embar-rassed at ourselves, we hadn't the slightest reason to be there, none of us, each one, confused, vaguely alarmed, felt in the way in relation to the others...To exist is simply *to be there;* those who exist let themselves be encountered, but you can never deduce anything from them... Existence everywhere, infinitely, in excess, for ever and everywhere. I sank down on the bench, stupefied, stunned by this profusion of beings without origin: everywhere blossomings, hatchings out, my ears buzzed with existence, my very flesh throbbed and opened, abandoned itself to the universal burgeoning. It was repugnant... Every existing thing is born without reason, prolongs itself out of weakness and dies by chance." Existence, according to this view, is essentially gratuitous or excessive for the very reason that there is no ulterior reason for it: there are no gods to endow it or afterworlds to redeem it. It just *is*, and the astonishing thing is that even without meaning or reason it replicates itself with the abandon of weeds or bugs or cancer cells. "Nausea" is thus an ontological counterpart to overeating: it occurs in the realization that being is *de trop*, a banquet in celebration of nothing.

Although Sartre may have cared little for the question of extraterrestrial beings, he thus discovered a profound inversion of it: the problem of *terrestrial extra-being*. At stake is not the existence of beings beyond the third planet from the sun, but the gratuity of existence as such. In the case of earth, certainly it is the gratuity of terrestrial existence: barring religious explanations, in which human life is the creative choice of a divine being, why should man exist? Is he not superfluous precisely because he could just as well have remained in the undifferentiated nothingness of non-being? That which is extra is over and above the necessary, and as there is no necessity to the existence of man, he is an "extra-being"—a "terrestrial extra-being" insofar as he happens to dwell on earth. Furthermore, if it is existence as such that is superfluous, the implications of this conception do not restrict themselves to the inhabitants of earth. We often ask *whether* aliens exist, but must we not also ask *why* they should exist? After all, why should they? The universe would fare just as well—perhaps even better, if the havoc man has wreaked on earth is any indication—without life. Is the entirety of life not thus an instance of extra-being? And is all life not thus subject to the quandaries of meaning that are a cosmic extension of the existentialism elaborated by Sartre? If science has taken over the question of the existence of extraterrestrial beings, perhaps it is now the task of exophilosophy to ponder the necessity of extraterrestrial extra-beings.

In his elaboration of the "categorical imperative," Kant analyzed morality in terms of a means-ends relationship and basically concluded that moral behavior consists in treating human beings not as means to an end but as ends in themselves. It is "wrong," in short, to use people. Certainly this would pertain to extraterrestrials as well. If you want to fuck an alien, you shouldn't lead it on, declare undying love, promise everlasting devotion, and then dump it the moment you get between its tentacles. That's the Kantian position, and the ethics of Mercury de Sade are clearly an inversion of this. He disposes of other beings as means to a singular end: the satisfaction of his fetish. Girls are to be used as aliens. Aliens are to be used as sex objects. Sex objects are to be used—period.

But what of morality in such a situation? Is an inverted morality "immoral" or "amoral?" Is it a new kind of morality, one opposed to the "moral majority?" Is morality just a skirmish between a majority and the minorities it oppresses? If morality is to be more than a mere clash of belief systems, if justice is to be served, judgment must be made free of interest—it must be made *objective.* But here a profound problem intervenes. Mafiosi are not allowed on the jury when a Don is brought to trial, for the obvious reason that there is a conflict of interest: if the Mafiosi are from the Don's clan, they'll free him, if not, they'll indict him—for reasons having nothing to do with justice or morality. Similarly, if a man were brought to trial for actions resulting from a sexual fetish that implicitly disparages the entirety of mankind, would humanity as such not comprise an interested party? Were Mercury de Sade brought to trial, would humanity itself not have to be disbarred from the jury? And would this not require that non-human life forms be called for jury duty? Because plants and animals lack the requisite intelligence, it stands to reason that only extraterrestrial life forms could judge Mercury de Sade with the objective disinterest necessary for justice. However, even this conclusion falls short, since the existence of extraterrestrials is itself at issue: if they do not exist, they cannot form moral judgments, and if they do exist, then they are the objects of Mercury de Sade's fetish and thus become interested parties as well. Consequently, an extraterrestrial sex fetish is incapable of being subject to a truly moral judgment. Mercury de Sade is therefore neither amoral nor immoral but rather *exomoral*—beyond good and evil.

The warden conducted Mercury de Sade through the minimum-security unit, where compliant sexual objects were to be seen undertaking acts of goodness and charity, before arriving at the maximum-security sector. Here there were jail cells full of children. "Not just children," said the warden ominously. "*Virgins*." Mercury de Sade found himself observing some of the most hardened virgins in the galaxy: virgins who had stabbed pregnant mothers in the stomach, virgins who had set fires in hospital wards full of paralytics—and then giggled at the thought of so many paraplegics striving to crawl, flop, or wiggle themselves to safety. Mercury de Sade watched as these pubescent terrors spent their day grouped around television sets or building biceps in the weight room. In the work program area virgins repaired radios and pressed license plates. In the waiting room parents spoke to their children through thick panes of bulletproof glass. In the yard a fight broke out between competing gangs of virgins, and Mercury de Sade watched as prison guards hosed them down with pressurized jets of ice water. In a solitary confinement cell another virgin lay on the hard metal floor wearing handcuffs and leg irons. "A would-be escapee," the warden explained. "She tried to scale the razor wire topping the airlock. When they brought her in she looked like she'd tried to win a wet T-shirt contest with her own blood." Noticing the warden looking at her through the slit in her cell door, the hard-nosed virgin gave him the finger. "Sometimes I think that no amount of sex could reform a child like this," he sighed, shaking his head.

On Psi, virgins were the enemies of society. Whereas on earth the virgin was thought to be innocent and therefore good, on Psi it was the opposite: it was not loose morals that encouraged sexual behavior, but rather sexual behavior that resulted in good morals. Fucking enhanced the virtue of the fucker, and thus on Psi saints were invariably sluts. A figure comparable to the earthly pope was a former star of pornography who had attained his hallowed status not through good deeds but through sexual endurance. Conversely, if fucking enhanced virtue, it only stood to reason that the celibate were the least virtuous. The worst crimes were committed by the celibate—by the impotent, the frigid—by religious enthusiasts who had taken vows of chastity—by children and other such "innocents." Gangs of virgins habitually roamed the streets terrorizing the sexually upright citizens of Psi. In response, alarmed parents would take extreme measures in an effort to prevent the innate evil of their children from expressing itself. They would slip aphrodisiacs into baby formula in an effort to sexualize their infants and thereby instill a bit of goodness in them. They would hire pedophiles to molest their children and thereby fuck a moral sensitivity into them. But still, there were sometimes parents who failed to deflower their children. There were sometimes unrepentant virgins who would devote themselves to crime as to a cult. Invariably these would rob a convenience store, set fire to a house of worship, beat a babysitter to death—and thereby end up on a police rocket bound for the prison satellite of Psi.

"Here's the one we want you to work with," said the warden, gesturing to another solitary confinement chamber. Peering through a slit in the door, Mercury de Sade saw a wild little virgin with stringy blonde hair and a defiant gaze. She had tattooed the letters spelling "pure" on the fingers of her left hand, and the letters spelling "evil" on those of her right. She had also scratched a swastika onto her forehead with a can opener. "This is an unrepentant virgin as bad as they get," opined the warden. "I don't envy you trying to fuck some moral sense into her." No sooner had the cell door clanked shut behind Mercury de Sade than the vicious virgin leapt on him and tried to claw his eyes out with her fingernails. He managed to throw her off, knocking her head against the metal floor. "This is for your own benefit," he shouted, struggling to pin her and pull her skirt down over her thighs. "Sex teaches us interconnectedness," he snarled, pushing himself into her dry, tight vagina. "It causes you to *feel*"—he thrust with his hips—"the necessary connection you maintain with your society." This was his specialty: instilling virtue in virgins that had seemed incapable of reform. He would not stop fucking them until a flash of moral insight would appear in the thunderclap of an orgasm that had been building for days. They would lie there beneath him in a state of enlightened bliss, ready to perform any sex act for the greater welfare of mankind. "That was *good*," they would moan. "No," he would correct them, "that was *goodness.*"

"What the hell's this shit?" asks Wesson. He pokes with a spoon at a small porcelain bowl full of small dark lumps. "I think it's caviar," says Smith. "Jesus," exclaims Wesson. "It looks like congealed blood. What is it? Some kind of beans?" Smith takes a piece of fruit from a silver tray emblazoned with the hotel's monogram. "Caviar is fish eggs," he says. Wesson wrinkles up his face. "Can't room service get us an omelet or something?" He takes the hotel's directory of services in hand and leafs through it. "When you stay in the best hotels," says Smith, "you get nothing but the best food." Wesson grunts, picks up the telephone and pushes the button for room service. "Then I want the best burger. I don't care what *he* wants." Wesson nods toward Mr. Goddard, who rasps heatedly into a cell phone and punches at the keys of a laptop computer. Although Smith and Wesson order food better suited to their essentially cop appetites, they do not hesitate to sip at the expensive champagne that came with the caviar. They plunk down on the edge of the bed, the delicate champagne flutes balanced dangerously in their strong, hairy hands, and sift through channels on the television. Finally they arrive at ESPN and willingly allow a college football game to engross them. They would far prefer to debate the finer points of Penn State's rushing and passing than pay any further attention to their host, or their master, or their employer, or whatever Mr. Goddard should be called. For Mr. Goddard is beyond debate: not because he is deranged, exactly, nor because he is powerful, but because he is both. The deranged can be incarcerated and the powerful can be ingratiated, but a powerful lunatic—what can you do but humor him? They couldn't arrest him when he murdered his wife. What can they do to him now?

Seated in his wheelchair like a king on a throne, Mr. Goddard wears all white: his head is wrapped in gauze, and his body is concealed by a plush white terrycloth bathrobe provided by the hotel. Although white often symbolizes good, in Mr. Goddard's case it becomes something else, something difficult to define precisely. It's not as simple as evil. It's more akin to an unbridled lubriciousness, a white the color of a rapist's erection, and yet at the same time it has a crazy vengeful quality to it, a white the color of a Ku Klux Klan hood. Then again, because of his injuries, there is also something limp about his coloration, a white like a boiled egg. All together, these qualities give Mr. Goddard the aspect of a lewd, nasty Humpty Dumpty—except that, if his wheelchair were to tip over, he wouldn't break into pieces, but would lie there quivering like Jell-O, his bathrobe open and his limp sex lying like a worm across his thigh. Smith manages to ignore the man, but Wesson finds himself watching, appalled.

"Triangulate that signal, you ass," Mr. Goddard barks into a cell phone, watching the sweep of a radar across his laptop. He notices Wesson watching him and mistakes it for interest. "Thanks to the marvels of modern technology," he pontificates, "it is now possible to track the progress of a hymen across the open space of a desert. Right now, technicians in New York are homing in on the pert poontang of my pernicious daughter. Once they triangulate the signal emitted from that hot humid hole in her hosiery—the vagina is a humidor in which the cigar of man is humidified—we will even be able to image her using the latest in remote sensing technology…" Wesson thinks he can make out the creases of a grin beneath the gauze encircling Mr. Goddard's head. Disgusted, he forces his gaze back to the football game.

As a green line traces itself across the radar display on Mr. Goddard's laptop, he bounces in his chair with excitement. "Look," he says, "they're leaving town." The green line, the geometric representative of Mercury de Sade and his chattel, heads east out of Flagstaff on Route 40. "Where do you think they're going?" Mr. Goddard pulls up a map of Arizona on the internet. "The Indian reservation? The petrified forest? New Mexico?" As the time passes, his white finger follows the green line across the screen, until finally it veers south on Route 233. "Are you idiots awake?" hollers Mr. Goddard into the cell phone. "Get me a video stream of Meteor Crater, as much resolution as possible." In another window on his computer, he soon has a feed of Meteor Crater. The grainy image shows Mercury de Sade's silver rental car pull up in the parking lot. He opens the door and leads Ninfa XIX by the arm toward the crater itself. "Oh boy," enthuses Mr. Goddard, his tongue pushing against the dry gauze at his mouth. As the two scamper down into the earthen hole, Mr. Goddard continually berates his technicians: he wants better focus, better resolution, the best image possible. He gives the impression of being frantic, desperate, demanding. Mercury de Sade spreads out a silvery blanket in the bottom of the crater, and then the two bodies tangle on top of it like water snakes. "Punish her!" Mr. Goddard screams, bouncing up and down in his wheelchair like a spectator at the college football game. Opening his robe, he reaches in and grasps his fat penis the way a farmer grasps a chicken around the neck. "Punish her!" he thrills, and though Smith and Wesson clearly see the motions of pumping and humping reflected in the glassy screen of the television, they utilize their twenty years of inculcated hardness to ignore it.

The modern flying saucer craze began in the United States in 1947, when a series of UFO sightings captured the imagination of a public already nervous about terror in the post-war skies. When Roland Barthes analyzed the "mythological" aspect of the phenomenon in the mid-1950s, he emphasized that flying saucers were not at first thought to hail from Mars but, in accord with Cold War tensions, from the Soviet Union. However, there was already something latently extraterrestrial about this attribution. It wasn't that flying saucers were more earthly for having hailed from the Soviet Union, but rather that the Soviet Union—seen from the west—already seemed to possess "the very otherness of a planet: the U.S.S.R. is an intermediary world between Earth and Mars." ("Martians," *Mythologies*) However, as it became clear that the Soviet Union was not the generative force behind the flying saucers, the meaning of the myth shifted. Although the UFOs were now thought to originate in outer space, still they came to participate in the Cold War conflict: Martians were emissaries preparing to arbitrate the perilous dispute between the superpowers, lest an atomic holocaust should destroy the planet and thereby threaten the entire solar system. Such a conception, according to Barthes, remained fundamentally mythological, except that here "we have shifted from the myth of combat to the myth of judgment." The flying saucers no longer represent a threat of military invasion, but have rather become a "celestial surveillance, powerful enough to intimidate both sides." Even the shape and form of the flying saucer symbolize a peace descended from the skies: Barthes speaks of "that superlative state of the world suggested by a substance without seams," referring to the sleek, streamlined design typically imputed to the UFO.

If both of these flying saucer myths call for a diagnosis of anthropocentrism—as though Martians only come to earth in order to participate in the affairs of humankind—others confirm it. When a scientist hypothesizes that Martians have come to survey the geography of earth, Barthes ridicules the prospect that the culture of Mars could have developed in such synchronicity with that of earth: "If the saucers are the vehicles of Martian geographers... it is because the history of Mars has ripened at the same rhythm as that of our world, and produced geographers in the very century when we have discovered geography and aerial photography. The only advance is that of the vehicle itself, Mars thus being merely an imagined Earth... Probably if we were to land in our turn on the Mars we have constructed, we should merely find Earth itself, and between these two products of the same history we could not determine which was our own." Even more ridiculous than this cultural synchronicity is the theory posed by a French religious newspaper. Arguing that spiritual and technological progress must proceed apace, the newspaper found it "inconceivable" that "beings who have achieved such a level of civilization that they can reach us by their own means should be 'pagans.'" Consequently, Martians would have had a Christ—and even, according to a further twist of argumentation, a pope. For Barthes, however, this casuistry serves to invest absolutely alien beings with a disconcertingly "ordinary spirituality" that reveals the myth to be not only fabricated but platitudinous. "Every myth tends fatally to a narrow and, worse still, to what we might call a class anthropomorphism. Mars is not only Earth, it is petit-bourgeois Earth." And the Martian, by this logic, is a projection not only of man but of a lower-class version of him.

For Barthes, a myth is defined structurally by the fact that it takes an object which already possesses a meaning or significance and adds a new meaning atop it. For example, the sense of the formula $e=mc^2$ refers to a complex relation between energy, matter, and light. To the extent that it comprises a myth, however, it sweeps up this primary or literal sense into a new meaning— perhaps "the universe is rational" or "Einstein was a genius." This mythical significance is an accretion or superposition of meaning, one which contains the literal meaning without explicating it. In the case of flying saucers and Martians, the myth is refined until finally it reveals its essence. First it appears, in the interpretation that UFOs are hostile vehicles from an enemy country, as a myth of combat. Next it appears, in the interpretation that UFOs are the black limousines of alien emissaries, as a myth of judgment. Finally it appears, in the interpretations of science and religion, in its most archetypal form: "this whole psychosis is based on the myth of the Identical... No sooner has it taken form in the sky than Mars is thus aligned by the most powerful of appropriations, that of identity." In short, although man dreams of contact with other worlds, the Martians he dreams are identical to humans. It's the "invasion of the body snatchers" inverted: it is not body snatchers who make aliens out of humans, but humans who make "aliens" out of themselves.

That there are styles in athletics as much as in aesthetics is not to be doubted. In tennis, for example, there is the player who sticks to the baseline. His performance improves with practice and is often called "robotic," since his demeanor is cool and his strategy not one of aggression but consistency: when he wins, it is by returning every ball until the other player commits an error. In contrast, there is also the player with "touch." His performance depends less on practice than on something mysterious as a whim. He is not robotic because he tends not to repeat himself: his wins are displays of utter novelty, shots incredible and saves inconceivable. When he loses, it is not because he is outplayed but because his talent seems to have escaped him, leaving him frail and swearing. Certainly such styles are able to be seen and admired in many endeavors, whether athletic, aesthetic, or otherwise. For example, if sexual acts were performed in public as openly as athletic contests, commentators would appraise the styles of these sexual athletes in the terms now reserved for centers, shortstops, and running backs. There would be the baseline players of sexuality, the robots intent on the production of orgasm as though it were the result not of a libidinal but an industrial process, and also the fuckers with "touch," the ones who alight on orgasm the way a little bird lands on a tender branch. There would be numerous other kinds of sexual athletes, and before long the greatest ones would become legends and role models in their own right. "Don't you want to be like Babe Ruth when you grow up, Johnny?" The mother smiles, brushing her boy's bangs from his eyes. "No, mom," says Johnny, pushing his mother to the ground and pissing on her, "I want to be a wild fucker just like James Brown."

The sexual style of Mercury de Sade is best characterized by two qualities. First, he prefers not to be touched. To be touched is to be passive, subject to the will of the other. Mercury de Sade, conversely, is always the one to touch, penetrate, or violate. Commands, verbal or gestural, enable him to control the way in which his body is touched, and thus his sexuality becomes a form of vicarious masturbation—it is Mercury de Sade who touches himself by means of his victim. In this respect, the sexuality of Mercury de Sade is also deeply technological, like a remote-sensing operation. Sexual partners are tools, instruments to be manipulated in order to bring about the successful completion of the procedure. And this completion for Mercury de Sade is always symbolized by the cum shot. The second feature of his sexual style consists in the tendency to ejaculate on the surface of the victim's body. Although he frequently sodomizes his victims, he is almost wary of an orgasm that he cannot see. When a programmer is learning a new language, the first exercise in any tutorial is invariably to program a little window with the output "Hello, world!" The cum shot is like this exercise: it is the "Hello, world!" of the orgasm program. It is almost as though the orgasm is of dubious ontological status until the white paste of ejaculate declares its existence across the face of the victim. The cum shot is the *cogito ergo sum* of the orgasm: I cream therefore I am. In this sense, Mercury de Sade's vision of ejaculating across the surface of an extraterrestrial being serves a dual purpose: the existence of the orgasm cannot be known until it reveals itself in the cum shot, and the existence of the alien cannot be known until it reveals itself in the close encounter. Might an absolute proof not consist in the union of these two certainties? Who would doubt the existence of an orgasm that shouted its existence in the face of an extraterrestrial? And who would doubt the existence of an alien so tangible that a man can ejaculate on it?

Mercury de Sade used the telescope in Casa de Sade to spy on the girls in the Omega satellite. Through port windows the size of television screens, he was able to catch meaningless, fragmentary views of daily life aboard the satellite: an Omega girl staring out at the stars while talking on the phone, her silhouette defined by the white light of the cabin behind her; a girl moving mechanically back and forth in front of a window, cleaning dishes and placing them on a shelf; a girl trying on various dresses, standing before a mirror and spinning her hips in order to watch the skirt billow and twirl. From this montage of glimpses and peeps Mercury de Sade saw that the Omega girls were elegant creatures, tall and smooth and aerodynamic, adolescent fashion models whose contours had been perfected in wind tunnels. Their skin was light gray, like the ash of a cigarette, and they moved with low-gravity grace, drifting and flowing rather than walking. The only peculiar thing about the girls was the ovoid head. On Omega it was not only breasts and genitalia that developed at puberty. An Omegan also lacked a face until she began to mature sexually. Prior to adolescence, a girl's head was egg-like and smooth, with broad oval contours uninterrupted by facial protrusions. Then, upon reaching puberty, eyes would start to form beneath the unbroken skin of the face, eventually pressing out like blisters. A mouth would slowly sprout, looking at first like scar tissue but then developing into a full round pucker with lips swollen as the pads of a lifejacket.

Precisely to protect these delicate girls against interplanetary invasions of lust, Omegans raised their daughters in heavily guarded satellites apart from all contact with men. Space-age boarding schools, the satellites circled Omega in orbits known only to computers. On occasion a transport came and went, bringing new students or packages from home, but even parents were not allowed to set foot inside a satellite itself. How, then, was Mercury de Sade to abduct one of the Omega girls? It would be suicidal to raid a satellite or a transport shuttle. Only ruse and stratagem could succeed, and to this end Mercury de Sade had managed to intercept radio signals coming from one of the satellites. These signals carried all kinds of messages—some essential to the vehicle, including the one that had revealed its cryptic orbit, others essential only to the girls. Like most boarders, the girls took delight in breaking the rules governing their little universe, particularly the rule forbidding contact with the planet itself. How were they to keep in touch with their girlfriends on the ground? And yet the girls should have known that the rules were really for their own benefit, for once Mercury de Sade had intercepted a signal, it was not a difficult matter to intercept a girl. Young girls are prone to romance, after all. And when they live in isolation, boys seem mysterious and appealing. Mercury de Sade easily cultivated a starry-eyed pen pal. "Meet me at opposition behind the bulkhead," she wrote, pleasurably aware of her nightgown against her sensitive suede skin.

Donning his deep-space camouflage suit—black with white points like stars—Mercury de Sade waited behind the bulkhead for his pen pal. When she came floating out the hatch, he quickly pulled the oxygen hose from her spacesuit and inserted a tube from his belt, which rendered her unconscious. Once safely back at Casa de Sade, he saw that his correspondent was a young Omegan: not only were her primary sex characteristics undeveloped, her face was still very egg-like. She did not yet possess a mouth or nose, although the gray skin where her eyes would appear had a translucent quality, like skin held up to the light. When she came to, she lay passively on a bunk while Mercury de Sade ran his hands over her gray body, which had the texture of rawhide. Pressing his lips against her head was like kissing an uncompleted statue or a dressmaker's mannequin. Picking up a lipstick, he drew a red mouth on her gray face, then added eyebrows and two dots for a nose. As he tongued the face he had sketched, its outlines blurred in the rivulets of his saliva, so he drew another: puckered lips like Betty Boop, big eyelashes, red blossoms on her cheek. Not liking this face, he deliberately spat at it and wiped it out. Subsequently he drew what he imagined to be the face of the prototypical alien and inserted himself inside the girl—but then, as he fucked her, it occurred to him that she already was an alien. Why parody himself by drawing a face learned from science fiction movies on top of her already extraterrestrial head? Spitting again, he wiped the fake alien face away and did no more illustration until ready to ejaculate. Holding himself above her, he spurted white gobs of semen onto the sleek shell of her head. Then, reaching out with a finger, he drew a final figure in the viscous goop, a smiley face.

Holding himself above her, Mercury de Sade spurts white gobs of semen onto the weak shell of Ninfa XIX's head. She lies there motionless on the ground while he stands above her like a warrior with his foot on the chest of a conquered foe. Arching his head toward the sky, he sees Venus and the stars—and in his mind's eye, he also sees the satellite he had so carefully triangulated with SATDATA. Does it record him in this posture of victory? Has he not broadcast a triumphant image, *Man Fucking,* into the solar system and perhaps beyond? Suddenly he remembers the space probe sent outside the solar system by NASA and laughs. On a metal plaque mounted to the spaceship was an engraving of a man waving "hello" with his palm in the air. *Man Fucking* is the antidote to this naïve image, he thinks. After all, what inspires sailors to stop at a port? The welcome wagon? The chamber of commerce? A lemonade stand? No—gambling, alcohol, hookers. If man wants aliens to come to earth, must he not promise them something more than a benign handshake? Should NASA not send another probe that shows a man with an erection and a woman with her legs spread? The important question is not "What do we look like from space when we're fucking?" but "From space, should we not look like we're fucking?" For a moment he feels primal, elemental, a Native American doing a rain dance for flying saucer gods.

But then the aura of triumph and orgasm fade, a victory parade marching into distant unconsciousness, and Mercury de Sade feels stupid and awkward. The thought of his own image serving as an invitation to outer space only reminds him that the body below him has failed, like the eighteen before it, to give him any real satisfaction. When a man wants to transform one girl into another, he thinks he just has to give her the same treatment that Jimmy Stewart gives Kim Novak in *Vertigo.* He puts a wig on her. He changes her makeup. He dresses her in certain clothes. It seems simple enough—but what if he wants to transform not just one woman into another, but a human into an alien? First he has to suppress all the outward signs of her humanity. This Mercury de Sade had hoped to achieve by forcing Ninfa XIX into an identification with technology, a girl with a monitor for a head. Then it would only have remained for him to impose the new signs of extraterrestriality. But had he not failed here entirely? What are the signs of extraterrestriality? Should he have painted her green? Attached a rabbit-ear antenna to her head? But aren't these just cheap tricks? After all, she would have remained stubbornly human beneath these trappings of weirdness. And that's just it, he thinks. She refuses to play along. And if she insists on being human, then she gets—she got—what she deserves. Aliens, most people would agree, are superior to humans. Mankind is inferior, and therefore ought to be treated the way it deserves—with cruelty. Any girl who clings to her own humanity asks for it.

Mercury de Sade presses his shoe into the face of Ninfa XIX, pushing at her nose with his heel in the hope of driving the bone up into the brain. He hears a damp, snapping sound, like stepping on a stick beneath a pile of soggy autumn leaves, and lifts his foot. Seeing his own cum on the bottom of his shoe, he wipes it on her forehead. Plopping down in the dirt beside her, he tries to imagine what he looks like from outer space, from the vantage point of the satellite, but all he can see is the crater—a hole. He imagines the religious man seeing the crater as an expression of the awesome might of God. He imagines the geologist enthusing over its interplanetary rock formation. He imagines the biologist seeking traces of animal life. He imagines the philosopher Sartre invoking his "lakes and puddles of non-being," which leads him to wonder whether holes have any real ontological status or whether "hole" is really a misnomer for a simple curvature of matter. Finally it occurs to him that the universal appeal of the crater resides in the simple fact that it is a point of contact between heaven and earth—a tangible, visible, undeniable point of contact. It is the realization in geography of what is only dreamt of in humanity: the close encounter. The thrill of the crater emerges from the unarticulated thought that, if it can happen to the earth, then why not to man? Why not to me? Reaching out with a finger toward the smashed head of Ninfa XIX, Mercury de Sade traces a figure in the blood and semen. Looking at the illustration in the viscous goop, he imagines it to be the face of the prototypical alien, but the resemblance is not remarked by the tour guide who discovers the body in the morning.

Over the course of the twentieth century exophilosophy has grown thinner and more tenuous within the body of philosophy. Considerations of extraterrestrial life have become increasingly infrequent and skeptical on the part of major philosophers. The Existentialists, for example, almost entirely disregarded the question of alien life on other planets—although not without inventing an astonishingly parallel discourse concerned with the Other. However, if exophilosophy has reached a state of crisis, it will not have exhausted itself without giving birth to an entire array of thriving exosciences. Although scientific (as opposed to philosophical) speculation about extraterrestrial life is not new—Galileo and Kepler both considered extraterrestrial life from the vantage point of science—in the twentieth century science has become the advance guard. In the physical sciences, Percival Lowell and his Martian "canals" took the early part of the century by storm, and in latter years Carl Sagan, Brandon Carter, John Barrow and Frank Tipler have formulated profound analyses of the implications of modern physics for extraterrestrial life. Nicolai Kardeshev developed a classificatory system for potential alien civilizations which approximates the perspective of a social science. And even in psychology, two of the century's major figures—Carl Jung and Wilhelm Reich—devoted entire books to consideration of flying saucers. In short, the same circumstances that give the appearance of crisis in exophilosophy point to a golden age in more specialized exosciences.

But is exophilosophy doomed to perish in the birth pangs of the exosciences? What prospects remain for exophilosophy? Categorically, the minimum requirement for exophilosophy consists solely of two brains, each alien to the other. Or perhaps not even: it would suffice for one brain to speculate about the existence of a merely conceivable other, rehearsing a cosmic soliloquy on an empty stage to an audience of none. Exophilosophy need not have an object in order to exist, much as theology need not have a deity in order to thrive. What depends on empirical confirmation is not the existence but rather the truth value and hence the legitimacy of exophilosophy. Much as a credible theophany would cause some religions to be true and some false, so too would a close encounter of the third kind verify at least a portion of exophilosophy. Even more important, while a theophany would falsify some religious beliefs, it would ratify the principle of religion as such. Similarly, a close encounter would dispel some alien myths, and yet it would justify the very principle of exophilosophy and thereby assure it of existence—or at least the right to existence. Martians, Saturnians, superior intelligences, rarefied bodies, stars that live and breathe—the existence of these strange and wondrous creatures therefore has a significance far surpassing that of science fiction come to life. Philosophically, what is at stake are modes of thought themselves. It is not just exophilosophy, a philosophical specialization, which is called into question by extraterrestrial life, but fundamental procedures of reason: the legitimacy of analogical inferences, the validity of inductive logic, even the propriety of self-contemplation as a mode of cosmological speculation. In a weird way, man's very ability to think therefore depends on the existence or non-existence of extraterrestrial life.

What is the probability that exophilosophy itself will undergo this close encounter with extraterrestrial life? Although exophilosophy and a host of other exosciences furnish arguments for both the existence and non-existence of aliens, there is almost universal consensus as regards one stipulation for contact: the theory of relativity establishes a maximum velocity for travel in space, and therefore the vast distances of interstellar space can only be crossed by a being with incredible endurance and longevity. Although starships carrying generations of astronauts are not inconceivable, far more feasible are robots—specifically "universal constructors" capable of repurposing cosmic material in order to repair and reduplicate themselves without material support from their planet of origin. The advantages of such robots are numerous: synthetic materials are more durable, more replaceable, and more replicable than flesh; robots are invulnerable to boredom and nostalgia and insanity and rebelliousness; programmed instructions could be beamed to them from their planet of origin. In fact, if extraterrestrials really possess bodies of metal, they will also possess minds of code. They will be not only beings of matter but beings of words—automata. But does this not also mean that, if exophilosophy ever does achieve contact, extraterrestrial life will not be living, and extraterrestrial intelligence will not be able to think for itself? It has long been thought that literature is immortal, but in alien beings it will be programming that vies for eternity.

Is it possible to develop conclusive proof of the existence of extraterrestrial life? Because of the logical nature of proof itself, all empirical or a posteriori evidence is in principle liable to doubt—after all, even if a Martian were to pinch a man, it would remain possible that the man had hallucinated it. How could he be absolutely certain that the Martian or that even he himself existed? A conclusive proof would have to be a priori, since only apriority has absolute necessity. But is such a proof even conceivable? Mercury de Sade obliged Ninfa XXIV to kneel on her hands and knees on the floor and, while he sodomized her, he also dictated a little parable which she was forced to type on a keyboard with her tongue: There once was a philosopher who, impressed by the Ontological Proof for the existence of God, sought to develop a parallel proof for the existence of extraterrestrials. To this end, he studied the traditional proofs and used various analogies to apply them to extraterrestrial life. Although the philosopher developed slick syllogisms and artful arguments, after a lifetime of effort he never managed to formulate a credible deduction, a conclusion so necessary that it would impose itself on every mind that came into contact with it. However, as an old man—broken in spirit, the best of his professional years having passed without success—he finally decided that the import of his work was not to bring the proof to completion. Rather, his very inability to complete the proof was in actuality the significant result, less an existential than an epistemological discovery pointing to innate liabilities of the human mind itself. "We like to think," concluded the old philosopher at the very end of his notebook, "that, if aliens exist, they must be smarter than man. But in truth, *even if they don't exist,* they are still smarter than man."

APPENDIX 1   The Programmatic Structure of the Case History

Because the case history is organized utilizing concepts from set theory, its structure displays a regularity that enables it to be manipulated by standard computer programming techniques. The history can not only be read—linearly, as is usually the case with the human reader—it can also be successfully parsed. For example, the entire history can be stored as a two-dimensional array in a global variable using code such as the following.

```
on declareArray

 -- declare the array
 global gBookArray

 gBookArray = [:]

 addProp gBookArray, #alpha, ["ASS": "Exophilia", "MOD":
 "Exophile", "LIE": "Exophilosophy", "DAT": "Parable of
 Human Vanity"]

 addProp gBookArray, #beta, ["ASS": "Most Raped Planet",
 "MOD": "Ninfa XIX", "LIE": "Plurality of Worlds", "DAT":
 "Philosophy & ET Life"]

 addProp gBookArray, #gamma, ["ASS": "Pornodrome", "MOD":
 "The Wiz", "LIE": "Cosmos and Soul", "DAT": "Programming
 Exercise"]

end
```

This code returns a two-dimensional array that looks like this:

```
[#alpha: ["ASS": "Exophilia", "MOD": "Exophile", "LIE":
"Exophilosophy", "DAT": "Parable of Human Vanity"], #beta:
["ASS": "Most Raped Planet", "MOD": "Ninfa XIX", "LIE":
"Plurality of Worlds", "DAT": "Philosophy & ET Life"],
#gamma: ["ASS": "Pornodrome", "MOD": "The Wiz", "LIE":
"Cosmos and Soul", "DAT": "Programming Exercise"]]
```

Once the sections of the case history are stored in the global variable gBookArray, they can be manipulated in various ways. The general structure of the case history can be obtained by stepping through the array with a repeat loop:

```
on encodeBook
```

```
-- uses the array to generate a string outlining the
structure of the book

if NOT listP(gBookArray) then declareArray
book = ""

repeat with i = 1 to gBookArray.count()
  repeat with q = 1 to gBookArray[i].count()
   put gBookArray[i].getPropAt(q) && i && \
   gBookArray[i][q] into line \
   (the number of lines of book + 1) of book
  end repeat
end repeat

return book

end
```

This function returns the actual linear sequence of the case history:

```
ASS 1 Exophilia
MOD 1 Exophile
LIE 1 Exophilosophy
DAT 1 Parable of Human Vanity
ASS 2 Most Raped Planet
MOD 2 Ninfa XIX
LIE 2 Plurality of Worlds
DAT 2 Philosophy & ET Life
ASS 3 Pornodrome
MOD 3 The Wiz
LIE 3 Cosmos and Soul
DAT 3 Programming Exercise
```

However, the data need not be parsed strictly in the linear manner of the case history. Using another function, for example, it is easy to extract a single section—designated by its index or Greek letter—from the array.

```
on getSection aLetter

 -- get a section (designated by a Greek letter) from the
array

 if NOT listP(gBookArray) then declareArray
 section = ""

 repeat with i = 1 to gBookArray[aLetter].count()
   put gBookArray[aLetter].getPropAt(i) && \
   gBookArray[aLetter][i] into \
   line (the number of lines of section + 1) of section
```

```
      end repeat

   return section

   end
```

When getSection(#beta) is called, it returns the elements of the second section of the case history:

```
ASS Most Raped Planet
MOD Ninfa XIX
LIE Plurality of Worlds
DAT Philosophy & ET Life
```

Another way of parsing the text is to extract not a section but a thread from the array. Rather than obtain the four elements of the second section, for instance, one might wish to obtain all the elements of a given thread (i.e. ASS, MOD, LIE, or DAT).

```
on getThread aThread

  -- get a complete thread (e.g. MOD or ASS) from the array

  if NOT listP(gBookArray) then declareArray
  thread = ""

  repeat with i = 1 to gBookArray.count()
    put aThread && i && gBookArray[i][aThread] into line \
    (the number of lines of thread + 1) of thread
  end repeat

  return thread

  end
```

When getThread("ASS") is called, it returns all the members of the "Alien Sex Scenes" set:

```
ASS 1 Exophilia
ASS 2 Most Raped Planet
ASS 3 Pornodrome
```

Although this is merely a tentative or cursory way of indicating how the case history can be parsed by computer code, its value is to demonstrate to the reader the benefits of reading like a machine—and, in the absence of extraterrestrials, the machine is as close to the non-human as the reader will ever get.

Why did I write *Extraterrestrial Sex Fetish?* It started out with two impulses: first, the vague desire to write a book called *Alien Fuckfest;* second, a romantic fascination with the possible existence of extraterrestrial life. Interestingly, neither of these impulses carried over into the text itself. The title I decided not to use, for the crass reason that having "fuck" in the title would make the text that much harder to distribute. And as for extraterrestrial life, the scientific and philosophical reading I did early on in my research convinced me that there is no such thing. Or to be clear, I think there may well be bacteria or extremely simplistic organisms on other planets, but I also believe that there is no conscious intelligence (other than man) anywhere in the universe. Coming to this negative conclusion obviously put a strange twist on the composition of the text. I had few choices. I could drop it altogether, but this I was loath to do. I could make the protagonist, Mercury de Sade, lust after bacteria or extremely simplistic organisms, but this he was loath to do. I could make the text a confrontation with the *myth* of extraterrestrial life—and this is really what I chose to do. ETSF is not a story about aliens, nor about a man obsessed with them, nor is it really even a story at all. It's more an "analytic," in the Kantian sense, but written in the montage style of modernist literature.

In particular, ETSF reverses two myths. The first is that of superior intelligence. Aliens are supposed to be smarter than humans? Then the protagonist, Mercury de Sade, gathers together some of the greatest minds in human history—Plato, Descartes, Kant, Wittgenstein—to demonstrate that an alien intelligence would have a very high bar to leap in order to show itself superior. This is reinforced in the "alienosophy" section, which asks: If aliens are superior in intelligence, should their communications to humans not reveal some fantastic wisdom? If human philosophers are capable of such profound formulae as "I think therefore I am" and "To be is to be perceived," should alien beings not be capable of even greater thoughts? A review of the "philosophical" pronouncements made by aliens in abduction accounts unearths no examples of a stunning wisdom. The intelligence of aliens turns out to be little more than the "philosophies" of trite human minds imputed to equally trite imaginary beings.

The second myth is that of abduction. Aliens come to earth to abduct, rape, and sometimes impregnate its inhabitants? Then the protagonist, Mercury de Sade, will do the reverse—he will seek out other worlds in order to abduct and rape their inhabitants. However, the difficulty that emerges here is that these two myths actually work at cross-purposes to one another. In order to abduct and rape extraterrestrials—or even to *want* to abduct and rape them—it is at least necessary to believe in their existence. And yet to perceive that their "intelligence" consists of human clichés is to admit that aliens are nothing more than fantasies, myths. This reduces Mercury de Sade to the unenviable position of wanting to rape something that he cannot believe exists. A "diary entry" that did not make it into the final draft of the text put it like this: "My mind may seek to know itself (hence philosophy), but my body seeks to know others (hence pornography). Sometimes a homosexual feels like a woman trapped in the body of a man. I feel like a solipsist trapped in the body of a nymphomaniac. (Strictly speaking, this would mean I go around fucking things the existence of which I deny.)"

The psychology of a character caught in such a dilemma will naturally be one of frustration. He is intelligent—or rather, intellectual—and yet his potency in matters cerebral is matched by a fundamental impotence in his sexual desires. As a character this does not make Mercury de Sade either likable or sympathetic. He is superior and, like many frustrated people, basically mean. Moreover, Mercury de Sade learns nothing, undergoes no revelations, experiences no reverses of fortune. He is one-dimensional—and yet this very flatness is the psychology typical of the fetishist. Unless he is caught, embarrassed, shamed, arrested, the fetishist is characterized by the subordination of his entire personality to a single-minded goal: the satisfaction of his "thing." This is why nineteenth-century psychologists called them *monomaniacs*. And unless you happen to share their "thing," it can also make fetishists rather monotonous.

This is where set theory comes in. Astute readers, perceiving that connections between the various texts of ETSF have the same contingent character as hyperlinks on the internet, will no doubt assume that it was my intention to write a "hypertext," to deform the novel utilizing the techniques of a web-browsing experience, or some such. Although I recognize the legitimacy of this interpretation, it was not in fact my intention. However deeply my professional life involves me in the language of machines, really it was not the computer but mathematics—in particular, set theory—that inspired the overall shape of ETSF. There were several reasons for this. First, on the level of content, I thought that set theory provided a powerful framework for describing fetishism: monomania is an obsession not with one thing but with variations on that thing—not one shoe, for the shoe fetishist, but a whole sequence of shoes of different types, qualities, colors, styles. Second, on the level of structure, I thought that set theory might provide new solutions to certain old problems of form and formlessness. Here my literary models were the serial structure of *120 Days of Sodom* and the collage structure of *Naked Lunch*. By writing in interleaved sets, I was able to obtain the best of both: reading within the sets is serial, reading across the sets is collage.

Finally, I would like to say that I expect ETSF to cause much consternation—not because it is intrinsically polemical, like an abortion debate, but because it defies genres in a way rarely done before. (Sade and Kierkegaard wrote similarly recombinant works, but who else?) Many will reject ETSF as pornography. Pornographers will reject it as philosophy. Philosophers will reject it as literature. Litterateurs will reject it as science fiction. Sci-fi readers might accept it, because they tend to be more flexible about these things—and yet, in spite of my enormous respect for science fiction, I don't think ETSF is that either. "Science" means knowledge, and knowledge by definition is true; "fiction" means counterfeit, and counterfeit is by definition false. The term "science fiction" is thus an oxymoron meaning something like "truth falsified." This is probably an accurate description of certain classic works of the genre: Philip K. Dick really had a way of fucking with reality, and is "fucking with reality" anything other than falsifying truth? Conversely, I think ETSF falls in a weird bastard category more like "pseudo-science non-fiction," by which I mean falsity—the belief in UFOs, Martians, grays, Little Green Men—exhibited and analyzed.